"An intriguing mystery and a heartfelt romance all in one, *The Matchmaker* is fresh, original, and utterly charming. You'll love this sparkling gem of a book."

—LIANE MORIARTY, #1 *New York Times* bestselling author of *Big Little Lies*

"Dazzling . . . I loved *every word* of this novel. I wish I could write like that."

—A. J. FINN, #1 *New York Times* bestselling author of *The Woman in the Window*

"Aisha Saeed expertly blends romance and mystery in this fun, fresh story that is sure to keep readers turning the pages. Smart, twisty and full of heart—you won't want to miss *The Matchmaker*!"

—AMY TINTERA, *New York Times* bestselling author of *Listen for the Lie*

"In the rarified world of the uber rich, a brilliant match-maker helps men and women find the partner of their dreams. But a mysterious someone is out to bring every-thing crashing down in this stunning blend of enchanting cultural traditions, sumptuous weddings, kidnap, and mur-der. *The Matchmaker* kept me enthralled and guessing until the very end. Don't miss this gem!"

—LIV CONSTANTINE, *New York Times* bestselling author of *The Next Mrs. Parrish*

"*The Matchmaker* combines a page-turning thriller with a sweet romance filled with palpable yearning, adds a dramatic family saga spanning generations, then plunks it into a *Crazy Rich Asians*–esque world of weddings and matchmaking. I loved absolutely everything about it!"

—MIA P. MANANSALA, author of the
multi-award-winning *Arsenic and Adobo*

"*The Matchmaker* is a mystery crackling with tension, both romantic and thrilling. I was swept away by the will-they-won't-they chemistry, and the cat-and-mouse mystery, all set amidst a gorgeous backdrop of lavish weddings. This page-turner pairs up the perfect match of romance and suspense."

—JULIA SEALES, bestselling author
of *A Most Agreeable Murder*

"*The Matchmaker* is a magical mix of romance, family saga, detective story, and teeth-chattering suspense. I was swept into the dreamworld of the super-wealthy—a world of beautiful brides, fabulous feasts, shimmering saris . . . and murder. I adored every page, and so will you."

—ROSE CARLYLE, internationally bestselling
author of *The Girl in the Mirror*

THE

MATCHMAKER

The Matchmaker

•

A NOVEL

•

Aisha Saeed

BANTAM
NEW YORK

Published in the United States by Bantam Books, an imprint of Random House, a division of Penguin Random House LLC, New York.

BANTAM & B colophon is a registered trademark of Penguin Random House LLC.
RANDOM HOUSE BOOK CLUB and colophon are trademarks of Penguin Random House LLC.

LIBRARY OF CONGRESS CATALOGING-IN-PUBLICATION DATA
Names: Saeed, Aisha, author.
Title: The matchmaker: a novel / Aisha Saeed.
Description: New York: Bantam, 2025.
Identifiers: LCCN 2024043750 (print) | LCCN 2024043751 (ebook) |
ISBN 9780593871157 (trade paperback; acid-free paper) |
ISBN 9780593871164 (ebook)
Subjects: LCGFT: Cozy mysteries. | Romance fiction. | Novels.
Classification: LCC PS3619.A3536 M38 2025 (print) | LCC PS3619.A3536
(ebook) | DDC 813/.6—dc23/eng/20240917
LC record available at https://lccn.loc.gov/2024043750
LC ebook record available at https://lccn.loc.gov/2024043751

Printed in the United States of America on acid-free paper

randomhousebooks.com
randomhousebookclub.com

1 3 5 7 9 8 6 4 2

Book design by Jo Anne Metsch

For K,
my perfect match

THE

MATCHMAKER

PROLOGUE

You still think there's a way out, don't you?

I see how your eyes dart around. To that pen on the counter. Your keys. You're desperate. For something, anything, that might deliver freedom.

Denial is normal. One of the five stages of grief or something, right? But time is of the essence here, so I'm afraid we're going to need to go ahead and skip to acceptance.

Because sooner or later, you're going to have to wrap your head around the fact that tonight, Nura Khan, you will die.

After a decade of trying to find "the one," I was over it. My friends said I was too picky. Of course I'm picky. What's wrong with having high standards for the person you'll spend the rest of your life with? Nura gets it. Within weeks of working together, she introduced me to Dev. And the rest, as they say, is history. We're getting married this summer. Nura Khan isn't just a matchmaker, she's a magician.

—AVANI PATEL

I'd been on Piyar's personalized matchmaking agency waitlist for years, and I'm here to tell you it was worth the wait! Piyar doesn't just help you find the one, they help *you* get yourself in gear too. Once I was ready, Nura introduced me to five people, and as soon as I saw Gavin, I knew he was the one. I don't know how she does it, but I'm so grateful she does.

—JONAH VOSS

I could have found someone on my own, but why? There are only so many hours in the day. Who has time to endlessly swipe apps and have meaningless first dates with people you may not see eye to eye with? *Piyar* means "love," and that's what Nura gave me. Saira and I have been married four years now. She's my best friend, we have two sons, and I couldn't be happier that I trusted this most important aspect of life to the expert.

—IRFAN MIAN

My anxiety makes dating a complete minefield. When I met Nura at age thirty-nine, I was at my lowest ebb, convinced it was hopeless to even bother trying—but Nura didn't blink. I'm about to meet my first match this Saturday, and for the first time I'm looking forward to it. I haven't met my perfect partner yet, but I couldn't wait to write a glowing review. Nura is not just your matchmaker, she's your life fixer. If I could give ten stars, I would.

—DEEBA MAKHIANI

you are cordially invited to

THE WEDDING OF

Saba

AND

Abid

Sunday, May 4th
Half past six o'clock in the evening

REISTA VIA GARDENS
653 NORTH VININGS ROAD
ATLANTA, GEORGIA

ONE

The bride beams for the cameras against a backdrop of blood-red roses framing the wedding stage. Her newly minted husband stands by her side in a cream sherwani and matching turban. She's in a golden lengha, hand-stitched with one thousand and one diamonds that shimmer beneath the lights. One could genuinely mistake them for royalty.

She scans the wedding hall. Every detail has been carefully arranged, from the long-stemmed moth orchid centerpieces to the twelve-layer wedding cake designed by Bontemps's very own head pâtissière. Her eyes land on mine.

The crowd parts like the Red Sea as she and her husband make their way toward me.

"You made it!" she exclaims.

"I wouldn't miss it for anything," I tell her. "Your vows were beautiful, and you look gorgeous." I gesture to the ballroom. "This is all a dream come true."

"Because of you." She pulls me into a tight embrace.

"She's right. Thanks, Nura." Her husband smiles at me.

The crowd that's been edging ever closer gasps. I've gone from just another of the seven hundred guests here to Nura Khan, matchmaker.

When the couple moves on, I'm quickly encircled.

"I can't believe you're *the* Nura Khan," a woman in a pink sari says. "I just read the article about you in *Vanity Fair*."

"Ah," I say neutrally, as though it hasn't been the bane of my existence since it was published last month. "It wasn't about *me*. It's about—"

"Lena Kamdar raved about you in it. I had no idea you matched Saba and Abid too."

"I use your Piyar app all the time," says another woman, gazing wistfully at the groom in the distance. "Still waiting for my Abid."

"Like she met him on the app," another retorts. "I'm sure she went the VIP route. Good luck affording it. *If* they even let you in."

I clock their stunned expressions and feel a pang of sympathy. "The app is also very effective. It has the highest success rate on the market," I reassure them. "I'm sure it's only a matter of time."

Excusing myself, I head toward my seat and run into the wedding planner. We embrace and exchange pleasantries.

"Always wonderful to see you," she says. "I can't thank you enough for the referral."

"I had a feeling she'd go with you. You've really outdone yourself tonight."

"Saba was a delight to plan for," she says, her smile shifting to a look of concern. "Tell me, how is your auntie? Is she recovering all right?"

"She's getting better every day," I tell her. "They finally discharged her from physical therapy last week."

"The latest stroke was such a shock. Thank goodness she has you."

"Well, her daughter is also—"

"Yes, yes, Nina's finally deigning to visit. But you're the one keeping it all together, aren't you?" She adjusts her sari and gives me a knowing look. "I remember when you first arrived all those years ago. You were what, ten?"

"Seven."

"Now look at you. Running the entire business. She couldn't have passed things down to a better person. Give her my love?"

I promise her I will. I glance around the wedding hall, missing Khala's presence all the more. Once upon a time, she would have been here with me. Charming everyone. She had a special eye for the people who needed our help the most. We'd have two dozen requests for matchmaking applications before samosas were served.

In the distance, the emcee announces the first dance for the bride and groom. A romantic ballad fills the space. I spot Azar at our table and settle down next to him. He's finally here. And I have to say, my best friend—and pretend fiancé—cleans up nice. No three-day stubble and blue scrubs today. He's in a gray Armani with a cream tie.

"You're late." I elbow him.

"Sorry." He looks at me bashfully. "Got tied up at the ER."

"You've been pulling a lot of long shifts lately. You doing okay?"

"We're just about done wrapping up interviews for the open position. Should be fully staffed by the end of the month. No more late arrivals after that, I promise."

"No worries. I was just networking a little."

"Any potential VIP clients?" he asks.

"Not VIP, *personalized*," I correct him. "Tonight was a slow evening. People were more interested in chatting about Lena's *Vanity Fair* article. I'm officially clocking out for the night."

"It sounds like Lena gave the agency some great word of mouth."

"There can be too much of a good thing. We're drowning in both inquiries and hate mail lately. Lesson for me about taking on a cosmetics heiress slash influencer."

"Lena should have checked with you before talking to the press."

"She meant well," I acknowledge. "It's not her fault the piece called us an 'arranged marriage throwback.' That's the line getting the trolls all worked up." I adjust the beaded embroidery on my sleeve. "Honestly, if I'd known I could wear scrubs to work, I'd have followed you to medical school instead."

"You sure about that?" He furrows his brows. "Because you'd also have to be equipped to grab a needle to suture a bloody—"

"Okay! Stop!" I squeeze his arm. "You win!"

He grins. "You know you love this work."

"I do." I return his smile. "And it's even better when you're here."

Azar's return to Atlanta from New York City three years ago was a game changer. I love matchmaking. Helping people find love is what I was put on this earth to do. But there's one catch in my line of work. A woman who matchmakes for a living and is thirty-one (going on thirty-two) years old and very much single? That raises eyebrows. Early on, I'd argued with Khala it wasn't necessary to pretend I was spoken for. *Those who don't, teach*—isn't that the saying? Besides, I got the desired results. As the years have gone by, though, I've had to face the fact that no matter how progressive the world gets, an unmatched matchmaker prompts whispers. To look the part, I need a partner by my side. Long live the patriarchy. Luckily, Azar doesn't mind filling in as my date, and with our busy schedules, weddings double as our chance to spend time together while eating delicious food.

"Are these wedding favors?" Azar lifts a Tiffany & Co. gold-plated clock next to his place setting.

"Engraved with their initials and today's date."

He eyes the tables stretched out in seemingly endless rows and lets out a low whistle. "How much did all of this cost?"

Azar's an old pro at lavish weddings, but he still can't quite process the wealth of some of my clients.

"Whatever these favors cost is nothing compared to the gift Saba got her blushing groom: a Bentley Batur."

"That car goes for two million dollars!"

"Two point *five*," I correct him. "It's completely electric, though. So good for the planet."

"Diamond heiress weds high school soccer coach. If Saba wasn't so private, the press would've nicknamed you a fairy godmother by now."

"Luckily, the press have their hands full documenting every second of Lena's wedding prep at the moment."

He leans back and folds his arms. "Speaking of weddings—"

"No, you can't get out of any you've committed to," I interrupt.

"Why do you assume that's what I was going to say?"

"Am I right?"

He laughs. "Good talk."

I push back a smile. He's so predictable. I guess that's what happens when you've known someone most of your life.

"I checked the calendar," he says. "You're booked nearly every weekend for the next few months."

"Wedding season is officially here, and I want to make it to as many as possible. It's how I get my best clients."

"But there are more weddings on the calendar this year than ever. You've got to pace yourself, Nur. How about you call in sick to the next one and play hooky with me? The botanical garden's got their light show going on—we could get a picnic dinner by good old flowery Medusa for old times' sake."

"Azar—"

"Or I can get us a table at Hayakawa? It's been ages since we've been there." He leans forward. His brown eyes lock into mine. "Downtime is important, Nur."

"The next event will have hand-carved Brazilian steak. And an oyster bar too. I know you can't say no to an oyster bar."

Azar considers this, then raises his palms in mock surrender. "You had me at steak."

I knew he'd never leave me hanging. I was seven years old when my mother died and I moved in with my aunt, drowning in a sea of change and grief. But when I met my neighbor Azar, six months older than me, scootering down the street, he became my constant companion. A steadying force in an unpredictable life.

Khala has needled me many times about why I only *pretend* to be with Azar. Azar of the dimpled cheek and curly hair. The crooked smile. I don't tell her how very much aware of his good looks I am. That we very nearly kissed. Once. A disastrous moment our senior year at Emory University when I found out he was heading to New York City for medical school. Azar made it clear: His feelings toward me were strictly platonic. After a few years of awkwardness, we managed to clear the air and agreed to pretend it never happened. Which is just as well. Azar's not one for commitment, and my life is too busy for complications.

My phone dings. It's an email from my tech guy: Y'all need to check out this creepy rant about the agency.

I'm about to click the link when a new song comes on; the pulsing bhangra beat fills the room. Azar's face lights up.

"Azar, no," I protest. "I'm officially wiped out."

He takes my hand. "It's illegal not to dance to this, Nur."

How do you say no to that face?

Walking to the parquet dance floor, my phone dings again. My assistant.

Did you listen to the recording? These are some vile accusations. Maybe even illegal. There's got to be a slander angle here.

My mood sours. I'm tempted to steal out to a quiet spot and see what headache awaits me. Except . . .

No. I slip my phone back into my clutch. Not tonight. I deserve a respite, however brief, from work drama. The truth is that people who don't get accepted through the vetting process for our matchmaking app or who aren't green-lighted to our pricier personalized services tend to get upset. Sometimes they lash out. It's the cost of doing business. I take in the newlyweds on the dance floor. The groom's arms encircle the bride's waist. They gaze into each other's eyes, lost in their own world in the middle of a raging bhangra beat. Some parts of this job leave a lot to be desired, but moments like this one, where I get to bear witness to the happily ever after that I helped make happen, make the headaches worth it. The music cranks up louder. I match Azar's dancing, beat for beat. Tonight is for dancing. For celebrating a beautiful union. I'll deal with whatever this is tomorrow.

L aughter and squeals drift over from a nearby playground as I pull my Audi into the reserved parking spot kitty-corner to our agency. Our office is a stand-alone one-story brick building in the chic walkable neighborhood of Inman Park, dotted with bookstores, cafés, and brunch destinations. My sunglasses fog up as soon as I get out of the car. It's not yet noon, not yet officially summer, but already the heat is rising. Checking my hair in my phone, it's confirmed: The faint frizzy halo is back. You can pay to have your slacks and blouses steamed and pressed, but desi hair—despite an army of professional products—is no match for Atlanta's sticky humidity. At least most of my clientele are also desi—they understand.

Swinging open the front door, the two-thousand-square-foot space welcomes me with its recessed lighting and creamy curtains fluttering in the air-conditioning. Darcy, my assistant, picked out nearly everything here not long after I leased the space, from the velvet-cushioned seating in the foyer to the handmade rug, custom cut, draping most of the marble floor, to the potted fern resting by the windowsill atop an old filing cabinet discreetly covered in satin damask. The team's been on me to get rid of that filing cabinet, but it's nostalgic—the only remnant of the old days when the business was just Khala and me working out of her basement. My office is in the back, next to the sleek, glass-walled conference room. Borzu, my tech guy, and Genevieve, my private investigator, have matching desks set up in the open space, as does Darcy. Hers is the biggest—double-wide and up front—to greet clients when they arrive and block those who have no business being here.

Darcy's not sitting at her desk right now. Instead, she's pacing back and forth, her hands clasped behind her back. Her slate-blue eyes flash with indignation. Based on the amused expressions Borzu and Genevieve just exchanged, she's been pacing for a minute.

"What do you mean, we can't shut it down?" Darcy exclaims to Borzu. He's sporting dyed red hair today, closely cropped. Darcy's in her usual buttoned-up professional attire—a cream blouse and gray skirt. Her white-blond hair is pulled back into a ponytail. "If anyone can do it, you can."

"Darcy," Borzu says with a sigh.

"Give it a rest," Genevieve says. "It's not like anyone's going to be tuning in to this."

"That doesn't make it any less problematic. We need to nip this podcast in the bud before it snowballs out of control."

"It's a podcast?" I ask. "How bad is it?"

All eyes turn to me.

"You mean you haven't listened to it?" Darcy stares at me.

"The wedding went late last night. Then I had that ridiculously early client intake this morning, remember?"

"Yoga Lady," says Genevieve. "Did she really make you join her on the mat?"

"Technically, she *invited* me to join her. But yes, I can confirm it's awkward to be in cobra pose while asking a client about their ideal dinner date."

"One sec. I've got it pulled up." Borzu squints at his computer screen. Presses play. A staticky masculine voice blasts through the speakers. The words clip in and out, but the final ones ring out crystal clear:

People call Nura Khan an expert. A magician. Are you kidding me? Here's the deal: Anyone can call themselves an expert. But I'm here to give you the straight facts. The Piyar matchmaking agency doesn't help people. It hurts them. You can post all you want about how magical the agency is, but at the end of the day, she's a fraudster. I know it. Soon the world will too.

The recording abruptly ends. My team watches me, waiting for my response. I look at Borzu's computer screen; the podcast, such as it is, is called *Piyar Confidential,* and this two-minute "episode" is the sole recording. Darcy has a mama bear attitude when it comes to me, but—

"Okay, that was a little creepy," I say. "But at the end of the day, it's an angry man, what else is new? I don't think it's such a big deal."

"You can't be serious!" Darcy's eyes widen.

"I'm with Nura," says Borzu. "This sounded more like a voice memo rant than anything else."

"He sounds as unhinged as Andrei," Darcy counters.

"This is a rando rejected client, not your obsessive ex-boyfriend," Genevieve interjects. "Nura's right. Would-be clients who don't make the cut get pissed. Looks like one of them just found a new way to express themselves."

"I'll take that over a one-star App Store review," Borzu adds.

"Shouldn't we at least try to figure out who we're dealing with?" asks Darcy. "It must be someone recent. We need to get to the bottom of this."

"Based on what information? I'm a PI, not a magician," says Genevieve wryly.

"I'll do what I can on the tech side," Borzu says. "But this was so low-budget, he probably got five clicks, if we're being generous. I only found it because of the alerts I set up."

"Even if it gets a hundred listens," I say, "we're talking about a teeny, tiny tide pool. With the way he was raging, he didn't exactly sound credible."

"What is it with guys like this?" Darcy shakes her head. "Do they throw temper tantrums anytime someone says no?"

"Probably," I say. "Remember Kaden Sineway?"

"I want to burn his name from my memory," Genevieve groans. "As if setting off fireworks outside the agency for two days straight because we dared to decline his application was going to change our minds."

"If we sued even one of these assholes, we could scare the others off. That'd tell them we have bark and bite," Darcy says.

I fight back a smile. Darcy dropped out of Duke Law School after her first year. She has just enough legal knowledge to be dangerous. We met five years ago when she was still figuring out her next steps and making ends meet as a barista at the coffee shop next door. We hit it off so well, I made the best decision of my life and asked her to join the agency.

"If we were to go after him—or any of these unhinged people—we'd draw attention to them," I remind her. "We'd amplify their message."

"It's the number-one rule online," says Borzu. "Don't feed the trolls."

"I don't want to feed them," grumbles Darcy. "I want to punch them in the balls."

But her anger's deflating—I can see it leaking from her like air from a punctured balloon.

"Fine. Maybe you're right," she finally concedes. "I guess I feel bad it's gotten this chaotic right as I'm getting ready to take my leave."

"That's still a few months away. Don't worry, these trolls will still be here when you get back," I tease. Hoping to change the subject, I ask, "How's wedding prep going? Picked out your invitations?"

"We did." Her eyes brighten. "I went for gold with a cream background. Can you believe these were on markdown? It's got a henna-inspired watermark beneath it." She pulls out her phone to show me. "Don't they look gorgeous?"

"Beautiful." As expected, given Darcy's impeccable taste.

"Darcy Jacobs, our very own Piyar success story," Borzu says.

"The perks of the job, I guess." Darcy grins.

Numerous articles speculate about the proprietary details behind the algorithm that Borzu developed for our app (which doubles as a pool of possible matches for our personalized clients). This time last year, though, there was no algorithm. It was just the four of us eating takeout and sifting through applications late into the night. It was before any of us had any idea how big our agency profile would soon become. One evening, I noticed Darcy lingering on one particular photo. Dark, inscrutable eyes. A well-chiseled jaw. Samir Bakshi.

"Can I make a profile?" She nodded to the picture. "He's cute. And I read his form. Seems like maybe we'd be a good fit."

I'd hesitated at first. Khala has strict rules about the matchmaking we do. Top among them is we never match people we're close to because it's hard to be objective. Except we weren't matching Darcy here, were we? She'd plucked his photo out herself. She was still smarting over her recent breakup with Andrei, a verified jerk who didn't seem to get that their relationship was over until she'd slapped him with a restraining order. Why couldn't she benefit from the services we provided? It turned out Darcy's instincts were right about Samir. They *were* a good fit. They dated for only a handful of weeks before he got down on one knee on the bridge overlooking the lake in Piedmont Park.

"I love that about desi men," she'd gushed when she flashed her rock to me. "They know how to commit."

I'd laughed at the generalization. Darcy knew very well that commitment-phobes come in all genders, sexualities, stripes, and colors. Darcy and Samir happened to fit, and luckily they'd figured it out quickly. She'd seen her share of hardships; she deserved this happily ever after.

"We should look into setting up a match profile for *you*, Genevieve," Borzu teases her.

"No thanks. Not interested in getting high on our own supply," Genevieve retorts. "It's like my dad always said: Boundaries are your friend."

"Well, *Nura* should definitely give it a go," says Darcy.

"Not this again."

"I don't understand how you have the best resources at your fingertips—that you *invented*—and you don't use them."

Darcy shoots me a look and I shoot one right back at her. Why does everyone see my single status as something to fix? I'm in the business of relationships. I don't have the time nor the inclination to go deeper down that rabbit hole myself. It's not like I've never been on a date. I gave it a go in my twenties, but dating is exhausting. Not to mention the time suck it involves. And for what? Even if I *did* give it an honest go, none of them would match up to Azar. Which is just as well. The more people you love, the more you risk breaking your heart.

Darcy follows me into my office. It's got all the outer appearances of cool contemporary with my glass desk, oversized iMac, and Herman Miller office chair. Customized floating shelves line the back wall with framed portraits of some of our successful matches through the years, but I have my personal comforts tucked away here too, like the stash of chocolate in the drawer to my left and my well-worn flip-flops from Target hidden out of sight beneath my desk to slip on between client meetings. I settle into my chair and switch out of my Louboutin heels as Darcy ticks off the day's agenda on her iPad.

"Water guy's coming in ten. We have Beenish this morning—the pastry order should be here any second now. I got the pistachio scones she likes. Her plane got in from Raleigh about ten minutes ago."

"Beenish Adeel . . . there she is." I pull out her dedicated notebook from my filing cabinet. I'd waffled on whether to take her on. She'd seemed stuck on her on-again, off-again ex for nearly a decade, but Khala had helped her parents find love many moons ago, and she was so sweet I decided to take a chance.

"The traffic looks clear, so I'm guessing she'll be arriving in about thirty minutes for her intake. Last I checked, she hasn't spoken to that abusive jerk of an ex in weeks, but she seemed a bit emotional when I scheduled her appointment. You might want to follow up on that, to see where she's at."

"Got it." I jot down a quick note in my spiral notebook.

"I know what you're going to say to the next item, but we got another interview request from *The New York Times*. They want to do a puff piece for their Lifestyle section."

"And that's a hard no, again."

"It's a profile with *The New York Times,* Nura! I'm sure your aunt wouldn't mind?"

I can't pretend it isn't tempting. Khala's always had a strict rule about not talking to the press, but a lot *has* changed at the agency since she stepped down. I've hired my team. Launched the Piyar app—a way to pay it forward and match those who may not be able to afford the far more selective and pricey personalized services we offer. Khala's never complained. She even gave me the financial infusions I needed to get the app off the ground. But a profile feels like rubbing her face in how much things have changed.

"I think the mystery keeps people hooked," I tell Darcy. "Besides, it's not like the agency is wanting for attention lately."

"So it's a no to the Bravo reality show inquiry too, then?" she teases. "I bet they'd pay a pretty penny to follow us around."

"A regretful pass."

"Next up." She checks her tablet. "I need to update you on Kaur."

"Uh-oh. That doesn't sound good."

"She's left four messages as of this morning. Wants to know when her intake interview will be."

"We only took her off the wait list three days ago!" Not that incessant calls or texts are unusual. People who possess the kind of bank accounts we deal with aren't used to waiting.

"I called her back this morning and asked her to be patient," Darcy says. "But, well, while we were chatting, she mentioned income brackets."

I fold my arms. "Let me guess. She thinks someone from

'lesser means' won't understand her lifestyle. It's a matter of compatibility. She's not snooty or anything."

"It's like they all passed around the same bad script, isn't it?"

"Send her the standard rejection template."

"You sure?" Darcy hesitates. "It was a crass thing to say, but we could go over the rules again? She seemed nice."

"She should have read the paperwork more carefully. My aunt spelled it all out in there for a reason."

The requirements for our personalized services are simple: trust the process (we don't just help you find the one, we help *you* become the one by getting your life on track so you're in a healthy place to take on a healthy relationship); be transparent during the vetting phase, warts and all; and understand that while we help the elite, we are *not* elitist. Any violation ends our agreement. I know Darcy thinks I could ease up a little, but Khala's standards have never steered us wrong.

"Got it. I'll shoot over the decline letter." Darcy jots down a note. "And last but not least." She hands me a manila folder. "My temporary replacements."

"Take that as far away from me as possible."

"Nura . . ."

"I'm telling you, we can manage on our own for a couple of months."

"You *need* the help."

I know I'm acting like the proverbial ostrich sticking her head in the sand, but I can't help but pout about the idea of several months without Darcy's help and company. After all these years working together, she's more than just my assistant—she's my friend.

"It's not a long list. November will be here before you know it." She sets it on my desk. "It would be ideal if you found someone while I'm still here so I can show them the ropes.

That inbox won't tame itself when I'm gone. It's been bonkers lately."

There's a chime from the front door.

"That's the water guy," she says. "Be right back."

I turn on my computer. My phone buzzes. It's Azar.

AZAR: What time is your birthday dinner?
ME: 6:00pm. Not Desi Standard Time.
AZAR: Shift ends at 6:00 :-/. Will try to slip out early.
ME: Don't leave me hanging! I need you there!
AZAR: (. . .)
ME: And yes, I ended up getting myself the Moccamaster coffee maker, so you'll have to think of something else for my birthday gift, which you should have started planning earlier considering it's in four days.

The phone buzzes again. An incoming call this time. Did I *really* guess his birthday gift for the third year in a row? But when I look at who's calling, my smile fades. It's not Azar.

It's Basit Latif.

He's facetiming me. Because of course he is. I consider sending it to voicemail, but he'll only call again. And again. State senators who also happen to own a billion-dollar car part manufacturing business aren't used to taking no for an answer.

I straighten my collar and accept the call. Today I'll get through to him. He'll have to accept that some things don't work out the way wealthy men want them to.

"Hello, Mr. Latif."

A man with graying hair parted to the side and a thin goatee wrapped around his lips gazes back at me. He's in his office. A concrete parking lot stretches into the distance through the window behind him.

"At last she answers."

His voice is smooth like silk—but I see the contempt lingering behind his eyes. I meet his gaze coolly. Men like him will never see me sweat. Discreetly, I slide my finger over my mouse, wake up my computer, and hit record. You never know.

"How can I help you, Mr. Latif?" I ask.

"You know exactly how you can help me. I *came* to you for help. Filled out your inane paperwork and signed all the releases. What did I get instead?"

"As I explained during our last call," I tell him, "our protocol is to work with the person *seeking* a match directly—"

"Fuck the protocol!"

His mouth presses into a thin line. He's half a continent away in Detroit, and I'm accustomed to toxic masculinity by now, but a shiver runs through me all the same. He looks as though he wishes he could strike a hand through the screen.

"Since when did helping your own child find a partner become taboo? I was matched with my own wife thanks to the help of my parents. They were the sound voices of reason guiding me toward the proper path. Sounds like someone has forgotten their ancestral roots."

My cheeks warm. "I understand how things were done, Mr. Latif, but that's not how I run my business. And not wanting to go behind a child's back to broker their marriage is not betraying my heritage. If you *and* your son wanted to reach out together to discuss options, that would be one thing. Most people do and—"

"Do you not hear me?" His fist slams on the table. "Farhan isn't ready."

"If he's not ready to discuss his own marriage, then he isn't ready for our services."

"Is this about money?" He pauses. "I'll double your asking rate."

I grip the edge of my seat. He's insulting me. And it's working.

"We are not the right agency for you, Mr. Latif. As a courtesy, our admin will reverse your application fees. I'm sorry it didn't work out."

"You're sorry?" An ugly smile spreads across his face.

My stomach twists. *Here we go.*

"Do you have any idea who I am?" He leans forward. "I could ruin you with a couple of phone calls. A few well-placed anonymously sourced stories about misconduct, and you're done."

"Any such story would be false."

"It won't matter. Ruined reputations don't repair as easily as you might think. Another nugget of cultural wisdom you probably haven't learned. Not yet, at least."

He leans back now, arms crossed. Like a self-satisfied fox from a Brothers Grimm tale. I take a deep breath. People imagine my job is all about attending lavish weddings, wearing saris and bangles, and partaking in private yoga sessions with a client while we hash out their ideal match. They don't see the moments like these, where you smile and stay calm instead of telling the other person what you really think about them. Luckily, I have a long-established protocol to keep me grounded.

"Mr. Latif, slandering me and my business will only end up hurting you."

"Sounds like you need some lessons on what slander is," he replies. "It's—"

"Spreading false information?" I tilt my head. "Knowingly?

Maliciously? I have this entire conversation recorded. One click and I could post this to social media—"

"You're recording me?" he bellows.

"You consented to it in the paperwork you signed. Honestly, I think your constituents would be interested to hear about our chat. If you call again, I'll make sure they do."

The vein throbbing at his temple is the only indication my screen hasn't frozen. He's there. Quietly seething. But he gets it now.

"Glad we could talk this all out, Mr. Latif. I have another appointment to run to." Then, with more steel in my voice: "You'd be well advised not to reach out again."

I end the call. He won't call back. They never do once they realize what they'll lose.

"Knock knock." Darcy enters. She sets a steaming mug of coffee on my desk. Taking in my expression, she frowns. "What happened?"

"Was Basit Latif one of the people we declined this morning?"

"I think so." She checks her tablet. "Yep. There he is. I emailed him along with five others. Why? Did he take it poorly?"

"He called me just now and tried to convince me to change my mind. Offered to double my rate, and when that didn't work, he tried to threaten me." I cradle my palms around the warm mug. "Some people think money can buy them anything, and anyone."

"Gross."

The front bell buzzes.

"That's gotta be Beenish." Darcy eyes me. "Do you need a minute?"

I shake my head. "Nah. Men like him are just the cost of

doing business. Besides, distraction will do me good. Why don't you get her settled in the conference room? I'll be there in a second."

She rests a hand against the doorframe. "Want a real distraction? You and I are overdue for a girls' night. How about some good old-fashioned axe-throwing sometime soon?"

Axe-throwing? I make a face, and Darcy laughs.

"Don't knock it till you've tried it! There's a place near me having a two-for-one special. You know I'll keep pestering you until you eventually say yes. It's my favorite way to get the feels out."

"Let's do it." I smile at her. "Thanks, Darcy."

"And hey, don't sweat that jackass," she says. "Helicopter parents gonna helicopter, right?"

Darcy's right. People like Basit arrange their children's entire lives from the moment they schedule their C-sectioned arrival into this world. The right nanny. The right preschool. Sidestepping other applicants with a healthy donation to a private school of their choice all the way to Harvard. This is what the wealthy do. They pay their way to the life they want. My help finding their child the perfect partner is one more thing they think they can buy. Rising, my silver bracelets clink against my arm as I switch back into my heels, gather my notebook and coffee mug, and head toward the conference room. The Basit Latifs of the world don't get to linger in my head. I won't give them the satisfaction.

THREE

I step out of the car and take in Khala's house. I'm in and out each week for Friday dinner—but with Azar coming over tonight, I linger in her cobblestone driveway, seeing the two-story stucco home with Spanish tiles through his eyes. Over-grown ivy tangles around the brick mailbox. Clumps of clovers and daisies litter the once perfectly mowed lawn. When did the shrubs lining the windows dry up? Khala had mentioned her landscaper retired last fall, but it didn't occur to me that no one had replaced him.

I glance at Azar's immaculate home across the street, a trail of freshly planted petunias lining his walkway—his *old* walkway, I correct myself. His parents have long since retired to Pakistan. How did Khala let it get this bad? And even if it had slipped her mind, what about Nina? *Nina has her hands full,* I remind my-self. *She's going through a lot.* But she moved in to take care of Khala, so couldn't she actually take care of things? I make a mental note to call around for lawn service quotes tomorrow.

The house smells like my aunt's favorite lavender-scented candles when I step inside. I set my purse on the ottoman in the foyer. At least the interior of the home hasn't gone to shit quite yet—it still looks exactly like it did when I was growing up. The walls are gray and there are framed art pieces by Jamali that Khala purchased at various auctions through the years. Handwoven Persian rugs decorate the dark hardwood floors in every room.

I hear the pitter-patter of small feet. My cousin Nina's four-year-old daughter, Lilah, emerges from around the corner. She's wearing a tiny apron tied at her waist, and wraps her arms around my leg.

"Happy birthday to you, happy birthday to you, happy birthdaaaaay, Auntie Nura, happy birthday to you!"

"Wonderful rendition!" Lilah's springy curls tickle my face when I give her a kiss.

"Me and Mama are making you a cake, but it was *my* idea."

"It smells delicious!"

A door creaks down the hall and Khala emerges from around the corner. She's wearing a turquoise shalwar kameez. Her silvery-gray hair is swept up. She looks as graceful as ever.

"Happy thirty-two, beta." She gives me a peck on the cheek. "I had not heard from you in a few days. I was beginning to worry."

My aunt's newest pastime: worrying about me. "Sorry, Khala. Didn't you get my texts?"

"I need to hear your voice to know all is well. How is everything at work?"

I tell her about the wedding last weekend. Saba and Abid's nuptials. Tidbits about some of our latest clients.

"You are balancing so many different things." She pats my arm. "Perhaps it's time to scale back the personalized matchmaking a bit? That app of yours is enough to keep a team of fifty on their toes."

"We *do* have a remote team of nearly fifty people who handle the app side of things," I remind her.

"Nevertheless, the ultimate responsibility falls to you."

"Khala—"

"It is merely a suggestion," she says gently. "Life is short. Look at me—health can turn on a dime, can't it? You deserve girlfriends and brunch. Vacations. I can't help but worry."

A stonelike sensation lodges in my stomach. Not this again. How casually she tells me to scale back what we've worked so hard to grow. The part of the work which makes us . . . well, *us*. It's not supposed to be like this.

I can still smell the antibacterial hand wash in the hospital room I'd raced into after her first stroke. I'd had to summon all my professional skills to stay calm. My once formidable khala with her designer shalwar kameez and gold bangles, diminished to a small frame in a thin cotton gown beneath starched sheets. It was like watching a superhero shed their costume.

"She'll be all right," the doctor had said. "As far as strokes go, this one was minor."

But the minor strokes continued over the next few weeks and months without rhyme or reason. Then came the diagnosis: stage three vascular dementia. Suddenly, I was thrust from being her partner at the agency to the only one in charge.

But instead of telling me she's proud of me, instead of being relieved that I'm carrying on the work that connects us from Atlanta to the flatlands of Punjab where the work began, she thinks I should stop. She means well. I know she does. But each time she makes suggestions like these, they land like a punch. My cousin Nina is to blame. I'm sure of it. All these little mentions of pulling back from our work began soon after she moved in.

"How is my dear Gertie doing?" Khala asks.

"Ridiculous as always." Thankful for the change in conversation, I pull out my phone and swipe through the photos of

Khala's senior Siberian forest cat, who's taken up residence with me since Nina arrived. Nina's allergic to cats. She'd probably say she's allergic to me as well, but I'm not about to be shaken out of Khala's life quite so easily.

"Gertie's getting the finest treatment any feline has ever received," I assure her. I wasn't exactly in the market for a pet, but Gertie's family, and the sweetest cat to boot.

"I would not have trusted her with anyone else." She glances at the front door. "Is Azar still joining us for dinner? It has been ages since I last saw him."

"He's running a little late, but of course he's coming. He's my closest friend."

"More like one of your *only* friends," Khala corrects me.

I'd protest this, but she's right. She knows better than anyone that this job requires complete devotion—outside of office hours, there's really only space for Azar. It's not as though *her* calendar was stacked with casual brunch dates while I was growing up. The only vacations we ever took had doubled as work trips—mornings watching cartoons with room service in a plush hotel room in cities like New York, Chicago, even Tokyo once, while Khala headed to intake meetings, after which we'd hit up a local zoo or museum. I can't get too worked up, though. She remembered my birthday. We've had an entire conversation without a single memory slip. I'm grateful for good days. There have been more and more of them lately. Maybe things *are* getting better.

"Can you help me with the crystal?" she asks. "I can't reach the glasses in the top cabinet in the kitchen and I want to make sure the dining table is all set up before Azar arrives."

"Am I already being put to work? Isn't this *my* birthday celebration?" I tease.

"I thought you loved helping your khala?" She winks.

As I entered the open and airy kitchen, the happy feeling fades when I see Nina.

"You're late," she says.

She's at the kitchen island in front of opened bags of flour and sugar. Her dark hair is newly pixie-short. Her slender shoulders are squared back, her jaw set firm. She looks so much like Khala that sometimes if I glance at her absentmind-edly, I feel a jolt to my system like I've traveled back in time. Like I'm looking at my aunt when I first entered her life at the age of seven. They have the same curved nose. The same doe-like brown eyes. If only she *acted* like my khala in any way. Lilah climbs onto the stool next to her mother.

"Work got busy," I tell Nina. "And Friday traffic was a monster."

"A monster?" Lilah's eyes widen.

"Yep. A ginormous snake that stretches for miles and miles!"

Lilah squeals. Nina acts like I haven't spoken at all. She opens a cabinet and pulls out cocoa powder. Grabs the tea-spoons from the drawer by the sink. She's been here four months at this point, but it still surprises me when I see her riffling through the kitchen. Like it's her house or something. *It is her house,* I remind myself. *This is her mother's home.*

"Are you all caught up with client intakes?" Khala asks. "The last time we spoke, you had mentioned quite the surge in ap-plications."

"Wedding season is definitely causing a bigger spike than usual. I'm racing to catch up," I tell her. "I had five back-to-back appointments today."

"Someone needs to get better with those boundaries," Nina mutters under her breath.

She's baiting me. She knows there are no weekends or holi-days in a job like mine. A job that pays the mortgage for this house, the water and electricity bills, and sends Lilah to Bishop Academy for a cool $2,300 a month. I don't see her complaining about any of that, do I?

Nina is currently on an "indefinite break" from her job as a curator at the Portland Museum of Modern Art to take care of Khala. A job she didn't need to leave, as I'd told her numerous times. Before she unceremoniously arrived, I'd started moving Khala's things over to my place. Some of her agency-related boxes stuffed with old notebooks, confidential documents, and the dated tape recorder she used to dictate notes are still wedged in my hallway closet. Then Nina stepped in and that was that. Now she's the one with the final say. She chooses the doctors. Decides which medicine is preferable and which physical therapist is best. I've learned it does not matter that this woman raised us both. At the end of the day, Nina is the daughter. I'm just the niece.

I grab the dusty crystal glasses from the top shelf of the cabinet. Flipping on the faucet, I rinse each one before patting them dry. *Why is Nina even bothering to make me a cake, anyway?* Her feelings about me are written all over her face. I tuck a strand of dark hair behind my ear. Even if she eggs me on, I'm not going to snipe back. We've had enough skirmishes to last a lifetime.

"Not *those* glasses, Billi. I meant the gold-rimmed ones behind them." Khala lifts and examines one of the drying stems.

Billi. My chest tightens at the nickname. My mother's nickname. My mother, who has been dead for over twenty years. Nina stops mixing the cake. Lilah looks up from her perch.

"I—I'm not Billi," I manage to say.

"Of course, *Bilqis*," she replies, smiling. "You are far too old for silly nicknames, aren't you? But no matter how old you get, you remain my little sister. Don't you forget it."

"Well—"

Before I can figure out what to say next, Khala gasps. Clasps a hand to her mouth.

"Nura. Oh, my sweet Nura." Her eyes fill with tears. "I am so sorry."

I rush to reassure her. Slipups happen. I try to keep my voice neutral and calm. To not show her how unmoored I suddenly feel. It's not as though she chose to forget me. Her memory lapses are minor enough—this one came and went in a matter of seconds, didn't it? But it's still a hard thing to witness. This shift in someone you love who'd once stood before you as sturdy and unshakable as a mountain, slowly coming undone.

Shakily, she sits at the kitchen table. I hand her a glass of water. She takes a sip. "Your mother is never far from my mind." Her gaze meets mine. "Look at you—you're the very image of her. On your birthdays, I think of her a bit more, I suppose. She would have been so proud of you."

I pull out the correct crystal glasses. I'm not about to contradict her, but I'm not so sure of how proud my mother would really be. I don't have as many memories as I'd like of her. Her almond-shaped eyes and oval face have faded to hazy outlines with the passage of time, so I cling to the few memories I do have, including the one conversation I can still recount word for word.

When my mother was tucking me into bed a few days after my seventh birthday, I'd asked her why we never visited Atlanta. My father had died of an aneurysm while my mother was pregnant with me. Khala and Nina were our only living relatives, and I hadn't seen them since I was two.

"Your khala and I . . . we don't see eye to eye on most things," she said, patting my arm. "It's better to keep our distance."

"Why not?" I asked.

"Honey, you're too young for all the details."

When I insisted on knowing more, she simply said, "Honey, she's so busy with her work, I doubt she would even have time for us if we visited. Her job completely consumes her. It's not healthy."

"She'd make time for us," I told her. "Can't we at least try? I want to see her. I want to see Nina."

My mother's expression softened. She leaned down and kissed my forehead.

"Let me think about it," she finally said.

Neither of us knew that in two weeks' time an atmospheric river would descend upon the Bay Area, causing her car to careen over a cliff on a wet and windy night. Suddenly, I was yanked from our one-bedroom apartment in San Francisco's Mission District and placed in a sprawling six-bedroom home set on half an acre in Atlanta, Georgia. Suddenly, Khala became my legal guardian and life as I'd known it was over. I look down at my silver bracelets. My *mother's* bracelets. Etched with flowers, they're worn with time, but they're all I have left of her.

"Mom has a two o'clock this Tuesday with the neurologist," Nina says, pulling me back to the present. "Can you take her, or maybe arrange for someone to take her? It overlaps with Lilah's pickup time."

"I can take her." Lowering my voice, I ask, "Did you ask Dr. Pang about the clinical trial at the last visit?"

"Nura, we've talked about this. She'd have to travel back and forth to New Mexico for years, and she might be in the placebo group for all we know. Mom and I discussed it, and she agrees it's too much for her."

"It's not a surefire cure, but isn't it worth trying everything we can?"

"She's getting older, Nura. That's how it is. You can't fix her."

"So that's it? We give up?"

"Nura, please. I don't want to relitigate this."

The oven beeps, preheated and ready, warming up the kitchen. Nina turns back to her mixing bowl. I jot Tuesday's appointment into my work calendar. I'm glad I'll be the one taking her to the doctor next. I'll see what Dr. Pang thinks. If he agrees with Nina, I'll get a second opinion. A third. There's got to be a way to help Khala get better. She's my aunt in name, but in all practical senses, she's my mother. I can't lose her.

I watch Nina pour the batter into the baking pan. Nina and I were both raised by the same woman. She should be more sister than cousin—instead, she feels like neither. Maybe that's what happens when you're twelve years apart. By the time I arrived, she was at Stanford, as geographically distant as she possibly could get, visiting for the occasional Thanksgiving holiday. I once thought her coolness toward me was because I'd taken on the family business instead of her. But she turned it down long before I entered the picture. She hated how all-consuming the work was. She derided it as archaic. She'd adamantly told Khala she wanted no part of it. Still, the only explanation for the way her eyes flash toward me when she thinks I'm not looking is jealousy.

The doorbell rings. When I open it, Azar is standing at the doorstep holding flowers. Seeing him, I feel my jaw unclench.

"Happy birthday." He kisses my cheek.

"Azar! Beta!" Khala embraces him.

Even Nina cracks a smile when Azar retrieves a vase from beneath the sink for the flowers. He pulls a miniature stuffed Pikachu from his pocket and presents it to Lilah for her collection.

Dinner, a few hours later, is lovely as usual. Khala ordered a veritable feast: Haleem with sliced ginger and serrano peppers. Mouth-watering goat biryani. Pan-fried shami kebabs. Later that evening, when I blow out the candles on the red velvet cake—which, I grudgingly admit, tastes moist and delicious— I start to relax.

Lilah hands me a card. Stick figures of the two of us and an enormous pink heart that takes up the entire page. Nina surprises me with a cream wristlet wallet with red trim. Khala hands me a wrapped box, which I assume is a necklace or earrings—her favorite go-to gifts—but tonight's gift isn't jewelry.

"A smartwatch?" I hold up the smooth white box.

"I bought one for myself a few months earlier—you really need one with how busy work is. Frankly, I am shocked you don't have one already."

Nina scoffs. That's exactly what I need, she says without saying. More ways to be connected to my work. She doesn't get it. Matchmaking isn't just a job for me; it's a calling. A part of who I am.

When I look at the cake she went to great effort to bake, I could almost convince myself she's trying to bridge the gap between us, but then the scoff and headshake—we are no closer to any meaningful connection at all.

"The watch buzzes when someone rings you, so no more missing my phone calls," Khala says. "We can also keep track of one another's steps. I hit ten thousand even on a bad day."

"Why does this sound more like a gift for you?" I tease her. "I love it, thank you."

When I open Azar's envelope, I gasp. It's a four-night stay at a Sofitel resort in Cartagena, Colombia.

"You've been wanting to go since college," he says before I can speak. "Plane tickets included, of course, but I figured we'd get to that once you've picked your dates."

"Azar . . . this is too much."

"You'd already gotten yourself a Moccamaster, so what was I supposed to do?"

"I can't go!"

"Why not?"

"Because . . ." I sputter. "It's . . . it's wedding season."

"Wedding season will pass," he says. "When's the last time you've been on vacation?"

"When was Italy?"

"Italy was three years ago, Nur. You're overdue."

Three years ago? I count back. He's right. It was right around the time he moved back. After we'd cleared up our years-long misunderstanding. Before Khala's most recent stroke. Before my life became quite this hectic.

"You're going to come with me to this one too?"

"Well, duh."

"What a thoughtful gift, Azar," says Khala. "I was just telling Nura she needs to take some time off and travel. Do something fun."

Azar could have plucked me a bouquet of dandelions from the lawn, and Khala would have declared it the perfect gift. Still—I look at the gift card—this *was* thoughtful, and I could definitely use a vacation. And uninterrupted one-on-one time with Azar—what's not to love about that?

My mouth is full of cake when Nina asks Azar, "Are you still her decoy?"

"Azar is her plus-one," Khala corrects her.

"There's steak next weekend," he says. "Oyster bar too."

"You should let Nura get started on matching you, Azar," Khala tells him. "Isn't it about time you found the one?"

My heart does an involuntary flip, but I go along with it. "Say the word. I'll even give you a hefty discount."

Azar laughs. Color rises up his cheeks. It's not as though I really would have. He knows we don't match the people we're close to, and he would never have actually taken me up on the offer, anyway. Serial dater Azar is too much of a ladies' man to settle down.

"Not everyone wants their lives engineered for them, Nura," says Nina.

I exhale. Nina can't let a visit go by without getting a dig in, can she? Before I can say anything, a hand glides over mine under the table. Azar's not looking at me, but he squeezes gently. *Let it go,* he's saying. *It's not worth it.*

I squeeze back. He's right. I'm here because of Khala. Because traditions matter to her, and so they matter to me. There's no point in getting into a slugfest with Nina.

"Can I work at the agency too, Auntie Nura?" Lilah asks.

Nostalgia tugs at my heartstrings. I'd asked my khala about joining the agency when I was still in grade school. I was mesmerized by her. Her perfectly polished nails. Her hair done just so. In the early days, as I navigated my grief, she let me follow her everywhere—her shadow, she'd teasingly call me. She didn't usher me out of the room when I eavesdropped on her conversations in the home office. The kids at school would talk about Disney movies, but what interest could they hold for me when I was living with a real-life fairy godmother? Time and again I'd see clients go from downtrodden and desolate to exchanging vows with their perfect partner a year later. When I'd asked to help, she'd gently tried to steer me away. She knew my mother hadn't approved and she was firm on honoring her wishes for me. *Go to college,* she'd told me. *Find your passion.* Except this *was* my passion. Eventually I wore her down. She saw that I wasn't only good at the work, I was born for it. Slowly she let me answer calls and transcribe notes. Over time, I helped her expand the business. We went from an exclusively desi clientele to serving a diverse and inclusive group of people. I still honored my mother's wishes and went to college. I gave it my all. Ran cross-country for Emory. Double-majored in psychology and business, and graduated with honors. Then I joined the agency and never looked back.

Before I can reply to Lilah, Nina sets her drink roughly on the table. "Not a chance, kiddo. You are going to have a balanced life, and you will definitely *not* be carrying on old-fashioned traditions that should have died out long ago."

Khala's expression falls.

"What is with you?" My voice rises, and even Azar's hand pressed against mine can't quell my frustration. "We've evolved with the times just like everyone else. You wouldn't know that, though, because you don't know anything about what we do."

She cocks her head and looks at her mother.

"Nura's right. I have no clue how any of this works, do I? Maybe you could enlighten me sometime about the godsend that is Piyar, the place where true love is guaranteed?" she says mockingly.

Khala fixes her gaze on her half-eaten cake slice. Her lower lip trembles. Anger rumbles through my core. Nina *is* jealous, isn't she? I lean forward to give her a piece of my mind. To let her know that if she looked down so deeply on us, she could pack up and be gone and leave us be. Just because her life hasn't worked out like she imagined doesn't mean she can take potshots at the one her mother and I have worked so hard to build. But from the corner of my eye, I spot Lilah. Her shoulders are hunched up to her ears. Her eyes water. My anger evaporates like steam.

"Sweetie," I begin.

"You won't believe what happened today," Azar interrupts.

He looks directly at Lilah. "Did I tell you about the patient who came in this morning because he swallowed twenty-five pennies?"

Lilah sniffles. "Not for real?"

"Completely for real."

He mimes the steps he took to help the improbably hapless patient. A metal detector. A fishing rod. Magnets. His antics do the trick. Soon, Lilah is howling with laughter.

I lift my fork. Only then do I realize my hand is trembling. But it wasn't because of our argument. And while upsetting Lilah disturbs me greatly, that wasn't it either.

It's the look.

The one Nina gave to my aunt. The wordless exchange that passed between them. The quiver of Khala's lower lip. The expression that crossed her face for the briefest of moments: fear.

FOUR

It's half past ten by the time I arrive at the agency on Monday morning. Genevieve's at her desk, typing. Her ginger hair is bunched up in a topknot, her brows furrowed in concentration. Borzu's reclined in his gaming chair, AirPods in his ears, wearing a pink polo shirt and sporting matching pink hair.

The front door chimes. Darcy walks in with a tray of coffees. Her four-inch stilettos click against the marble floor.

"Perfect timing," I tell her.

"Per usual." She grins, setting the tray on the counter. "How was the follow-up with Yoga Lady? Did you get on the mat again?"

"It was core yoga today." I groan. "Why is everyone multitasking lately? Surely she should be able to squeeze in a meeting without requiring me to don athleisure?"

"You got a two-for-one! A client meeting *and* core strengthening."

"Except I can't reach my drink now." I gingerly edge my fingers toward the steaming cup. "I had no idea downward dog would be part of the business."

"Everything can be part of the business." Darcy nudges the drink toward my grateful grasp. "And since when do you get sore doing yoga? You dragged me to that local studio for nearly half a year!"

"I lost the motivation once you moved in with Samir." I take a sip of the warm beverage. The foam from the latte tickles my tongue. "Why does he have to live all the way across town?"

"Aw, I'm sorry. I got priced out anyway after they raised their rates."

"It's fine. I barely have time to squeeze my run in these days, let alone a one-hour yoga session at the studio."

The front door chimes again. When I see who it is, I frown. Beenish? She's wearing oversized sunglasses and clutching a beat-up Prada bag. She'd flown in last week for her intake and to sign all the paperwork. Darcy sent her the list of therapist and life coach referrals on Tuesday. What is she doing here now?

"Beenish." Darcy startles. She moves toward her desk to greet her. "I didn't realize you had a meeting today."

"I don't." She looks at me. "I really need to talk to you, Nura. Figured I'd trek over."

From Raleigh?

Darcy shoots me a concerned look, then turns to Beenish. "I need to check Nura's schedule to see if she has time right this—"

"Oh God. I just barged right in." Beenish bites her lower lip. "I didn't even stop to think that you might be busy. I can go. I'll—I'll leave."

"You didn't barge in," I tell her. "Why don't you come on back? I want to know what's going on."

Once the door to my office shuts, Beenish collapses into the chair across from me. When she pulls off her sunglasses, her eyes are puffy from crying. I ping the button on my desk. In thirty seconds, Darcy's at the door with a glass of mint water.

Beenish takes a few sips. When she sets the drink on the table, her shirtsleeve shifts, revealing a bruise the size and color of an autumn maple leaf along her wrist. She sees my stricken expression and quickly folds her arms.

"He didn't mean to do it."

They never do. I shift my face to neutral. Nod encouragingly for her to continue.

"I thought we were over. I swear." She takes another sip of water and steadies herself. "Austin called me last night and said he wanted to come by and talk. He wanted closure. You should have seen his face. He was completely devastated. He was crying, Nura. He begged me to forgive him and promised he'd do better. He looked like he really meant it—it was like a lightbulb finally went off in his head. Then after we ordered takeout and were settling in for the evening, he lost it because I wasn't in the mood to watch basketball."

"Is this typical? For him to pick fights over small things?"

I keep my voice gentle. Curious. Though it's not easy. What I want to do is grab her by the hand and tell her she can't let him keep doing this to her. That she needs to kick him to the curb and not look back. Because that bruise on her wrist won't be the last mark he leaves. There will always be another apology. Another excuse. Another angry explosion. With my years of experience, I know I can't say any of that, though. Beenish has to reach this conclusion for herself. She has to see for herself—and believe—that there is life after Austin.

"Oh yeah. Freaking out about the littlest things is, like, his playbook." She takes the tissue I hold out for her. "Austin's the crowned king of petty, but it's like his fuse is getting shorter and shorter these days."

"Was it during the argument that he hurt you?"

"He didn't mean to," she rushes to correct me. "He just grabbed me harder than he realized."

"Beenish, if it was hard enough to leave a bruise . . ."

"I know. You're right." She dabs at her eyes with a tissue. "I gave him an ultimatum. I told him he had to go to anger management or we were done. When I woke up this morning, he was gone. No note. No text. So I guess I have my answer."

"That's another pattern of his, isn't it?" I ask. "He picks a fight, gets physical with you, then storms off, only to come back a few days or weeks later with apologies?"

"It's not going to work out with us. I get it. I know that in my brain." Her lower lip quivers. "I just love him so much. . . . Yes, he's got his flaws, but I can't resist him. It's been that way since we met in freshman-year bio. It's like . . . there's a magnetic pull between us, drawing me to him. I know *soulmates* can be a corny term, but as imperfect as he is, that's what he feels like to me."

There's a special kind of mythmaking people do when it comes to love. This belief that if we're continually drawn to someone, it's because we're meant to be. In my experience, the reality isn't all that deep. It's simply that the other person has become a habit. Like snacks with a movie. Smoking. Biting your nails. Just as hardwired and just as simple—or not—to quit.

"I get it, Beenish," I tell her. "Really, I do. You have history together. Which means even his bad traits, they're familiar, right? There's something comforting about knowing someone that deeply. But that means you also know this cycle won't end. Reaching out to us was a brave first step. It means deep down, you know you want to move on. You wouldn't have gone through the interviews and the intake and the vetting process if you didn't believe you could find happiness with someone else. From everything you've told me, Austin sounds like a bad habit you need to kick once and for all."

"He's more than a habit. He's an addiction."

"Did you end up talking to any of the therapists on the referral list Darcy sent you?"

She shakes her head. "I've seen a million therapists at this point."

"These ones are truly the best of the best, though," I tell her. "I really think Dr. Higdon might be a great fit. He's more than a therapist, he's like a superhero. Give it a few sessions? The acupuncturist I suggested is also great for stress relief, and not too far from your home. Invest in yourself, Beenish. Give this whole thing a real chance. It's critical to let go of the past to create the better future that you deserve."

"I think what'll really help me move on is *actually* moving on, you know?" She sniffles. "There's an Austin-sized hole in my life now. That's how he keeps getting back in. If I met someone new, I'd finally know it in my heart that we're history. When can you start matching me up?"

"Soon," I promise. "But we need to close certain doors before we can see which ones to open. Austin is a pretty big door we need to make sure is properly shut."

"It's closed now." She traces a hand over her bruised wrist. "I'm going to block his number. I'm serious."

"Beenish—"

"Please?" Her voice cracks. "My mom said your aunt went straight to matching for her. There was no wellness aspect to any of it back then."

I take in her tear-filled expression. Beenish is certainly not the first person to walk through our doors begging us to introduce them to their rebound relationship. The end of any relationship is hard, even if the end was long overdue. But even if Khala didn't have an official self-care aspect to the matchmaking agency when she was in charge, she never set people up if they weren't ready. Beenish's parents were in the right head- and life-space for their happily ever after. But I'm not here to chide Beenish.

"You swore you were done with Austin weeks ago," I remind her. "That's okay! Backsliding happens. We want you to start whatever new relationship you embark on without the baggage of the past, though. A clean slate. I know this is difficult, Bee- nish. Really, I do. Please trust the process. You're in the midst of the toughest part right now, but it *will* get easier."

"Maybe you're right," she says. "It's just . . . it's a lot."

I soothe her. I assure her the effort spent investing in herself will be well worth it. That when the time comes, we will do everything in our power to help her find the exact right match she deserves. When she leaves, I look at the clock with a start. Forty-five minutes passed in the blink of an eye. This is the part of the job that brings me the most personal satisfaction. The part of the job that truly centers me. Helping people like Beenish is why I do what I do.

Once Beenish leaves, Darcy hurries inside.

"I can't believe she showed up unannounced like that," Darcy says. "I'll have a chat with her. This sets a horrible prec- edent."

"She was really hurting. I think we made some good prog- ress today. How's the rest of my day looking?"

"Lighter than usual." She scrolls her tablet. "You've got a cli- ent call at noon, and Genevieve told me she needs thirty min- utes this afternoon to chat with you about a few cases."

"Can you send out a calendar invite for us at four o'clock?"

"You got it. Oh—and good news! We have another matrimonial success! Sheraz proposed to Fatima. It was a basic 'on one knee at a restaurant' deal, but hey, a proposal's a proposal. She said yes."

"That was quick!" I perk up. "We should celebrate soon. You were instrumental in pairing them up. I can see if they have an open table at Meta Sushi on Friday. I keep meaning to take you there—they have the best nigiri I've ever had."

"You're busy Friday night," she reminds me. "It's Avani and Dev's mehndi."

"Right." Darcy brought my sari from the cleaners this morning for the elaborate dance-filled night preceding the actual wedding day. It's pressed and hanging behind my door. Avani was a personalized client whom we found a great match for through the Piyar app database. Dev's laid-back style was a perfect complement to Avani's type A personality.

"Are you going to miss the constant check-ins from Avani's entire extended family?" Darcy winks.

"They're great, but yes, very involved." I laugh. The time between engagement and nuptials is often fraught with logistics and the myriad of emotions that can arise. While we don't plan the weddings, we're there for our clients from start to finish, whether as a listening ear, to help mediate disagreements, or to give references for whatever they might need. "I'll need to swing by the bank to grab a jewelry set sometime this week. Not sure I'll have time, but—"

"It's already in the office safe. Pale gold always looks good with pink. I figured I'd save you the trip."

"Darcy, really? I'm going to miss this level of service once you're married."

"I'm not going anywhere, silly."

"I know. But Samir's got his entire extended family in town. You'll be exhausted from the million events you'll be busy with after your big fat desi wedding." I give her my best pout. "Samir isn't all that great, is he?"

"He's even better."

Darcy in love. I smile. "After everything you went through with Andrei, I'm so glad you found someone as fantastic as Samir."

"I wouldn't wish Andrei on anyone." She shudders. "But I guess sometimes you have to taste the bitter to appreciate the sweet."

Bitter was one way to describe Andrei. They were dating back when I first met Darcy, when she was a barista at the coffee shop next door. I remember how he'd skulk about by her car after closing, arms crossed, while Darcy and I finished up our conversations. He didn't take their breakup too well, either. Refused to take no for an answer. He began leaving threatening voice messages on her cell and, eventually, at the agency, which turned out to be a blessing in disguise because it got Darcy a restraining order against him once and for all. I'd never understood what she saw in him in the first place, but I guess love can blur the rough edges off of anyone.

"How's wedding planning going?" I ask her. "November will be here before you know it."

"We're tasting cakes this evening. Even though I've already decided which one we're going to choose. I'm getting the—"

"Three-layer chocolate mousse from Ponce Café," we finish together.

"They're the best priced, too, but when else do you have an excuse to hit up all the best dessert spots?" She settles down on the chair across from me.

"You might be the only person I know who can make wedding planning look fun."

At this, her smile fades. "Cake tasting will be fun, but the rest of it, not so much. Weddings are expensive, even when you're trying to go budget. Samir's been great about covering most of it. He knows how much having a proper wedding means to me, but he just survived a round of layoffs at work, so he's being a bit more cautious than he'd otherwise have been."

"Oh, Darcy—"

"It's fine." She shrugs. "I guess I'd been hoping Samir's parents would have come around by now and offered to pitch in, but no dice. Not like *I* have parents to turn to for help."

Poor Darcy. She didn't have a stable home growing up, but despite her difficult circumstances, she was determined to make something of herself. She worked hard all through high school only to discover, while applying for college, that her mother had stolen her identity and run up tens of thousands of dollars in credit card charges in her name. Even a Zen master would have a hard time moving past a betrayal like that. Thanks to her mother, Darcy had to juggle three different jobs in college and take out predatory loans just to make it through. My mother died when I was young, but at least I know she loved me dearly and had looked out for me. And when I became motherless, Khala was there for me—she had been my soft place to land. Darcy had no safety net. She'd had to make one for herself.

"Have you heard from your mother recently?" I ask her.

"She called me a few months ago to catch up, and then, of course, she just happened to mention that she needed to borrow money." She rolls her eyes. "Like she hasn't taken enough from me? Samir insists I should consider inviting her to the wedding, but I didn't even tell her I'm engaged. She'll find some angle to work me. He's afraid I'll regret it if I don't. But she's lost the right to make me feel bad about anything."

"Absolutely."

"He doesn't get it. His parents set up a Roth IRA for him

when he was five. They paid for his full ride through school, just like your aunt did for you. *My* mother saddled me with debt that will follow me to my grave. If you hadn't done me a solid and rescued me from my dead-end job, I'm not even sure where I'd be right now."

"Hey, you did me the favor," I remind her. "And look, about your mother, your wedding day is about you," I tell her firmly. "You and Samir are creating a brand-new life together and you should be able to savor your special day like you deserve. You can always make the call to invite her last-minute. There's no rush."

She dabs her eyes and smiles at me. "Hey, if we can't choose our family, at least we can choose our friends, right?"

"That's right." I reach over and pat her hand. I pay my team nearly twice the going market rate, but even then, I know Darcy's debts loom large. I make a mental note to touch base with my accountant to see if I can disburse at least part of the year-end profit share earlier this year.

"Speaking of weddings." She clears her throat and shoots me a nervous smile. "I've been wanting to talk to you about something kind of important."

"Don't tell me you're extending your sabbatical," I say half-jokingly.

"I want you to be my maid of honor."

"Darcy?" I set down my pen. "Really?"

I'm not sure why I'm surprised. We've known each other for five years—six if you include the small talk we did when she was the barista who made the best lattes. Outside of Azar, she's my closest friend—I can't imagine life without her—but I'm her boss too. I'm aware of the lopsided power dynamics.

"You can think about it," she says quickly. "But I didn't want to ask anyone else but you."

"Who knew my caffeine addiction would lead to such a

beautiful friendship?" I grin. "I'd be honored to be in your wedding party."

I walk around the table and give her a hug.

"Glad to hear it." She hugs me back. "First thing will be bridal outfit shopping."

"Fun! Where are you looking? Styles by Simone? Aperti's?"

"Savita's."

"Samir wants you to go desi?"

"He doesn't care. If it were up to him, we'd elope at the courthouse. Which might be the financially advisable thing to do—but I'm only getting married once, right? I'm thinking I might have a white dress for the vows, and then a lengha for the reception. Desi jewelry comes out really good in pictures too. Maybe your aunt could loan me one of her sets?"

"I'm sure she'd be happy to lend you whatever you wanted."

She pulls out her phone and shows me kundan earrings that dangle practically to the shoulders. I live and breathe weddings, so I've seen it all, and I've always cringed at the bride entering an intercultural marriage who can't wait to play dress-up. Darcy isn't doing it for the 'gram, though. I know Samir's mother hasn't been thrilled that her future daughter-in-law isn't the Indian bride she'd dreamed of. Darcy must be hoping this is a way to help her come around.

Her phone vibrates. Darcy looks at it and grimaces. "It's Lena." She sends it to voicemail. "I need a shot of something stronger than caffeine for that call."

"Their wedding's almost here, so at least we're nearing the finish line."

"Hopefully the wedding's still on."

"Now what?" I groan.

"It'll be okay. She's just upset at the wedding venue."

"Is it about the elephant?"

"It's about the elephant." Darcy nods. "She's threatening to cancel the whole thing over it. Tanvir had his heart set on arriving that way to the wedding hall. I'm sure the wedding planner is tearing her hair out as we speak."

"Wait until that leaks out to the press."

"It's already out there, unfortunately. Lena posted about it this morning. I'm sure it'll spark a lovely wave of emails to the wedding venue *and* us. Why are we the scapegoats for everything our clients choose to do? We introduced them to each other; we didn't plan the wedding."

She leans back in the chair and massages her temples.

"How bad is the general inbox these days?" I wake up my computer. Clicking out of my emails, I open the general tab.

"You don't need to see all that." Darcy hurries to my side of the table.

Too late.

Now that I'm in here, all I can do is stare. There's a flood of general inquiries. Impatient would-be clients. Journalists requesting interviews or comments.

Then the *other* emails come into focus.

GO BACK TO WHERE YOU CAME FROM

NURA WILL PAY

MESSAGE FOR NURA AKA BITCH

YOU OWE ME.

ARANGED MARRIAGE ASSHOLE

FUCK YOU NURA KHAN

A chill passes through me. It's not just that the subject lines are angry—some racist, and others who can't properly spell—it's the sheer volume.

"Seriously, Nura, I wouldn't open them. You can't unsee it. These days, I just delete without reading."

"How long has it been this bad?"

"The haters swarmed after the article," she says. "It was like an infestation. It's eased up. The inbox looks better than it did even a few weeks ago."

This is "eased up"? I balk at the subject headings. "It's the one line they had to put in for clicks," I say. "Calling us an 'arranged marriage throwback.'"

"Like Bumble and eHarmony don't exist."

"Exactly. They wouldn't say any of this if I wasn't desi."

Of all the options, my agency offers the least shallow matchmaking service out there. Even our app is careful to dig deep, with a comprehensive questionnaire to ensure proper pairings. Yes, marriage is about attraction, mutual interests, and the undefinable chemistry that mixes it all together—but none of these on their own are enough, are they? Not even love is enough to guarantee a successful marriage. My team at the agency work like coaches, guiding our players to victory. We ask the questions better explored before one has two children and is staring out the window onto their concrete cul-de-sac wondering whom they signed up to spend the rest of their life with. Our goal is simple: We want you to be happy. Cheesy? Yes. The truth? Absolutely.

"I need a palate cleanser," I mumble.

I skim through the media requests. Darcy's right about us needing a temporary replacement while she's out of the office. Managing the inbox looks like a full-time job. There's an invitation to headline an app makers summit. A request for an

Insta live with a lifestyle influencer. The interview requests from journalists are practically identical. A profile would be "a great free advertising opportunity." . . . They'd love "a few moments of our time." . . . Promises of a full Nura Khan spread . . . Direct appeals to my vanity . . .

As I'm reading, a new email dings.

"If it isn't Logan Wilson," I say. "Again."

"From *Rolling Stone*, right?" Darcy rolls her eyes. "He just won't quit."

Hi, Nura,

I was checking in to see if you might have changed your mind about that interview? You've done what so many dream of doing but few actually accomplish. Your assistant explained to me that you don't do profiles, but after listening to the latest disturbing episode of the podcast, I can't help but reach out and try one more time to see if you might change your mind. Everyone who works with you has nothing but rave reviews about the personal touch you provide, but then there's this other side: Those not chosen. Those who feel resentment. I would love to do an in-depth profile that paints the full picture about you and your business and puts it in a holistic light. I'm in town for a few days and would love to speak with you about what a profile might look like. Hope to hear from you soon.

Best,
Logan

"'Disturbing'?" I glance at Darcy. "Is there a new podcast episode?"

Darcy winces. "We were going to tell you. I kept trying to figure out the right time."

I pull up my podcast app—there *is* a second one. This one is also short, a few minutes in length, and harder to make out than the last one. It's like he's recording it from inside a wind tunnel. His words clip in and out.

Fraud . . . shady . . . egomaniac . . .

But his final words ring out clear as day:

You want to call the agency "magical"? That might be right. Magicians are the masters of illusion, and let's be real: Piyar Matchmaking Agency is just a mirage. They don't help people. They fuck with people's lives. Nura won't quit UNTIL SOMEONE STOPS HER.

The recording abruptly ends. His final words reverberate through me. For a moment, neither of us speak.

"I'm sure he's all bark and no bite," I say slowly. "But you were right, Darcy. We should try to figure out who this is."

"Definitely." She looks visibly relieved. "This is too creepy to ignore. I bet Borzu or Genevieve can get to the bottom of it. There's got to be a way to figure it out, on the dark web or *somewhere*."

"Logan. Now this. They're all coming out of the woodwork, aren't they?"

"Well, don't worry about Logan. I'll tell him to kindly go fuck himself. In a professional way, of course. He'll get the message."

When she leaves, I look at the two-minute recording on my phone. I shouldn't, but it's like an itch you can't help but scratch. I press play. The man's voice quivers with rage. I can practically feel the spittle flying from his mouth. I play it again.

And again. Straining for some sort of clue as to who it could be, even though I know: He's a pissed off would-be client. There's no getting around this unsavory reality. It happens.

Still. Those words: *She won't quit until someone stops her.* Khala taught me to let things bounce off me like oil on water, but this is impossible to ignore.

THE FAMILIES OF

Avani Patel

AND

Dev Kasturi

CORDIALLY INVITE YOU TO

A MEHNDI CEREMONY

FRIDAY, MAY 16

SEVEN O'CLOCK IN THE EVENING

FOUR SEASONS HOTEL

34 MIDTOWN STREET

ATLANTA, GEORGIA

The mehndi hall overflows with lanterns and brightly colored flowers. When it comes to desi weddings, I try to make an appearance at the mehndis, the henna party the night before the actual nuptials, when things are a bit more casual and everyone's nerves are slightly less frayed than on the actual wedding day. Tonight, the walls practically pulse to the beat of the bass. I press my fingers to my own throbbing temples. Music and mehndis have been inextricably tied together since the beginning of time, though they didn't always feature deejays blasting pumped-up Bollywood tunes that make the floor vibrate. My head pounds in sync to the rhythm. The bride and groom have not yet made their appearance, but I'm hoping they arrive sooner than later; with this impending migraine, I may need to make my exit earlier than expected.

I head out of the hall and bypass the black-clad security guards monitoring guests entering and exiting the festivities. I need to find a quieter place, at least for a little while.

"Nura!" The bride's mother sidesteps security and hurries toward me. She looks stunning in a silver sari. "I thought I saw you."

She wraps me in a warm embrace.

"You are glowing," I tell her.

"Inside and out. Truly," she says. "You know how high-strung Avani can be. The life coach you suggested changed everything. And then—Dev. He is the best thing that's ever happened to us. It's like my daughter says, you really are magic."

"Avani and Dev are a great fit," I tell her. "All of us at the agency wish them both a lifetime of happiness."

"From your lips to God's ears." She looks at me anxiously. "You're not leaving yet, are you? My sister is dying for you to meet her daughter. Avani's success churned up a lot of interest in you. After the rasms are taken care of, we can make some connections with a few interested parties?"

After the rituals? I try to not wince. At the rate things are going, I'll be here past midnight.

"I nearly forgot." Her eyes light up. "That journalist who came by to interview us was absolutely lovely. Of course we sang your praises to him."

"Journalist?"

"The one from *Rolling Stone*. He reached out last night to see if he could get some quotes on our experience working with you."

"He's here?"

"He *was*." She glances around, then back at me. "Is that all right? I'm sorry—I assumed you knew."

"It's fine," I lie.

"*Rolling Stone*. Well done, dear. Avani was thrilled."

My headache pierces my temples. One more thing to deal with. I promise her I'll be back, and cross the hotel lobby. When I enter the lounge, the hoopla drifts down to a faint rumble, and the lighting is blessedly dim. I take a seat at a barstool, retrieve my emergency stash of Advil, and ask the bartender for a club soda.

Pulling out my phone, I text Azar.

You're late.

His reply is immediate.

On my way!

I purse my lips. He was supposed to be here half an hour ago. Three dots appear on the screen again and then:

AZAR: I'll make it up to you. Promise. Save me some Brazilian steak?

NURA: They haven't even served appetizers yet.

AZAR: So I'm NOT late! Ha! Be there in a sec ☺

I down my medicine and hope it kicks in soon. Once Azar's here, I'll feel more settled.

I type *Rolling Stone, Logan Wilson* into my phone's search engine as I flag down the bartender.

"Another club soda. With lime, please?"

"Why not an actual drink?" a voice says.

There's a man three stools down. I hadn't noticed him before. He's white, with brown hair parted to the side and piercing blue eyes.

"Last time I checked, this is a drink." I raise my glass.

"You like lime?" He motions with his shot toward my glass. "How about a mojito, then?"

I don't bother to reply. Instead, I busy myself with my phone. I don't drink. Never have. But I don't owe him an explanation. That's one thing so many of our clients fail to realize, especially the people pleasers: Folks can ask you for your time, but they are not entitled to it. Until Azar arrives, I can occupy myself.

When I glance up a few moments later, the man is staring at me with an expression I can't decipher.

My search results load just as he says, "Nura Khan?" A grin spreads across his face.

Logan Wilson. Of course it's him.

"I was hoping I'd run into you." His demeanor shifts. Like he went from black-and-white to full color. "I'm Logan Wilson. I emailed you earlier this week. Not sure if you saw it, but—"

"You didn't mention you'd be following me here."

"I'm in town wrapping up a piece but couldn't resist a chance to sidebar with you. I saw Avani's client testimonial on your website and figured I'd reach out and get a chat in with her as well. She had nothing but glowing things to say. What you're doing—what you've accomplished—it's incredible. Non–Silicon Valley startup. Zero venture capitalist funding. Grassroots app to the core. An in-depth profile could be huge for both of us. I did that Brad D'Angelo profile. If you like, I can share my process and how it works?"

I look at his eager expression and shift in my seat. I don't love that he took it upon himself to show up uninvited, but I can grudgingly respect his resolve. I think of the inbox over-flowing with hate mail after the *Vanity Fair* piece. If I said yes to an interview in a high-profile magazine like this, it wouldn't be to advertise the agency, it would be to set the record straight. A piece with a journalist like him would certainly be definitive. Maybe . . .

"And I must say I'm impressed," he continues. "You've made arranged marriages all the rage again."

Aaaaaand there it is.

"Do you label other relationship services the same way?" I ask. "Or only when the founder is a Brown woman?"

His face reddens a touch. "I—I didn't mean . . . Okay, yes.

That *was* inappropriate of me. I apologize. This is exactly why you should talk to me, though." He rushes to add, "People have misconceptions. This would be your chance to correct them."

Oh, to have the confidence of a mediocre man. I stand up. It's time to face the bass-filled mehndi hall, migraine be damned. I put a twenty-dollar bill on the counter and move toward the exit.

"That recording was something else, wasn't it?"

My stomach turns. Logan's eyeing me steadily. "Whoever it is, he has a real vendetta against you. So much pent-up aggression. Any comments on that? Off the record?"

"Men feeling angry they didn't get whatever it is they wanted isn't news, is it?" I say. "If you want clickbait, you can move along. You won't get any from me."

A hand grazes my shoulder. Azar. Handsome as ever in his fitted black sherwani.

"Sorry to interrupt," he says. "Quick word, love?"

"You are interrupting nothing," I tell him.

"I was just heading out." Logan sets his shot glass on the bar and drops a few bills. "Nura, it was nice to meet you. I'm sorry for putting my foot in it. I do hope you'll consider getting in touch."

He walks out of the lounge. I watch the automatic doors slide apart as he exits the main hotel in the distance. Only then do I exhale.

"What was that about?" Azar frowns.

"A reporter. He's gone from calling and emailing to stalking, apparently." I fill him in on our conversation.

"That's obnoxious." He looks at the space where the man had been moments earlier, then back at me. "Do you think you'll sit with him for an interview?"

"Azar!"

"I know! But that's *Logan Wilson*. He's practically a celebrity. You know that profile about Brad D'Angelo, the reclusive tech guru, that came out last month? That was him! Even *I* read it." He laughs at the side-eye I shoot him. "Okay, okay, if not a profile with him, maybe a piece somewhere else? A quick Q and A? You have your pick, don't you? Answer their questions about the mysterious Nura Khan, and people will finally move on."

"I may have to, sooner or later. But not with him. He was completely full of himself."

"I understand." He lifts my hand and kisses it. "Only a suggestion, my dear fiancée."

My skin tingles where his lips pressed against it. He plays the part of loving fiancé so well. Too well. Sometimes I can forget it's all pretend. Sometimes, like now, with our shoulders brushing as we walk back to the mehndi hall, admiring the appetizers the caterers are hurriedly setting up, I want to take his hand in mine. Draw him closer . . . And just as quickly, my mind flashes back to that night at Emory. The way he'd pulled back when I leaned forward. The mortification spreading across his face. That split second of terror coursing through me that I'd lost my best friend and there would be no fixing it. Instantly, all such thoughts disintegrate. I did lose him. For nearly seven years. I'll never risk losing him again.

"Looks like the appetizer line is opening," Azar says.

"I'm famished." I flush, grateful for the distraction.

I grab a bite-sized samosa and masala shrimp. I arrived an hour late, as is proper protocol for a desi event, but now it's nearly two hours past the official start time. I'll need to settle in for an especially long night ahead.

When we sit down at our table, I take a bite of the shrimp and quickly grab a glass of water. "This has got a kick to it. How was the samosa?"

He doesn't reply. He's looking over my shoulder. Following his gaze, I see a slim desi woman in a silk sari approach our table.

"Dr. Shah?" She smiles at him, then quizzically at me.

"Halima, this is Nura—my childhood friend. She's the matchmaker behind the nuptials this evening," Azar quickly says. "Nura, Halima is the best nurse on the face of the earth, bar none."

They talk for a few more moments. When she leaves, I tap his elbow. "That's a first, running into someone you know. I'm kind of surprised it hasn't happened before."

Azar doesn't reply. He studies his uneaten food.

"Azar? What's wrong?"

He takes a deep breath, then looks at me. "I can't keep doing this. I can't keep being your pretend fiancé."

"You told her we were friends." I give him a funny look. "I've never explicitly told anyone we're engaged; your presence just wards off the inevitable questions."

"It's not that. I'm just thinking. . . . At a certain point, we have to stop this, right? I mean, how do I explain this to someone?"

How do I explain this to someone? Tiny fireballs of terror go off inside of me.

"Are you . . . are you seeing someone?"

I wait for him to laugh. Mr. Hasn't Ever Been on More Than Two Dates with the Same Woman. But he's not laughing. He's fidgeting.

"I wouldn't say I'm seeing her. It's only been a few weeks. It just got me thinking, you know?"

A few weeks. My insides feel like they're seizing up.

"Do I know her?"

"Her name is Zayna."

"She works with you, right?"

He nods. I think back to the little Azar has told me about her. She joined his ER a few months ago. Which means Halima will likely be telling her all about running into the two of us at this wedding.

"Why didn't you tell me sooner?" I ask.

"There's nothing to tell." He shrugs. "It's all really new."

A few weeks isn't new. Not when it comes to Azar. Besides, they work together. They've known each other even longer. I take in a deep breath to steady myself, but this sensation passing through me—it's like I'm free-falling.

"I—I'm glad you're hitting it off with Zayna," I finally say. "She won't mind your being my plus-one to weddings, will she?"

"I have such little free time as it is, it just doesn't feel fair to her." He shakes his head. "I'll be thirty-three this November. We can't keep doing this forever."

Somewhere deep down I had to know this would eventually happen. That there would come a moment when he'd find someone. Fall in love. I should count myself lucky we've lasted as long as we have. There's no partner in the world who would be okay with her boyfriend spending every weekend going to weddings with another woman. There probably aren't very many who would be okay with our friendship at all.

He searches my eyes for a reaction. I swallow. All those years ago at Emory, I blamed our near kiss on sleep deprivation from a week of pulling all-nighters. Or the hookah we'd snagged from his roommate, passing it back and forth while we sat on his bed watching our favorite survival show, *Wild*. He'd just told me he'd gotten into NYU medical school moments earlier, and the news was still sinking in. We'd known each other forever. We'd been in and out of each other's homes growing up. Hanging out at the creaky kitchen table at Khala's. Or the overstuffed leather sofas in his family room, the scent of his mother's potato parathas wafting over to us. Through college, it had been a new setting but the same Nura and Azar. We were in and out of each other's routines. We *were* each other's routines. That night, it had hit me: Come August, he'd be gone. That night, I'd taken in the heart-shaped curve of his mouth. The stubble against his jaw. I'd leaned forward. A sudden desire to hold on to him. To be with him. I'd realized a truth so real it had taken my breath away: I loved him. I remember how he recoiled. He'd looked at me like a rabbit caught in a snare. Desperate to undo the damage I feared I'd done, I'd rolled my eyes and laughed. Teased him for his stunned expression. Then I'd begged him to pretend it never happened. Turns out, though, you can't pretend a moment like that away. We kept in touch over the years—phone calls on birthdays, memes texted back and forth—but it was never the same again. It took years, until he moved back to Atlanta and we officially cleared the air, to put the past behind us. I've moved on. I completely accept that we're just friends. But he was always meant to be a friend I would lose, wasn't he? Sure, we will always know each other. I'll attend his children's birthday parties. Send gifts on holidays. But it won't be the same. These days of easy togetherness are numbered.

I clear my throat. I know I'm jumping to a million conclusions. Who knows what'll happen between him and Zayna, though the fact that she's outlasted every woman who came before her tells me things are more serious than he's letting on. Still, I'll be his friend as long as I can. And I'm going to find out everything there is to know about Dr. Zayna Chaudhry. My best friend's love interest warrants a healthy perusal to make sure everything checks out, doesn't she? Azar deserves the best.

From my peripheral vision I see the mother of the bride heading toward me.

Good. A distraction. Except—

As she grows closer, I realize she's not walking so much as she's *marching* toward me. Her sari is bunched in one hand. Her eyes are swollen and puffy.

I jump out of my seat and hurry toward her. "What's going on? What's the matter?"

Her response tilts my world completely off its axis:

"The wedding is off."

SIX

"You can go," I whisper to Azar. "Party's over."

"I'll wait for you," he replies, his expression lined with concern.

Wordlessly, I follow the mother of the bride out of the mehndi hall. Down a nondescript corridor. She hasn't said a word since the bombshell revelation.

I slip into the luxurious bridal suite. Plush sofas. A makeup table with ten different lights spotlighting a singular velvet chair. Which is empty.

"Where's Avani?" I ask. "What happened?"

Tears spring to her mother's eyes. She tosses me a balled-up paper.

I unfold it as Avani's father storms in. The door trembles when he slams it shut behind him. Prying apart the sheets, I see two pieces of paper. The first is a mug shot. Dev, the groom, stares blank-faced into a camera. A booking date from three years earlier is listed beneath it. Felony assault. The next, a court order showing a two-year sentence, commuted to six months for good behavior.

What the hell?

Avani's parents stand in front of me with their arms crossed. Waiting. The silence in the room amplifies the sounds outside. It's a loud din, like the roar of the ocean crashing against a cliff—a cliff the three of us inside this room have already fallen off.

I flip back and forth between the papers. I understand anyone is capable of unspeakable actions. Seemingly debonair gentlemen with battery charges sealed away by powerful parents—they exist. But my job is to shake out the skeletons. To ensure that there are no surprises, that moments like this do not happen. And they never *have*. Until now. And now the people standing before me want an explanation. I can't explain why these documents are in their possession, but there is one thing I know above all else: These papers are fake. They must be. I trust my team, and I trust our process.

"Well?" Avani's father asks. "Aren't you going to say anything?"

His Adam's apple quivers. He won't believe me. I know before I even open my mouth, but I tell him the only thing I can: the truth.

"These documents are fabricated."

"Fabricated." He looks at his wife, who is clutching her waist as though she might vomit. He glares at me. "You're going to pretend you didn't miss critical information?"

"They can't be real." I try to keep my voice steady. It doesn't matter that I'm shocked and shaken—I have to keep it together. "A mug shot and a court order are both public information. If they were real, we would have found them immediately."

"Or they are real, and you missed something glaringly obvious and put my daughter in danger." He turns and barks at his wife, "How much did we pay her? Because you *knew* she got results? Because Asha's daughter is *so* happy?"

I need to stop this from spiraling out of control. I need to fix this.

"Where did you get these?" I ask.

"What does it matter?" The mother lets out a sob. "There are five hundred people out there. My mother flew in from Toronto last night. She's eighty-three. She'll have a heart attack. How are we supposed to show our faces to the crowd out there?"

"Nothing has to happen," I say as gently as possible. "I understand how scary this is. I'll ring up my people. They can figure out who is behind this, and we can fix it. If I could speak with Avani—"

"Maybe these papers were sealed by court order," the father interrupts. "Maybe *that's* how you missed it."

Except we pay Borzu handsomely to get around such seals. To find whatever doesn't want to be found. *Especially* what doesn't want to be found. There's no use arguing with the father, though. He is terrified. Humiliated. He is suffering and wants someone to blame.

"Where did you find the papers?" I ask again.

"Avani said they were left here, in the bridal suite," the mother says.

"Did you see anyone acting strange around this area? In the hallways? Someone who seemed out of place?"

"I hardly have time to observe every stranger passing by."

Except, for someone to have done this, they couldn't have been a stranger. Before I can press further, the bridal suite door bursts open. Avani's in an orange-and-green ghagra, her neck layered with ancestral gold. Angry rivers of mascara trail her cheeks.

"He's denying it!" she shouts. "He had the nerve to get mad at *me*. I told him if you can't be honest now—then what are we even doing?" She sees me and lets out a shriek. "Nura. What the hell?"

"The papers aren't real," I tell her. "Let's get Dev in here, and I'll call my team over. We can resolve this right now."

"Resolve this?" She collapses onto the sofa. "There's no resolving this."

"How did you come across the note?"

"It was on my makeup table when I arrived to get ready. I thought Dev had left me a present." She lets out a trembly laugh. "I was hoping maybe he'd snuck in plane tickets for our honeymoon. He's been keeping it a surprise and knew it was driving me nuts."

"And when you confronted him with these papers, he denied it?"

"Of course he denied it," her father scoffs.

"He's a scammer," the bride whimpers. "Who knows how many people he's done this to? He acted all insulted when I showed him the proof. Stormed out like I was the crazy one. Classic gaslighting. Like *he* has anything to be upset about."

Avani's mother slides next to her daughter on the couch and puts an arm around her.

The father glances at the two of them and then me. "I was against this from the start," he says in a low voice. "When she told me about this ridiculous idea to work with you, I told her it would be more trouble than it was worth. I had said to both of them that we were better off seeking matches within our own class."

"This has nothing to do with class." Heat floods my cheeks. Dev is a Cornell grad and a software engineer at a successful startup, yet he'd barely passed muster for her father.

"Of course not. How dare I not be politically correct? After all this work. All this effort—" He breaks off. I know what he's thinking. They paid me to avoid problems. What bigger problem could there be than this?

I hurry out of the suite. Down the hall. Azar catches up to me. He matches my stride. "What happened?"

"It's a mess." I fill him in on the pertinent details.

"Nura, that's awful."

He frowns in the way he always does when he's at a loss for words, his eyes full of concern that doesn't need to be expressed verbally to be felt. Not between the two of us. He gives me a hug instead, and for only a moment, it feels like everything will be all right.

By one o'clock in the morning at our emergency meeting in Borzu's fourth-story walk-up in Midtown, it's confirmed—as I knew it would be—that the documents are fake.

"Check out these details." Borzu leans back in his chair. The light flickers above, reflecting against his newly green hair. He stabs a finger at the mug shot. "This is total amateur hour. They superimposed his driver's license over a mug shot backdrop, see?" He pulls up Dev's driver's license. The photos are an identical match. The same deer-in-headlights expression. "The cut-and-paste job is so basic it hurts my eyes."

"Whoever did this was counting on them to freak out first and ask questions later." Genevieve yawns.

She's right. Back in the bridal suite, though I had known the mug shot couldn't be real, with my pulse beating so loudly in my head, I couldn't prove it as easily as I can now, clear-eyed, in the still of night.

"It's the same with this court document." Borzu nods at the

paper. "Someone switched out the names. You can see where they cut and pasted his information onto the document from someone else's trial."

"Whoever did it wanted to call off the wedding," Genevieve says.

"Well, they succeeded," I say.

Genevieve pulls out her laptop, encrypted in ten different ways. She types furiously, then—"It looks like Avani only had one boyfriend before Dev."

"Sunil Gupta." Borzu squints at his own screen. "I'll see what he's up to."

"They'd broken up years before we signed her," I say. "She said the relationship had no spark—it dissolved into a friendship. I'm pretty sure she invited him to the wedding."

"He was there tonight?" Genevieve raises her eyebrows. "All the more reason to look into him."

"I'll dig into Dev's past to make sure I didn't miss anything," Borzu says. "But he was cleared when we did the deep scrape."

"Who, then?" I murmur. I regret not waking Darcy up. She's not an investigator, but having her here to spitball ideas would have been helpful.

"It could have been anyone." Borzu pulls up Avani's social media profile. "She was posting details of the festivities constantly, and it was a Four Seasons, not some remote location. The mehndi hall itself had security, but the rest of the place didn't. Her bridal suite obviously didn't."

"Can we go over camera footage of the event?" I ask. "Something's got to have been captured on there."

"I'll see if I can grab that in the morning," Genevieve says, exchanging a glance with Borzu.

"What is it?" I ask.

Borzu hesitates. "You know this isn't part of your job, right?"

"We are supposed to give them a turnkey partner. A happily ever after. I'd say we failed on that front."

"But we didn't," he says.

"Avani and Dev *were* a perfect match," says Genevieve. "He didn't actually do any of the things he was accused of."

"This was an Act of God event," says Borzu. "You're not responsible. I'll dig some more, and we'll get to the bottom of what happened sooner or later, but you can't beat yourself up over this."

Except it wasn't an act of God. It was the act of *someone*. Someone went into the hotel and left a ticking time bomb. Did they sit in the audience and watch as the mehndi imploded? Did they cackle with delight to see true love go up in flames?

Did Logan catch wind of any of this? I swallow. One fire at a time, but the sooner we fix this, the better for everyone.

Hours later, my body is stiff from hunching over Borzu's computer.

"Want some coffee for the road?" Borzu asks. He saunters over to a sleek device resting on the kitchen counter.

"I'm wired enough as is." I glance around his place. The walls are newly sage green. And I do a double take at the sofa—the white contemporary sectional across from me is a far cry from the lumpy futon he used to have. "You've really done this place up."

"You mean I finally tossed the cinder block shelves? According to my mother, I needed to grow up at some point. She forced me to do a whole renovation. The kitchen cabinets are resurfaced too."

"The cabinets look great, but I miss the cinder blocks!" I protest. "They had personality."

Khala used to get on my case all the time about my own bungalow with its original wood flooring and creaky front door. *Just get a few upgrades,* she used to insist. But as contemporary and modern as my office might be, as expensive as the purses and shoes I own to keep up with my clients, when it comes to my personal life, I keep things simple. If life has taught me anything, it's that things can turn on a dime. Besides, I like my cozy cottage with its original chimney and exposed-brick kitchen. I have so few memories of my childhood before Atlanta, but I know my mother and I had lived simply. Maybe that's why simplicity is what always makes me feel most at home.

"Before I forget"—Borzu yawns—"I looked into the podcast."

"Yeah?" With everything else going on, I'd nearly forgotten all about it.

"Whoever it is, they made a crude website for it. It's a basic account. The IP address puts them in Texas somewhere."

"That's a relief. It's not someone local," Genevieve says.

I think of the anger in that man's voice. "How accurate is the location?" I ask.

"I'm guessing it's pretty accurate," he says. "The site didn't appear to be the work of an online sophisticate."

"Like you," Genevieve says dryly. She's never had any patience for Borzu's tech talk. She just wants the results. "Darcy and I will go through the database tomorrow to rule out any potential rejected client. And Borzu, you can hack into the website and take it down, can't you?"

"It'll be down by tonight. That's way easier than removing the podcast files, but I'm not giving up on that either."

"There is one more person I'd love to look into," I say. "I ran into a journalist tonight."

I give them a quick summary of my conversation with Logan

Wilson. "He couldn't have done this to get a good story, could he?" The question seems absurd as soon as I say it aloud.

Borzu types his name into his computer. "Wait. We're talking about *the* Logan Wilson? Not that this rules anything out, but he *is* a journalist. One of the best tech reporters out there. I can't believe you actually *met* him." Borzu's no longer looking sleepy. He's downright perky. "Look, he's got eighteen bylines on here alone. A Wikipedia page. The Brad D'Angelo piece went viral."

"Who's got time to read a ten-thousand-word profile?" Genevieve retorts.

"When he discloses that D'Angelo sleeps on an eighty-thousand-dollar bed and has a panic room outfitted with a movie theater, I've got time. No way he's behind this. Logan doesn't make up stories, he breaks stories!"

"I'll track his whereabouts on the hotel security footage when we get it." Genevieve shoots Borzu a withering glare. "Doesn't hurt to rule things out."

The sky has shifted overhead by the time I reach my home and pull into the driveway. Flecks of pink and purple fill the horizon. I rest my head on the steering wheel. The wired feeling from earlier has worn off. Now my eyes feel scratchy like sandpaper. I want nothing more than to unbuckle my seatbelt, crawl into bed, and sleep the day away. But my work is not yet done.

Entering the house, I turn off the beeping security alarm and sidestep my running shoes lying askew next to the front door. Gertie hops down from her cat tree and hurries toward me. Pressing against me, she purrs.

"Sorry I'm late." I scoop her up and snuggle her. "It's been a *day,* and it's not officially over yet."

With a free hand, I pull out my phone and sink into the

couch. It's five o'clock in the morning, but I doubt Avani is sleeping given the night she had. I need to tell her what happened. She needs to know as soon as possible that Dev was exactly as advertised: a perfect match. My agency did not screw this up. She picks up on the first ring.

"It wasn't real," I tell her. I explain how the mug shot was fabricated. The court record cut and pasted from someone else's. "It was a prank. A cruel and horrible prank."

There is silence on the other end.

"Avani? Are you still there?"

"So he isn't a criminal." Her voice breaks. "So what? I already accused him of being one. I accused him of lying to me. It's not like he's ever going to forgive me. I can't even blame him, can I?"

My chest tightens. I want to fix this. But how *does* Dev get over the fact that his fiancée accused him of felony assault? That she hadn't taken him at his word, her trust in him dissolving in an instant, like salt in the sea?

After some halfhearted reassurances, I hang up with Avani and bite my lip. Running a hand through Gertie's fur, I look down at her. "What would Khala have done in this situation?" I ask her. "She'd have sorted it out, wouldn't she?" Gertie leans up and licks my chin with her rough tongue in response.

I refill Gertie's food bowl. Replenish her water tray. Glancing at my sneakers, I'm tempted to go for a quick run. It's always the surest way to clear my head. But this isn't something a simple jog will sort out. My team thinks I should let it go, that I shouldn't take it personally. Maybe they're right. Contractually, I'm not on the hook. But there's no getting around the reality that there were people at the mehndi eager to meet the "world-renowned matchmaker" and who instead watched a disaster unfold. How exactly am I supposed to let it go?

SEVEN

I nearly canceled my weekly Friday dinner with Khala. Even if Nina and I somehow get along beautifully tonight, I'm a coiled-up ball of stress. But on hearing Khala's voice when I called to postpone, all my excuses evaporated. I thought of my birthday. Those six or seven seconds when she looked at me but didn't see me. The memory still lands like a gut punch. I need to be with her as much as possible while she's still the woman I know. While she still knows me.

But now that I'm here, sitting in my car in her driveway, taking in the cream shutters, the bright-blue front door, the scent of basil filling my car, I debate dropping off the Thai food takeout and heading home to Gertie.

It's been exactly one week since Avani and Dev's wedding fell apart. A week of using every method we know to figure out how the fake documents reached the bride and, just as important, why. If I can find out who did this and for what reason, maybe there could be a way to help Avani and Dev find their way back to each other. So far, nothing's turned up. Even Logan proved to be a dead end. Footage showed him entering the hotel lobby. Interviewing Avani. Swinging by the bar for a drink. It even captured our conversation in silent-movie fashion, after which the grainy footage confirmed that he really did grab a rideshare and leave the premises. I'd have loved an easy answer—an ambitious reporter out to make the story he wanted to see in the world. Too bad nothing is ever quite so simple.

There's an incoming text.

GENEVIEVE: Finally heard back from my contact at the Four Seasons. No security cameras in the back walkways.

NURA: What about the interior hallways? I saw cameras there.

GENEVIEVE: They're broken.

I slump back against the seat. Through the windshield I see a ceiling of gray clouds sliding overhead. *Snap out of it,* I chide myself. No amount of beating my head against a wall will make this situation untangle itself. There's nothing I can do about this right now.

Balancing the two bags of food, I make my way up the pathway to Khala's house. I note with a small feeling of satisfaction that the lawn service I hired has spruced the place back up. The scent of freshly mowed grass still hangs in the air. The dried-up shrubs against the windows were pulled, new ones planted in their stead.

Nina's in the family room scrolling on her phone when I enter.

"Auntie!" Lilah hops up and gives me a hug.

"I come bearing Thai food," I tell them.

"Mom's sleeping." Nina doesn't look up.

I set the food on the kitchen table and glance at Khala's bedroom door, which, sure enough, is closed. So why am I here? I could claim an emergency and bow out—but seeing Nina hunched on the sofa, pecking away at her phone, I steel my resolve. I won't let her run me out. I'll park myself on the screened-in porch off the kitchen to catch up on my emails until Khala wakes up.

There's a tug on my pant leg. Lilah. Her light-brown curls bounce against her shoulders. "I'm making a puzzle. Want to help?"

I hesitate. It's not that I don't want to hang out with Lilah. More that I don't want to be in the vicinity of Lilah's very grumpy mother. "What about kicking the ball around in the backyard?" I offer.

"No way." She wrinkles her nose. "It's too hot. Puzzles! I can teach you."

How do you say no to those sweet brown eyes?

I join her at the coffee table.

"Do you like Bulbasaur and Pikachu?" She holds up a 100-piece puzzle box.

"I love anything Pokémon," I tell her. "Charmander's my favorite."

"He's my favorite too!"

As I pick up a piece of yellow Pikachu tail, I hear a sharp exhale. What now? Am I wrong to like Pokémon? But when I look at Nina, the phone is pressed to her ear. Her jaw set in a firm line.

"No. I can't hold. I need to speak to someone right now. I was already put on hold and hung up on twice." Nina rises. She paces the length of the room.

Whatever the person says in response makes her eyes water. Her voice becomes softer, a little kinder, but still assertive.

"I ordered these transcripts weeks ago. I have a confirmation number and—" Her voice breaks. "Okay. Thank you. What's that number?" She scribbles something on a yellow legal pad.

"Transcripts?" I ask when she hangs up. "Is there an issue with Lilah's school?"

"Lilah's four, Nura. She doesn't have transcripts yet."

Serves me right for trying to have a conversation. I turn back to the puzzle.

"I'm sorry," Nina says. "That was rude."

An apology? From Nina?

"I'm trying to get my credits transferred to Oglethorpe," she explains. "They're making me run around in circles. I check one thing off the list and something else gets unchecked. I feel like I'm going crazy."

"I didn't know you were back in school."

"I'm just a few credits short of finishing my master's in communication, but apparently, I can't manage to communicate with anyone. Portland State promised to send the transcripts three times, and now I'm about to miss the deadline."

I try to keep my expression neutral, but this brief stop while Khala recovers is starting to look like a permanent move.

"Thank God for different time zones. Their offices are still open," Nina says, scrolling her phone. "I'll see if the fourth time's the charm." The phone vibrates in her hands. Nina's expression darkens.

She doesn't need to say who it is. I can tell it's her soon-to-be ex.

Nina's face scrunches. Like she might cry. Khala's confided in me that she worries Nina is struggling, but all I've ever seen is her stoic demeanor. Watching her in this moment, I feel a pang of sympathy. Sure, Nina acts like a martyr about being here to help out when I could have handled matters fine by myself, but it doesn't mean this hasn't been difficult for her.

"Nina, if you want to get the call, take it. Or toss it to voicemail and follow up with the transcripts office. I have an eye on Lilah," I tell her.

"I can deal with it later."

"Do what you need to do. We're having fun, right, Lilah?"

Lilah beams and nods.

Nina looks at the phone, which is buzzing again, then at me. "You sure?"

"Yes, Nina." I try not to sound exasperated. "I can handle putting together a puzzle with your child. We'll be here when you get back."

Her voice is a whisper. "Thanks."

Her footsteps pad up the carpeted stairs.

Lilah and I finish the puzzle and move on to her pile of library books. She settles next to me on the oversized couch, her little body curled up next to mine. We read *The Ugly Vegetables*. *Pluto Gets the Call*. *The Pig on the Hill*. And then we read them again. She squeals when I imitate the pig.

Snuggling, I realize this is the closest to normal I've felt all week.

When I reach out to grab another book, I see Khala. She leans against the wall, watching us.

"Well, isn't this a pretty picture?" she says.

"I got takeout from the Thai place you love."

"Did you bring mango chicken?" Lilah asks. "I'm getting hungry!"

"Of course I brought mango chicken. I'll warm everything up closer to dinner."

"It seems a good nap gave me a good appetite as well, Lilah." She eyes the wall clock. "Looks to be a bit early for dinner, but I'll go ahead and set the table. We can eat in an hour." I move to get up, but she puts out a hand to stop me. "Stay with her.

This is good for both of you." Khala heads to the kitchen. "By the way, dear, I checked your steps this morning. I'm afraid you are falling behind."

"It's been a sedentary few days." I check the step counter on my watch.

"You can't forget about your health; work is not the only important thing. And"—she wags a finger toward me—"I could use some real competition."

"Ouch!" I grin. "Message received." She's right, it's been a while since I've run. I *could* go for a jog later tonight.

I hear cabinets creak open and shut. Porcelain serving trays clink as they're set on the granite counter. I've told Khala countless times that one of the benefits of takeout is fewer dishes to clean up, but she insists things be done properly. And properly means nice plates and bowls and silverware.

I glance at my watch, then wistfully at the hallway. Once upon a time, we shared more than our step counts. Once upon a time, I'd have walked over, settled onto one of the kitchen stools, and parsed out every detail of Avani and Dev's disastrous mehndi. I miss those days. When fixing things was someone else's issue. Or at least a burden to be shared. But this is my agency now. It's my problem.

My phone and wrist buzz simultaneously as Lilah and I finish up the last book. It's Darcy. I decline the call as Nina rejoins us in the family room. I'll call her on my way home.

"Well, that went longer than expected," Nina says. "But I had a chat with the *right* person, and new transcripts are finally, *hopefully* on their way. And the other thing . . ." She glances at Lilah. "That'll sort itself out."

Nina doesn't talk about her separation much with me, but I know part of the reason for the move was to get as geographically far from her husband as possible. Apparently, she stumbled upon his suspicious text message exchanges with a co-worker when they were buzzing on a stray iPad on the counter. Which led to checking his credit card bills and discovering the charges to hotel rooms that lined up with overtime hours, followed by her "surprise" run-in with him at said hotel's lobby one fine evening. Nina may not approve of the agency, but she'd grown up with Khala as her mother, so she learned how to investigate from the best of them. No one's filed for divorce, but if she's transferring her credits, things can't be going well.

She leans against the wall and squeezes her eyes shut. I feel a wave of sympathy toward her. If this is barreling toward divorce, her headaches are only beginning. Soon there will be court filings. Custody battles. Property division. I can offer my team's assistance in cutting her ex down to size. But looking at the circles under her eyes, I can help in the way she actually needs right at this very moment.

"Nina, go on and get some rest. We have an hour until dinner. I've got Lilah."

She bites her lip, considering. "You sure?"

"She's sure!" Lilah sings.

I give her an encouraging nod.

"I'll be in my room," Nina says. "Get me if anything comes up. And . . . thanks, Nura."

The stairs creak. A door closes upstairs. Lilah turns to me and claps.

"Guess what? We painted a mural in school today! I did the trees!"

"Did you make the redwoods we read about last week?"

"No. I made skinny trees. I can show you?"

"I'd love that."

"I'll get paint!" She races to her room, and I grab the butcher paper. Unrolling it, I tape it to cover the coffee table as I hear her rattling her paint box for the right palette.

Settling onto the couch, I reply to a few messages and text Darcy that I'll ring her once I'm in the car. Then I glance around the empty room. I shouldn't do this. This is the exact sort of thing I tell my own clients *not* to do. But I can't help it. I click Azar's inactive social media profile. It's still gathering dust, as it has for years. When I go to Zayna's profile, there are loads of photos. She's at a cooking class with girlfriends. Posing in a forest with hiking poles. Raising a medal in the air— the New York City Marathon banner billowing behind her. Suddenly, my heart feels like it's stopped beating.

There's a photo of them. Azar and Zayna.

She has well-executed winged liner and a pretty red dress. Brown layered hair falls past her shoulders. Azar's arm is around her. She's gorgeous. *They* are gorgeous. My chest constricts at the tagged location: Hayakawa.

That's our favorite sushi place. He'd spotted an article about it our last year of college and had saved up for months so we could go. Even though the bill amounted to more than two weeks of tutoring gigs, we'd pretended money was nothing but a number that last night.

Was it the afterglow of that dinner that had emboldened me as we unwound later that evening in his dorm room, sitting on his bed, watching television? Was that the reason I'd nearly kissed him?

I laughed when he jerked away. "Oh my God, the look on your face."

"What look?"

"You thought I was going to kiss you, didn't you?" There, I said it.

"Nur," he began. "We should talk about it."

"But maybe we don't have to." My cover of cool cracking.

"Nur," he began.

"Please, Azar?" Tears formed in my eyes. "You're . . . you're like a brother to me. Can we pretend this never happened?"

He looked at me for a moment. Blinking. Thinking. My heart felt like it was seizing in my chest. The terror I felt in that moment—that I might lose him, that our friendship could be over—that free-falling feeling can still grip me now.

He slowly nodded. "Consider it forgotten."

All these years, it had been one thing to accept that Azar was simply not one for relationships—but it turns out I had it all wrong, didn't I? Azar wasn't a commitment-phobe. He'd just been waiting for the right person.

"I got the paints!" Lilah sings as she heads down the stairs.

I exhale, grateful for the distraction.

"I can't wait to see your masterpiece," I tell her as my phone buzzes. A text reply from Darcy.

We really need to talk.

I frown. This must be serious.

"Lilah, I have to take a quick call," I tell her. "I'll be back in a second."

"Can I start painting?"

"Make sure you wear your apron. We don't want to make a mess."

"No mess!"

I sit down on a wicker chair on the back patio. Darcy answers on the first ring and cuts straight to the chase.

"I was checking our messages. Logan called."

"Logan? I thought it was something serious. I'm at my aunt's."

"This *is* serious." Her voice is strained. "He wants a comment on Avani and Dev's wedding implosion."

My stomach turns. This was inevitable, wasn't it? "Do you know if Avani's talking to him?" I ask her. "I know she posted a few days ago about the wedding getting canceled."

"I just went online, and it looks like she's deleted all her social media accounts. She must feel horrible. I doubt she'll be eager to talk to the press."

With or without her comment, though, Logan's got a certifiably juicy story now. A Piyar agency match implodes on the eve of the wedding. That'll blow my reputation to smithereens.

"We should keep the PR agency in the loop. Sounds like we might need them," I say.

"Good idea. I'll give Sherri a call," she says. "I'm so glad you're not panicking. It's making me feel a little less manic."

I *am* panicking. It's bubbling inside of me like water in a boiling pot. But I'm the boss. I'm in charge. I must stay calm.

I put my phone away as a flash of lightning slices through the sky, followed by the distant rumble of thunder.

It's terrible how things went down for Avani and Dev, but it's like Genevieve and Borzu said: Our agency did nothing wrong. Still, just to be sure we didn't miss anything, I'll swing by the agency after dinner. I'll grab the paper files for Avani and Dev from my desk. Maybe there's a stray thought or note in there that I wrote down. Maybe it'll jog my memory. Help me figure out who could have had the motive to destroy their wedding. This is too important to leave any stone unturned.

The scent of mango and garlic greet me when I get back into the house. My shoulders relax a little. I'm glad I stuck around this evening, despite my misgivings. I made progress with Nina. Got some much-needed downtime with my niece.

"How's the painting coming?" I hurry back to Lilah. "I can't—"

Stepping into the family room, I freeze. Lilah is painting. Not on the white paper I'd set out on the coffee table. A brown tree trunk drips down the gray living room wall. Green streaks swirl off branches. She turns to me and grins.

"We painted the mural like this!"

A mural. How did I miss that key word? She'd created a wall painting at school, and now she's re-creating it. Here. On Khala's wall. Inches from a framed Jamali worth over five thousand dollars.

Before I can respond, I hear footsteps. Nina emerges from the hallway, her hair wrapped in a towel.

"A shower was exactly what I needed." She walks into the family room. "Lilah, can you . . ."

Her words die on her tongue. She takes in the scene before her. Speechless, she turns to me. I want to sink into the floor. I want to vaporize.

"I had a quick call I needed to take, and . . ."

"Right. A call." Her expression shifts.

"I'll get a sponge." My chest stings. "The paint's water-based, isn't it?"

"I've got it, Nura. Thanks for your *help*."

The words land like a punch. I deserve it. I screwed up. Instead of helping my cousin get some downtime, I added more to her plate.

I've never felt so relieved to leave Khala's home after dinner. The wind has picked up, and the thunder that was rumbling in the distance earlier is growing louder. My hair whips against my face. As I turn on the car, thick raindrops splash against the windshield.

I can't stop kicking myself. I'd extended a fragile olive branch toward Nina, and then I'd carelessly stepped on it and snapped it in two. Why hadn't I waited and called Darcy back later? Sure, she said it was important, but watching Lilah was important too. Now the peace I barely glimpsed is gone.

I turn out of Khala's neighborhood and head toward the agency. The rain is coming down heavier. I press my wipers to their highest setting.

After parking the car, I jump out, shielding my face with my arm against the onslaught of rain, and dash toward the front door. *In and out,* I promise myself as the sky thunders. I do not want to be stuck in this storm.

I'm so preoccupied, I almost don't notice it.

Not as I duck under the awning and pull out my keys. Not as I stick them into the lock.

The note.

It's wedged into the door. I pull it out. It's a flyer. Advertising a new eco-friendly dry cleaner. Opening next to the overpriced taco fusion restaurant, adjacent to the barre studio.

I'm about to crumple it when I see the message scrawled on the back side in marker. Ink trailing down like mascara. The words barely legible, yet unmistakable:

NURA KHAN, I SEE YOU.

EIGHT

Wind howls through the forest across from my house. Lightning illuminates the sky, followed by the sound of a thunderclap. As soon as I'd glimpsed the note, I ran back to my car and hit the accelerator all the way home. But even now, safe inside my house, Gertie circling my legs, I don't feel much better.

"Is Borzu coming?" asks Azar. I'd called him from the car, and he arrived just after me.

"He's ten minutes away."

"What about Genevieve?" He moves to the window, parts the sheer white curtains, and gazes out at my driveway.

"I'm guessing she's flying above the Colorado Rockies right now. She's attending a family reunion in Utah."

"I forget some of your team members have lives outside of this agency." Azar sits down on the couch next to me. I'd told him he didn't need to come over—what could he do in this situation? But as the wind howls and the streetlights flicker, I'm grateful he's here.

We study the note on the coffee table, as though looking at it long enough will reveal some sort of clue. But there's nothing to be gleaned from bleeding marker pressed against paper.

Thunder rumbles, rattling the windows. "I should tell Borzu to turn back. It's getting worse out there."

"You really don't want to call the police about this? This is serious stalker shit, Nur. What if it's . . ." His voice trails off.

The podcaster. I know what he's thinking. But what good will reporting this note do? The police barely blinked when Kaden Sineway lit fireworks in the agency parking lot to express his displeasure with us. They won't care about this. We'll handle it on our own.

Raindrops pelt harder against the skylights above. Thunder sounds, crackling like popcorn. Gertie yowls and leaps into my lap, burrowing her head into the crook of my arm.

"Silly girl, I won't let the storm get you." I scratch her behind her ears. I wish my own worries were as simple as Gertie's.

Azar leans down and studies the note on the coffee table again. I take in his profile. He's in a salmon polo shirt. Stone-washed jeans.

Oh no.

"Azar. Were you on a date?"

He shrugs. "It's fine."

"You *were* on a date." I clamp my hand over my mouth. His face is clean-shaven; his hair has an undeniable hint of gel. "Those are your out-on-the-town jeans. Admit it. If you don't tell me, I'll just find out on her Instagram later."

"Keeping tabs on me, Nur?"

"Hi, have we met?"

"It wasn't anything big. *Les Mis* is in town. She's already seen it a couple of times."

I blink. "Let me get this right. You were watching a *musical?*"

"What's wrong with that?"

"Nothing, other than you've said you'd rather eat squid than watch a musical. And you're deathly allergic to squid."

"What can I say? Things change, Nur."

Yeah, I think. *I guess they do.*

"Is it serious between you?" I ask, shooting for casual. "Is she your girlfriend?"

"Girlfriend?" His forehead crinkles. "It hasn't even been that long."

"A few weeks is plenty. A lifetime in Azar years."

"I don't know. Maybe. It just felt like it was time," he says. "You have to get on with the next part of your life at some point, right?"

Get on with the next part of your life. The part of your life that doesn't include me. Maybe it was inevitable, but that doesn't mean it doesn't hurt.

"What about you?" he asks.

"What *about* me?"

"I know, I know—you've sworn off all that." He rests his elbows on his knees, his gaze intently on mine. "Do you ever think about it? A relationship?"

There's that question everyone asks. It feels different coming from him.

I try to brush him off with a laugh. "Not this again!"

"Gertie's sweet as can be." He leans over and rubs her head. "But I figured eventually you might want a relationship of the human variety."

Yes, I want to say. *I did think about a relationship. Once. With you.*

I remember the day he moved back to town. The doorbell rang, and there he was. Like a mirage. At my doorstep holding takeout from Lee's, my favorite pho place. Decidedly over the

gray-skied winters of New York, he'd quit his toxicology fel-
lowship and moved back to Atlanta. We'd sat side by side on
this very couch, our steaming bowls of soup resting on the
coffee table. I'd chattered on and on about the agency, funny
client interactions, trying to fill the room with words, to pretend his liquid brown eyes gazing into my own did nothing to
me. That despite our best efforts, the past did not hang heavy
in the air.

We finished eating. I warmed a pot of water on the stove for
chai. He'd turned to me. Stuck his hands in his pockets—his
tell for when he was nervous. For when he was debating if he
wanted to say what came next at all. Then—"I was thinking.
Since I'm back in town, maybe we should talk about . . ." Azar
gestured to the space between us.

I stiffened. There it was. He'd named the tension in the
room.

"I know I promised I'd never bring it up again, but it was so
good to see you last month at my parents' going-away party."
He looked down, studying the wooden floorboards. "It hit me
how much I've missed you. We were such good friends, Nur. I
can't remember a time we weren't friends, and it just hasn't
been the same for so long. Now that I'm back . . ." His voice
trailed off, searching for how to finish the sentence, but he
didn't need to. I heard how he emphasized friendship—twice
in one breath. I also heard what was left unspoken: *Let's make
sure we don't have any misunderstandings again.*

"Our friendship means so much to me too," I quickly told
him. Hoping he didn't notice the heat rising up my neck.

"Nur, that night, in the dorm—"

"Can we just . . . never talk about that night ever again?
Please?" I tried to smile, but my eyes watered. "You've been
away for years, and I'm so glad you're back. I've missed you. So

much. I want our friendship back too. The way it was." And to make sure he knew I understood, I added, "That is *all* I want."

The chai pot had bubbled over on the stove while he regarded me. I tried my best to appear calm, though my nerves pulsed through me like a live wire. Then he smiled. "That sounds perfect, Nur."

Just like that, the tension had vanished into the ether. I'd accepted his terms. He was my friend again, and we could go back to the way we used to be. We could leave the past where it belonged.

"Nur?" Azar taps my leg, jarring me to the present.

"Sorry." I clear my throat. "Nothing's changed on the relationship front for me. I'm good as is. Tell me about Zayna. What's she like?"

"She's—she's fantastic. Hilarious. She loves to travel and try new restaurants. I think you'll really like her."

He's downright chipper, which isn't a typical Azar mode. He seems so happy.

"She sounds amazing. If you like her, I know I will too. Hopefully I get to meet her soon."

He looks visibly relieved. "Definitely. Let's make it happen."

Suddenly, it dawns on me. "Did you leave Zayna *at the theater* to come here?"

"This was important."

"Azar . . ." I lean back into the sofa. Zayna's going to *love* me now. "I should have texted to see if you were busy before unloading on you."

He locks his gaze into mine. "I want to be here, Nur."

Headlights brighten the living room. Borzu. I head to the door. I think of what happened with Lilah. The look on Nina's face when she realized I'd taken a call instead of watching her daughter. She hadn't even been surprised. Just resigned. Because she knows I put myself first, doesn't she? I hadn't even considered that Azar could be busy. I had simply launched into what happened as soon as he answered the phone. For that matter, had I asked Borzu if *he* was free before asking him to come over? Is this who I am? Someone who prioritizes myself over others?

"Thanks for coming," I greet Borzu. "I hope I didn't pull you from something important."

"Not unless you count rewatching *Breaking Bad*. It was wild to finally try out my new Tesla in a thunderstorm. The lightning flashing through the glass ceiling was surreal." He pulls out his laptop and sets up shop on the coffee table as I press my rickety front door shut with a shove of my shoulder. On windy days like today, it can have a mind of its own. "Should we get Darcy?"

"She has an early-morning consult with a wedding photographer. Not like she can do anything about any of this anyway. I'll fill her in tomorrow," I say as rain beats harder overhead.

"Now, I hate to say I told you so," Borzu says, "but I've been on you for years to get security cameras installed around the agency."

"The paperwork and red tape to get clearance was endless," I remind him. "The city has their own network, anyway."

"Apparently whoever left this note knew all about their cameras. Or at least how to get around them."

"What do you mean?" My stomach drops. "There's no footage of who left it?"

"Kind of?" He glances at me. "You have to see it for yourself."

He loads a video of the intersection across from our agency. Rain bouncing off concrete. A car zips by. And then—

A hooded figure wearing all black, including a black face

mask—practically blending into the night. They raise a hand toward the camera. I lean forward to make it out when there's a splash against the screen. I flinch. The screen blurs.

For a moment no one speaks. Goosebumps trail my arms.

"What . . . was that?" I ask in a half whisper.

"I'm guessing foamed-up detergent." Borzu expands the feed. Lightens it. "Whoever did this knew someone might look at the cameras and decided to get ahead of it."

"We might as well be looking for Bigfoot," I murmur.

"*Someone* must have seen this guy." Azar points to the frozen image. "Look at him! He's wearing a hoodie, long sleeves, and a face covering and wandering around in the pouring rain. There's no way he wasn't spotted spraying the cameras!"

"It's not a busy intersection," Borzu reminds him. "Plus, it's dark out with the storm."

I think of the taunting voice on the recordings. "Any luck unearthing the podcaster's identity?"

Borzu shakes his head. "Darcy went through the database twice this afternoon. Genevieve cross-checked all our applicants. No one stands out."

"What about the disgruntled personalized clients from the past? Maybe Lindy or Jamaal? Things really went south with them."

"Lindy was on a Tinder date in San Diego. Jamaal's married with a kid, and living in Slovenia."

"Your inbox might have some clues," Azar suggests. "You said you've been getting a ton of hate mail lately. Maybe there's something to uncover there."

"We delete them as soon as they come in," I say. "The subject headings are hard enough to stomach."

"I can retrieve the deleted messages," says Borzu. "I'll get on it first thing tomorrow. Darcy can help me comb through them."

"Wait." A sick feeling washes over me. "Basit Latif. He's beyond furious with me. I don't think he's the podcaster because we had our argument after the first recording had already posted. But I wouldn't put it past him to threaten me like this. Or at least have someone do it for him."

"Basit Latif? . . . Hang on a sec." He types the name into his search engine. He taps a few more times, opens and closes several new windows, and then—"He's in Jakarta right now. I can keep tabs on him if it helps you feel any better."

"It would. Thanks, Borzu."

The next couple of hours are rainy outdoors and useless indoors as we try to work out who the masked man is. When I walk Borzu to the door, it's well past midnight. The rain has eased to a misty fog.

"The weather looks like it's holding for a bit," I tell Azar. "You should head out, too, before it starts coming down again."

"I don't know." He eyes the skylight. "Looks like we could have a downpour at any moment."

"Don't you have work tomorrow? It's your five o'clock shift."

"Exactly." He grabs a throw pillow, tucks it against the sofa arm, and lies back. "I pulled a double yesterday. Catching as much shut-eye as possible is strongly advised."

"Azar—"

"You don't want me to get caught in a storm, do you? They've got extra scrubs in the office."

Gertie climbs onto his chest and settles in, giving her own opinion on the matter. I shake my head and stifle a smile. We both know the real reason for this sleepover. He wants to keep an eye on me. I can't say that I mind.

I head to the hall closet. Maneuvering around my aunt's old boxes, I grab a blanket and toss it to him.

"I remember this one from college." He pats it and yawns.

"It's old, but clean." I settle onto the love seat across from him and kick my feet onto the coffee table. I wrap a throw from the sofa around myself. Rain starts to fall again, plinking against the skylights. Echoing against the wooden floors. Soon it's like an avalanche of water is pouring down—I look outside at the blur of rain. You'd think we were in a boat, lost at sea.

"I forgot to tell you," he says. "I talked to my mother today."

"How's she doing?"

"She's coming for a visit in August. She wanted me to ask if you needed any new clothes from that boutique near Anarkali Bazaar that you like. She's going there later this week."

"Always. Your mom has great taste. I'll call her tomorrow. When are you going to Pakistan to visit *them*?"

"Work's been so erratic lately, it's easier for them to come here. Last summer they were here for three months, remember? There's no way I could ever take that much time off."

"Nina's doing it," I say sardonically. "She's here going on five months, and it looks like she's putting down roots." I tell him about the transcripts.

"A permanent Nina presence?" He looks at me. "What do you think about that?"

"Khala's thrilled to have her home."

"What about you?"

"It's complicated. I'm glad Khala is happy. But every time I go over there now, it's like I'm a stranger in my own home. Nina's a gray cloud hovering over everything. She can't let a moment go by without a snarky comment about the agency." I think about our last interaction. The paint-streaked walls. "Though she's right, I can mix up my priorities sometimes."

"Nina can be difficult," Azar says. "When you're as unhappy as she is, it seeps out toward other people."

"More like it spews out like a broken water main."

"On the bright side, if they're staying, that means more Lilah time?"

"That's a definite perk. I've gotten pretty attached to her." Lilah is a few years shy of the age I was when I moved into Khala's house, not fully processing that my life had forever changed. Maybe I can help her navigate her own huge transition. I look at Gertie snoozing on Azar. Her temporary relocation to my place is probably permanent now. She's adjusted great, but Khala misses her dearly. I make a mental note to bring my aunt by ASAP for some time with her beloved feline.

"Auntie's doing okay health-wise, though?" Azar asks. "No slipups since your birthday?"

"She's better lately."

"Did you tell her about the wedding implosion?"

"No way. We need to *keep* her in a good place. Dr. Pang said at her last doctor visit that stress is the worst thing for her. It's hard, though. To see her so changed."

"Her last scans all looked good."

"No one, not even her neurologist, will get on board with the clinical trials." I remember Nina's dismissiveness. "She is getting older. It's not like she could've kept up the pace she used to keep forever. But why not try to see what could work?"

"What about Khala? What does she want to do?"

"It's like she's given up. If Nina would be open to having a real conversation with me, we could team up and convince her to keep on trying. We can't lose hope that something might cure her, or at least give her more time with us."

"I'm sorry, Nur. This is all so hard."

"It's not like I have that many people in my life. I want to hold on to the ones I *do* have."

"You have me," he says.

"For now," I say lightly.

"For always, Nur."

We'll see, I think.

"I just wish I could visit her without having to walk on eggshells around Nina," I say. "It's exhausting."

"You know what you all need?" He yawns. "A family bonding experience. Something to pull you out of your routines."

"Got any ideas?"

"A basketball game. Everyone gets a Hawks jersey and roots for the home team."

"Next."

"Doesn't your aunt love those Bollywood flicks? A trip to the movies could do the trick."

"Azar." I toss a throw pillow at him. "Can you imagine Nina sitting through a musical romp?"

"What do you think she's into?"

"I don't know. Horror?"

"Might do her some good to watch something lighter together."

"Maybe." That's one major difference between me and Azar. When someone treads over me once, I remember and act accordingly. Azar? He always sees the good in people. He makes excuses for their foibles. I guess I'm grateful for it, because he also sees the good in me, even when I feel wanting.

"Do you know where *The Office* might be streaming?" Azar yawns again. He nods to the television.

"It's nearly two in the morning. You have to be at work in a few hours."

"But I haven't seen it in ages."

"At this point you've got the entire series memorized word for word."

"And you don't?"

"I do. Which is why I've moved on to other shows."

"You can't ever move on from the shows that you imprinted on as a teen."

But neither of us makes a move toward the remote. We keep talking. As time ticks forward, I try to follow the threads, but pretty soon I'm not sure what we're talking about; I'm just grateful to have my best friend here with me. We speak until our eyes grow heavy, our words slower and more nonsensical, until he's telling me about the tastiest burger he's ever had in his life and, mid-sentence, his words trail off. He's asleep.

Exhaustion wraps itself around me, but sleep is harder to come by. I turn onto my side and watch him. He's lying on his back, his hands clasped together. His blanket's askew.

I walk over and straighten it, tucking it up to his chin. He lets out a gentle snore. I give Gertie a quick head rub and then move as quietly as possible, taking care to use the runners to avoid creaking against the wooden floors, and head to the kitchen. Grabbing a glass of water, I lean against the fridge. I can't stop thinking about that man. His dark sweatshirt. Arm raised toward the camera.

Pulling out my phone, I click the podcast app. Hit refresh.

My breath catches. There's a new post. Time-stamped to less than one hour ago. I grab my AirPods from where they're charging on the counter. I slip one into my ear. Click play. There's that same deep masculine voice. He's not angry today. He's downright giddy. And tonight every word comes out crystal clear.

Guess who's not getting married? Avani Patel and Dev Kasturi, that's who! Two lovebirds hand-picked by none other than, drumroll please, Miss Khan herself. Don't believe me? Check out Avani's Instagram. Oh wait—she's deleted it! Doesn't want the world to see her shame after all these months preening on and on about being one of the chosen few to be matched by the perfect matchmaker. Well, how perfect is your magical match looking now, Avani? I see you, Nura Khan. Now the world does too.

The recording cuts off.

Somewhere in the distance, a coyote howls. I trace a finger over the phone screen. His glee at the cancellation of Avani's wedding is chilling, but it's the words in the middle of his rant that take my breath away: *I see you, Nura Khan.*

The same words that were dripping down the note.

I shiver. The note. The sabotaged wedding. They're connected. They tie back to him.

They tie back to me.

avita's bridal boutique is the ultimate mirage. From the outside it's just another unassuming space in a nondescript strip mall filled with desi clothing stores, restaurants, and cafés. But the shop shifts to nearly otherworldly beyond the gauzy curtained entrance. Classical Indian music plays on low, and the walls are lined with folded lenghas and silk saris. Bolts of fabric lay folded and elegantly stacked for anyone interested in custom-tailored traditional gowns.

"Thank you for getting me squeezed in," Darcy says. We stand by the entrance as Savita finishes up with another client. "Last I checked, the waitlist was backed up for months. I'd given up any hope."

"She owes me. My aunt and I set her brother up years ago."

"Well, now *I* owe you," she teases. Looking at me, her expression shifts. "You're all right, though? It's okay not to be fine given everything that's been going on."

"I'm fine. Really. Just wish we could figure out who was behind this. I thought for sure we'd know something by now."

"At least we have a motive."

"At least we think we do. . . ."

"It's obvious! He's clearly a deranged stalker obsessed with

Avani," she says. "I don't know why we didn't piece it together before. He alluded to her testimonial in his first podcast. Remember when he said you're not a magician? Avani's the one who'd called you that. And then his whole rant about social media posts—Avani was the one posting every minute of her marriage prep. The way he cackled about their wedding falling apart." She shivers. "He was fixated on her."

"He seemed equally fixated on me."

"My guess is he blamed you for matching them up," she says. "There hasn't been any hint of him in weeks, has there? I bet he left that note as a sick victory lap."

I hope Darcy's right. Thanks to the note and the footage of the masked man, we were able to file a police report and rush the clearance process with the city to install security cameras at the agency. The office feels like Fort Knox now. And to Darcy's point, it *has* been nearly two weeks since that note was left on our door. Nothing else has happened. Every wedding I've attended since Avani's has been blessedly uneventful. Maybe it's finally behind us.

Or am I simply in the eye of the storm? The walls of the hurricane could be churning in the distance, inching closer. Each morning I promise myself I'll go for a run, determined not to let him spook me, and each morning I look out at the deserted stretch of road from inside my house and think: *Whoever left that note, they're out there.*

I remember feeling this same edgy sensation after my mother died. A lot of the details have faded with time, but the memory of how I felt remains vivid. That feeling of waiting for something else to come crashing down. Would Khala decide I was too much trouble and send me packing? Would something bad also happen to her? And if it did, what then? My thoughts used to run in loops back then. The aftershocks of trauma leave your body tense and bracing for what comes next. But as my aunt told me when I finally let her in—shared with her my deepest fears—even if the feelings are real, it doesn't mean the fear is justified. Just because you think the other shoe is about to drop doesn't mean it will. Maybe whoever was trolling me has moved on. Maybe I should move on too.

Darcy watches me worriedly. I feel a pinch of shame. We are here to pick her wedding outfit, and somehow I've made this moment—Darcy's moment—about me.

"I'm fine, Darcy. Promise. And I'm *really* happy to be here with you for this special moment."

"We're okay with time?" She checks her phone. "Don't forget, you have a two o'clock video call with Beenish."

"I moved it to this morning so we wouldn't have to feel rushed."

"That's great! How's she doing? Any more contact with Austin?"

"Things are going well—she really did block his number and his social media accounts across all platforms. The therapy and coaching are working like a charm. She's further along than I'd have expected. It's going to stick this time."

Darcy's eyes sparkle. "When do we get to introduce her to possible matches?"

"It's time to start pinning down some good options. Jahanzeb might be a good match for her, what do you think?"

"Nayab could be a fit too," Darcy says. "He seems just her type. I'll double-check whether he's still single."

"Ladies, no more business talk." Savita walks toward us. "My apologies for keeping you waiting, but it's officially wedding time for *you*, my dear."

We're ushered into a back room. "It's like I'm Alice in Wonderland," Darcy marvels.

She's right. I've never ventured this way before. Sitar music plays low in the background. There's a tea table flanked with two matching chairs. Piping hot chai sits in a teapot in the center with porcelain cups and a tower of bite-sized sandwiches and scones. Two dressing rooms flank the back wall with identical floor-length mirrors on either side of them, as well as even *more* bridal gowns. Rows and rows of multicolored ghararas and elaborate lenghas and saris stretch out into the distance.

Darcy walks over to a blank-faced mannequin dressed in a lacy gown. She traces the delicate fabric with her finger. Lifting the veil, she examines the price tag. Her smile falls.

Ugh. I'm glad I could help make this moment possible, but there's no denying that Savita's bridal gowns are pricey.

"I'll talk to her about a discount," I whisper. "Desi shops are always up for good old-fashioned bargaining. In all my years, I've never paid sticker price here."

"Even with a discount . . ." Her hands drift to the tag for the gown on the next hanger. She subtly shakes her head. "It's fine." She clears her throat and shoots me a smile. "If I don't end up buying something from here, it'll still give me some good ideas."

Hours pass in the blink of an eye as Darcy tries on different outfits. Now she swings open the door to her dressing room, revealing a beautiful two-toned lengha.

"That one's absolutely perfect," I say.

"You've said that about every outfit I've tried on."

"I mean it about this one!"

"You think?"

"I know. The cut is very flattering."

She checks herself out in front of the floor-length mirror. The champagne of the frock brings a flush to her complexion.

The silver embroidery along the edges adds a touch of elegance and complements the platinum in her hair.

"I agree with Nura." Savita collects our teacups and nods approvingly at Darcy. "It brings out your eyes."

"The price is right too," she murmurs, examining the tag attached to the veil.

"I can give you a good discount on that one," Savita offers. "We have a bit of an overstock."

"We have a winner, then!" Darcy grins. "It's a *tiny* bit snug around the waist, though. Could I get it taken out?"

"Let's get you a size up instead. It's easier to tailor it down."

When Savita reappears, she brings the right size, along with six different outfits.

"Oh noooo," Darcy says. "Savita, my problem isn't finding the perfect dress. It's that you have *too many* perfect dresses."

"Glad to hear it." Savita hangs the new gowns and saris on a hook against the dressing room door. "These arrived last night. Best to be absolutely sure for the most important day of your life."

Darcy purses her lips and examines them. She takes one and hands it to me.

"Try it on," she says.

I raise my eyebrow. "This seems sacrilegious."

"We're basically the same size, aren't we? Come on. Help a girl out. I have so many to try on. Let's call it wedding party duties?"

I can't argue with that. I try on a raw silk dress. A traditional red gown. They're both pretty, but we agree they're not quite right. Next, I try on a periwinkle-colored sari.

"I like that one!" Darcy says when I step out of the dressing room.

"This is a gorgeous sari. But not bridal."

"It's not supposed to be." She gives me a sly look. "It's your maid of honor outfit. I called Savita before we came and asked her if she had a sari in the right color, and I have to say, she really came through."

"Darcy!" It's soft and silky. I walk up to the floor-length mirror. "I love it."

"I'm going with a unifying color theme instead of matching dresses for the bridesmaids, so everyone can choose something they'd actually want to wear."

"I'd definitely wear this again," I tell her. "You know I'm always on the lookout for new wedding attire."

"I hadn't realized." She winks. "Let's do a selfie. I want to remember this moment."

She pulls out her phone. The light flashes and I look at the two smiling women on the screen. In just a few months she'll be married. She'll be traveling the world with Samir. And even when she's back, she'll be busier than before. Her priorities will shift, as they should. I'm happy for her, but between Azar and Darcy, I'm grateful at least Gertie can't get married and move on without me.

As we wrap up, I take my sari to the counter to pay.

"It was going to be a gift for you," Darcy protests. "It's part of the budget."

"Darcy." I shoot her a side-eye.

"It's my way of saying thank you. For that advance on the year-end . . . and for everything, you know?"

My heart swells with affection. She is stressed about money and working so hard to pay down her debts, but here she is earnestly wanting to buy this for me.

"Thanks, Darcy, but it's way too generous when you have so many other important things to spend your money on." I hand Savita my credit card.

After we finish up, we exit the bridal shop. The sun beams bright overhead. Cars rush past us on the busy four-lane road across the way. I peek at the silky outfit in the bag. "Would you mind if I wore this to Lena's mehndi? It's lovely, and I know the perfect jewelry set to go with it."

"Of course you should wear it," Darcy says. "I can't wait for that wedding to be behind us, though. I'm forever paranoid it's not going to happen."

"Has there been any progress with the elephant situation?"

"It's a proper standoff at this point," Darcy says. "Tanvir won't budge, and Lena's standing by her man. The folks at the wedding venue said the liability risk is too high. And they worry it sets a bad precedent."

"I can't argue with them there."

"Me either," she says. "I had no idea Tanvir would turn groomzilla on us. I spoke with Lena's mother yesterday. She's fed up."

Uh-oh. That's not good. It's the children I'm setting up in these arrangements, but it's usually the parents who settle the bill. We aren't planning Lena's wedding, but Tanvir's temperament definitely remains within our professional purview. I make a mental note to give him a call today. Weddings can make us lose perspective. I'll see if I can't talk him down.

As we make our way toward our parked cars, my stomach rumbles.

"Want to grab a bite to eat before we part ways?" I ask her.

She doesn't reply. Her gaze is fixed on something in the distance. A lone car stopped at the red light at the intersection.

"Darcy?" The light turns green. She clutches her purse. The car—a white Mercedes—zips past us. Darcy's shoulders relax.

"You okay?" I ask.

"That's the same car Andrei had," she says bashfully. "But

it's also the same car as a million other people in the metro Atlanta area, so I basically have a mild freak-out multiple times a day."

"He hasn't bothered you since you got the restraining order, has he?"

"Not a peep. I still get jumpy, though. Old habits die hard. I'm fine," she says in response to my worried expression. "Really."

Before I can say more, a familiar voice calls out.

"Nur?"

Azar. He's walking down the sidewalk in blue scrubs. His curls are tamed and brushed back. And— Oh. He's not alone. Alongside him is a woman wearing matching scrubs. There's no winged eyeliner or red dress like the Instagram photo. But it's definitely—

"Zayna?" I blurt out as they approach.

Her easy demeanor shifts as she takes me in. "You must be the famous Nura Khan."

"It's nice to finally meet," I say. "I've heard a lot about you."

"Yeah? I've heard a lot about you too," she replies.

I give Azar a quizzical look. He flushes. "What are you both doing in this part of town?"

"Wedding shopping," says Darcy, after she introduces herself to Zayna. "I might have found the perfect dress."

"That's great," Azar says. An awkward silence falls over us.

I clear my throat. "What about you two kids? Up to anything fun and exciting?"

Kids? Fun and exciting? I cringe. Why am I being so awkward? Also, how does she manage to look drop-dead gorgeous in blue scrubs and orthopedic footwear?

"We took a break to grab some dosas," Azar says. "Zayna introduced me to a hidden gem."

"We were going to check it out a few weeks ago, but I think something came up for you, Nura," she says. "Some kind of emergency?"

"Sorry again about that, Zayna," Azar says. "I shouldn't have gotten up and—"

"No, *I'm* sorry," I interject. "I called him and made it seem like it was a big emergency. It was a strange—"

She waves a hand and cuts both of us off. "It's fine. Water under the bridge."

When they leave, I look at Darcy. "That was . . ."

"Awkward?" Darcy finishes. "Um. Yes. A little bit."

I watch them walk toward Azar's SUV. The last time I met someone he dated for any length of time was our freshman year in college. He and Amara lasted barely two weeks, parted amicably, and she's still my friend. But I get a sinking feeling Zayna won't be interested in a friendship with me. His hand rests on her lower back as he opens the passenger door. This is as serious as Azar's ever gotten. It won't matter how long I've known him. How deep our roots go. If she hates me, the door between me and Azar will close forever.

"I'd say, given that her boyfriend doubles as your pretend fiancé," Darcy says, "if she's a bit cagey around you, it's understandable."

"She doesn't need to worry about that anymore. He officially dumped me."

"What?" She looks stricken. "She told him he couldn't attend weddings with you anymore?"

"He said it was eating up too much of his free time."

"There's no shortage of people to pair you up with for a plus-one. Samir's got a really cute best friend, and he's single. Maybe you could even go on an *actual* date."

"I don't want anyone else. Azar was enough."

"Oh?" Her eyes shine.

"Darcy! Not like that." Heat rises to my face.

"If you say so." Darcy purses her lips, considering. "Okay. Fine. How about I accompany you to Lena and Tanvir's wedding? I'll be your date."

"You're overloaded as is right now. I know I'm throwing myself a pity party here, but I can handle attending a wedding by myself. I do it all the time. Maybe I'll buy a wedding band and say my dashing husband is putting our kids to bed. That could be my new routine going forward."

"Honestly, I'd love to go. It'll be nice to see them off. It's supposed to be the wedding of the decade, right?" She hooks her arm through mine as we near our cars. "Plus, I like spending time with you."

I squeeze her arm. "The feeling's absolutely mutual."

I slow down in front of the chaat house across from our vehicles. The scent of coriander and cumin wafts through the air. I scan the glossy menu pasted against the front door. Per usual, the place is packed with people. I eye the crowded tables. Maybe I can grab an order to go.

Wait.

I inch closer. I look at the man sitting by himself near the window.

It's Logan Wilson.

He's alone. His eyes are fixed on something on the table. It's likely he's watching something on his phone. He doesn't notice me watching him.

Ever since this chaat house got Zagat rated, the place draws just about everyone. If he's in town for business, it's not out of the question that he'd hunt down one of the best eats around.

But to be in the exact same area at the exact same time as me? Atlanta isn't some quaint pastoral village. We're a sprawling urban development nightmare. Why is he here?

"What's the matter?" asks Darcy.

"That's Logan." I point him out. "Kind of a weird coincidence, right?"

"That *is* weird." She looks at me. "You think he was following us?"

"Who knows? Since that note I feel paranoid about everything."

"I can't blame you. I'm glad you cleared your schedule for this afternoon," she tells me. "You need to take your mind off things."

Logan is not following you, I chide myself. He did *not* leave that note. He had no reason to. It's like Darcy said, whoever left it proved their point. Spooked me within an inch of my life and moved on. I need to clear my head. Get out the adrenaline pumping uselessly in my system. I'll stop for groceries, and then I'll lace up my sneakers and hit the track near my house. The park is always packed with soccer practices and baseball games around this time of day. It's safe. A run will do me good.

I get in my car and turn on the ignition. The small space fills with welcome air-conditioning. Before I pull out of the parking spot, I text Azar.

Let's get this out of the way: Zayna hates me, right?

Three dots immediately appear.

What? She loved meeting you!

Mmmhmm, I reply.

We need to all grab dinner ASAP, he texts. You'll love her.

Is that what you're starting to feel toward her, Azar? I wonder. *Love?*

As I made my way down the highway, my phone rings. I move to decline, but I pause at the name blinking on the screen: *Stark Residential Security Services.*

The woman on the other line asks me to answer a host of verification questions, then—

"We received an alert that your house alarm has gone off."

I draw a sharp intake of breath. "I—I'm not home."

"It looks like Zone One was activated. There may be no need to worry. Alarms go off for all kinds of reasons. We have an officer en route to check out the property."

I take the first exit off the interstate. *Chill, Nura,* I try to tell myself. That rickety front door triggers the alarm even when it's snugly secured, though it's never done it when I wasn't home. Gripping the steering wheel, I accelerate through a yellow light and roll through each stop sign until I turn onto my street.

It's fine. Nothing is wrong. Stay calm.

But calm, I realize once I pull into my driveway, is something I'm not sure I'll ever feel again. The alarm screams. It pulses through the sleepy street as though warning of an impending air raid.

My front door is open. Flapping back and forth in the breeze.

Unsteadily, I stumble out of my car. Wind tousles my hair. I inch closer to the opening. From the foot of my steps, I scan the door for signs of damage. There's no way I'm getting any closer. I'll wait for the police.

Then my blood goes cold.

Gertie.

Rational thought vanishes. I take the front steps two at a time and stumble into the foyer. I rush into my living room and survey the scene. My television. The expensive speakers that Azar gifted me two years ago. My spare MacBook rests on the bookshelf. Everything is still here.

"Gertie!" I call out. I grab the tin can with her favorite salmon treats. The ones that coax her from her coziest of hideaways. I rattle it as I hurry through the rest of the house.

I scream her name until my voice goes hoarse, flipping open cabinets, scanning beneath my bed, but as police lights flash outside the windows, I already know.

Gertie is gone.

TEN

It's been three days and there's been no word on Gertie.

"Did the police have any updates?" Genevieve asks when I arrive at the agency.

"I'm not sure why I bothered to swing by the station again. They're still insisting my rickety front door flew open on a windy day."

"That's bullshit," says Borzu.

"They're stuck on the fact that nothing was taken. Like Gertie doesn't count? But they insist no one's breaking and entering to steal a senior cat. I *know* my door can be stubborn. That's why I'd elbowed it shut that morning like I do every day, to make sure."

Didn't I?

Or was I so lost in my thoughts that I failed to properly pay attention? Maybe the door *wasn't* closed all the way. Maybe it's easier for me to blame an intruder than to blame myself.

Azar and I have put up signs everywhere. We handed out flyers with Gertie's photo and my contact information to every local café, restaurant, and store within a ten-mile radius. There have been no sightings. Not that I'd expected any. Gertie lived indoors her entire life. She never expressed a remote interest in going outdoors. Khala couldn't even coax her into the out-door catio she'd had built for her. Someone took her. Someone who wanted to hurt me. Who wanted me to know that they were still out there.

Khala. Tears fill my eyes. I need to tell her what happened. But how? She entrusted her beloved pet to me for safekeeping, and now she's missing.

"Too bad there's woods across the street from you, or we could have had a chance to at least grab a neighbor's camera footage," Borzu says. "I ordered you video surveillance. I'll install it as soon as it arrives."

"I'm sorry, Nura," Genevieve says. "This is too much to take back-to-back."

"Any updates on Basit's whereabouts on the day Gertie went missing?" I ask.

"Basit has been in Malaysia all week," Borzu says. "His search history is clean."

"His search history." Genevieve shakes her head. "I don't know why I'm surprised."

"I only hack for good, but there's nothing shady in there—or rather," he amends, "nothing shady pertaining to you, Nura. I'm still digging in on the podcaster's identity. My contact said they're going to introduce me to someone who knows someone. Waiting to hear back. Sooner or later we'll get to the bottom of it, I promise."

I know my team is doing their best to figure out what's going on. I know things take the time they will. It's what I counsel my clients on practically every time we speak: the importance of patience. But it's harder for me to follow my own advice. How is it possible to keep on hitting dead end after dead end? How much longer do we have to wait until we know what's

going on? I think of Gertie and push back tears. The not knowing is physically painful.

"While we figure things out . . ." Genevieve glances at
Borzu, then me. "We were thinking that maybe it's time for
some personal security for you. Just to be on the safe side."

"Borzu ordered surveillance equipment," I remind her.

"Nura." Genevieve rolls her eyes. "I'm talking about real security."

"She means a bodyguard," Borzu interjects.

"Or maybe if you had a gun," Darcy begins.

A gun? Just the word gives me goosebumps. I look at their
concerned expressions. "I get it. I'm worried too. But you all
know how I feel about guns. I've got my Mace. And we took
that self-defense class last year, remember?"

"All the self-defense in the world won't help if the other
person is armed," Darcy insists. "After that whole Andrei mess,
I feel so much safer now that I have one."

"A gun is a nonstarter. Lilah goes through my things all the
time. I can't take any risks."

"At least let me check in with our contacts for a good personal security agency," Genevieve says. "It can take some time
to get things set up."

The thought that I might need a bodyguard makes me
shiver. My phone trills a reminder alarm.

"Can we table this for now? I have a virtual appointment
with Beenish that I need to prep for," I tell them.

At this, Darcy perks up. "Any idea how her date with Nayab
went?"

"She flew up to New York last night to meet him. She texted
me this morning and sounded thrilled."

"I have a feeling about those two!" Darcy exclaims.

"You have that matchmaking eye," I tell her. "I *am* going to insist she meet the three other potentials we lined up. It's good to explore all options. But Nayab definitely seems promising."

"This is the best part of the job, isn't it?"

She's right. It's hard to beat that feeling when you realize that you might have helped steer the trajectory of someone's entire future in a better direction. Even with all the heaviness around me, at least there's this bright bit of news.

I settle into my office as the phone rings. It's a few minutes early for our chat, but when I check the number, it's not Beenish.

"Nura?" the woman on the other line asks once I answer. "This is Patti—your neighbor from three doors down. I saw the flyer for your kitty taped up over at Java Nut. I think I might have spotted her on my way home."

"You saw Gertie?" I sit up straight.

"It was definitely a white-and-silver kitty. I tried getting closer, but she got spooked. Slipped behind The Tavern next door."

I grab my keys. Skirting my desk, I tell Darcy to reschedule my call with Beenish, and hurry out the door. Maybe the police had it right. Maybe the door really did blow open, and then Gertie freaked and bolted. Maybe I can find her. Maybe Khala won't ever have to know what happened.

But three hours of searching the nooks and crannies around The Tavern prove fruitless. There's no sign of her. No trace at all.

"Any luck?" Patti asks when I pull into my driveway. She's standing across the street, her beagle on a red leash.

I shake my head. "She may have fled by the time I arrived."

"I wish I could have grabbed a picture," Patti says. "She moved quickly."

I hesitate. "Patti, did you happen to see anything unusual the day Gertie went missing? Any strange cars or people on our street?"

"That was Tuesday, wasn't it? I babysit the grandkids on Tuesdays and Thursdays. I was gone for much of the day. I'm sorry, honey. If I'd seen your door open, I'd have shut it. I'm happy to share my handyman's information so you can get it fixed right up."

"Thanks, Patti."

"Don't worry, hon, she'll turn up. I bet she didn't go far. Those woods across from us, they're a dream come true for a cat to explore."

I look at the shadowed woods in the distance. Pine and poplar and brush ten acres deep. I imagine Gertie slipping out my door to frolic among those trees, chase squirrels, and catch mice in her twilight years. A final moment to reclaim her Siberian forest roots.

If only this was the image that stuck. Not the other thought that runs in a loop in my mind's eye. Of that man. The one in the dark hooded sweatshirt. His face obscured by a mask. Drifting down my street. Skulking about my house. Who knew that grabbing Gertie, Khala's treasured pet, was the exact right way to bring me to my knees.

I blink back tears. If that's his plan, if that's what happened, if he's behind this, then it's working.

ELEVEN

"Are you sure Darcy's still on for the wedding?" Azar asks over the car Bluetooth.

"Why wouldn't she be?" I stop at a red light. I'm on my way to Khala's to get the jewelry set to go with my sari.

"I'm just saying, I can be there."

"I thought you broke up with me."

"Fine. I can admit that I'm jealous. Darcy getting to eat all that amazing food? How's that fair?"

"You turned it down!" I make a right onto Long Island Drive. Sunlight wanes through the trees.

"Sometimes you don't know what you have until it's gone."

"I'm fine, Azar."

Besides, I think, *I'm pretty sure Zayna would* not *approve.*

"And you have the Mace?" he asks.

"For the thirteenth time, yes." This is the real reason he's calling. The real reason he's allegedly craving wedding food. Like everyone from Borzu to Genevieve to Darcy, he wants to pop me into a protective bubble. "There are ten different cameras around the agency and my house. Pretty sure the neighbors suspect I'm on some kind of reality television show," I say.

"Borzu made sure my phone and car were clear of trackers. I'm okay, really."

"Have there been any more cat sightings?"

"None." My voice breaks. "I don't know how to live with myself, Azar. Khala trusted me with her cat, and I lost her."

"Nur. Don't do that. Beating yourself up isn't going to make it better."

Even if I deserve it? Hoping to change the subject, I ask, "What are you up to tonight?"

"Not much. I might go for a run, but other than that, it's a television and chill kind of night."

"A *run?*" My eyebrows shoot up. "Since when did you pick up running?"

"I run sometimes!" he protests.

"That 5K I dragged you to sophomore year does not count."

"Well, forgive me for wanting to be a little more physically active."

"I can swing by after I'm done at the wedding. I'll see if I can finagle you a doggy bag. Running can build up quite the appetite."

"Uh, yeah. Sounds good."

I arch an eyebrow up. When you know someone as long as we've known each other, you know when they're not saying something.

"Is Zayna coming by?"

"Zayna? Not sure. Maybe."

Which means definitely yes. He's probably fluffing up the couch pillows and preparing a carpaccio dinner for two as we speak. Zayna's probably the reason behind his recent interest in running too. I think back to her photo holding up a marathon medal. I've been on him to run with me since middle school, when I begged him to join me on the cross-country team. I guess running wasn't a priority until he found the right person to make it one.

"I'm almost at Khala's," I tell him. "Talk later?"

"Have fun, and, Nur? Stay safe."

We hang up and I yank down the sun visor to avoid the sun's glare. I need to get my head in the right space—and trying to figure out Azar's love life is the exact opposite of the right headspace.

As soon as I pull into Khala's driveway, my pulse ticks up. What do I say if she asks about Gertie? It's been ten days since her cat went missing. I wake up multiple times a night at the scraping of a tree branch against my window. Hoping it's her. Hoping I can put this nightmare behind me.

I need to get it together. Get my game face on for Khala. It will be good practice for the game face I'll need for Lena and Tanvir's mehndi. For a few hours tonight I'll slip into the welcome relief of work mode. Darcy's coming to babysit me, but she knows how to have a good time too. It's not every day she joins me at weddings, and given her upcoming sabbatical and marriage, who knows how many more events like these she'll have time for. I want to make tonight count.

I park in Khala's driveway and attempt to maneuver out of the car in my bulky sari. Driving while wrapped in seventeen feet of fabric is more complicated than it may seem at first glance. Or maybe—I look down—it's exactly as complicated as it looks. Approaching the house, I check my watch. Even for someone who's usually on Desi Standard Time, I'm running a tad behind, but Khala's platinum set inlaid with diamond-shaped sapphires will match perfectly. Days when I feel the most vulnerable are when I need my armor most of all.

"You look like a princess," Lilah announces when she sees me.

She hops up from the couch where she was sitting with Nina, a puzzle splayed out on the coffee table. Nina barely acknowledges me.

"Thanks," I tell her.

I peek at the wall; to my relief, the stain from the ill-fated mural is completely gone.

"I don't like princesses," Lilah clarifies.

"Oh yeah?" I tickle her. "But you like this one, don't you?"

"No!!! Yessss!!!" She squeals with laughter.

"Mom's in her room," Nina tells me. Her eyes are on her phone. She's in sweatpants and an oversized T-shirt. Her hair is rumpled. "It's . . . it's not the best day for her."

"What happened?" From the looks of it, it's not the best day for Nina either.

She hesitates, then turns to her daughter. "Want to go watch TV?"

"Really?" Her eyes widen.

"One episode."

Lilah races upstairs—moments later, I hear the familiar opening notes of her favorite Pokémon show.

"Mom forgot to pick up Lilah from school," Nina tells me. "She left the house and came home an hour later without her. She was foggy and confused. I have no idea where she went."

My heart sinks. This is the biggest memory slip she's had. "Was Lilah okay?"

"She didn't even notice. The teachers put her in with the aftercare kids, so she was on the swings with her buddies when I got there. I had to pry her away. It's not like she was remotely in danger, but of course Mom's beating herself up over it."

Khala had been having a streak of good days, so many that

I'd let myself be lulled into thinking that maybe—just maybe—her mind was recalibrating. That the memory lapses would soon become a thing of the past, and not an inevitability like the doctors have spelled out time and again. But moments like these are only going to increase. This is one of the hardest things to accept with Khala's decline: Whether I like it or not, I am going to lose her.

"Let's look into getting a mother's helper for you to get Lilah from school," I say. "A housekeeper a few hours a day can't hurt either."

"Thanks, Nura."

I'm grateful that despite the mess I made of things last time I was over, we're able to have a conversation where I don't feel like I'm walking across a minefield.

"Normally, I would have noticed that it had been a while since she'd been gone," Nina says. "I've been distracted because I got served a few hours ago."

"Served? As in a process server came by?"

She holds up a manila envelope that had been resting on the coffee table. "Divorce papers. He beat me to the punch."

"Nina . . ."

"Want to know the best part? He didn't ask for custody. Even as a backhanded way to fuck with me." Her voice cracks. "He wouldn't have won, but he couldn't be bothered to try. Guess he wants to start over new and pretend this part of his life never happened. That kills me for Lilah. He *does* want the house, though. I know how to pick them, don't I?"

She wipes her eyes with the backs of her hands.

"If it helps you feel better, Khala and I never liked him."

She looks at me, then lets out a laugh. "That does help, actually."

"We can figure out a way to make him back off without putting up too much of a fight."

"Like what?"

"We have private investigators at our disposal at the office," I remind her. "You already know why he wants a divorce. We can see what else is going on with him. If there's anything that can help you, count us in."

Nina doesn't say anything.

"Not everyone wants to dig deeper—it *can* get ugly," I quickly add. "I know you don't like what we do at the agency. But—"

"Let's do it. I want to pin that fucker so hard he won't be able to move. I'll be damned if he takes my house."

"That's the spirit." I've seen people in the midst of breakups like hers. I know there will be ebbs and flows to this journey—but it's good to see her in fight mode right now, as opposed to the teary-eyed, exhausted version from moments earlier. If she lets me, I'll support her however I can.

Khala's in bed when I enter her room. The tangerine bedcovers are draped over her. She pauses the Pakistani drama on the television—the actress freezes mid-pout.

"Don't *you* look like a movie star?" Khala smiles at me, but her smile does not reach her eyes.

"Are you all right?" I ask her.

"I abandoned my granddaughter. Surely Nina told you what happened."

"You didn't abandon her. Lilah's fine. She was never in danger."

"She was my responsibility." Her voice wavers. "Yet even this simple task was beyond me. If I can't even look after my own grandchild, I'm no help to anyone."

"Khala." I squeeze her hand. "It was one time. Things happen. You're a huge help to us just by being you."

I give her my most comforting smile. Inside, though, I am unmoored. My cool, calm, and collected khala—it's hard to reconcile her with the frail woman lying in this bed. I'm not accustomed to having to help her feel better. There's no way I can tell her about Gertie even if I wanted to.

She clears her throat. "You are here for jewelry, not to hear me prattle on and on. You see? My head is not set on straight lately."

I accompany her to the dresser, where she slides open the top drawer and runs her fingers over the varied boxes inside. The more expensive sets are in the bank—as are many of the heirloom necklaces and rings she brought over from Pakistan— but even the ones in this drawer are easily worth thousands of dollars.

She pulls out a velvet box. There it is: the platinum set. I trade out my silver bracelets for the chunky bangles. She unclasps the necklace from its brackets and hands it to me. "I must say, this one looks tailor-made for your sari."

"It's even more perfect than I remember," I marvel. "I've never seen anyone with a collection like yours, Khala."

"My trinkets pale in comparison to the sorts of jewelry our clients have."

"They may have higher-valued possessions, but they can't match your taste."

Even when I was a little girl, she'd indulge me with these rings and bangles. Let me slide open these drawers anytime I liked. She'd fasten a necklace around my neck and applaud as I modeled it in front of the vanity. These were among my earliest memories of moving here, when this home was too big. Too sprawling. The ceilings too high and echoey. The heft of the solid-gold bangles clinking against my wrist as I turned the pages of a book on the couch soothed me. Khala never stopped me. Never chided me or warned me not to handle them too roughly. Which I never did anyhow. Even then, I knew them for the special pieces they were.

I hold up my hair and she clasps the necklace around my neck. "I think I might have followed you into the family business just so I can have an excuse to wear these."

"Bilqis . . ."

A lump grows in my throat. I turn to look at her, to tell her I'm Nura, but her eyes are fixed on my reflection in the mirror.

"Your mother, she loved this set."

I trace the delicate platinum along my collarbone, now all the more precious. "Was this one from Pakistan?"

Khala nods. "I pawned many of the expensive ones early on, but I worked with everything I had to get this one back. It was her favorite. It will be yours someday."

Had my mother ever worn this necklace around me? Pictures only help so much for memories I was too young to hold on to properly. It astonishes me sometimes, how connected I feel to a woman I barely knew. Do I really miss her, or am I missing what could have been? The other life that could have existed with her as a part of it?

"Whose wedding are you attending?" Khala asks.

"It's Lena and Tanvir's mehndi tonight."

"Ah. The Karma Cosmetics heiress. She's the one who was featured in the magazine that spoke disparagingly of our work?"

"That wasn't her fault. She meant well when she highlighted our agency."

"Good intentions can only do so much," Khala says. "But Lena's praise for you was certainly well deserved. I am not sure if I say this enough, but I am so proud of you, Nura. For all you have done at the agency. I rest easy knowing it is in good hands. You have taken on so many responsibilities without a word of complaint."

I bite my lip, thinking of Gertie. I don't deserve her praise.

"Lena gave me a lot of credit in the piece," I say, "but Darcy was the one who worked with her the most. I'm grateful for her help, because Tanvir has been a handful lately. It's one of the few cases we worked on side by side from start to finish."

"Who knew a gori girl would so deftly handle the desi business?" Khala chuckles.

"She sees herself as an honorary desi," I say. "And she's my date tonight."

At this, Khala's eyebrows furrow. "What about Azar?"

"He said he wasn't up for being my pretend fiancé anymore."

"And you did not convince him otherwise?"

"He—he met someone." The words taste bitter in my mouth. "It looks like it must be serious if he's pulling back from being my plus-one. That boy loves his wedding feasts."

"I cannot believe it." Khala clucks her tongue.

"It's fine. He's still my friend. He always will be. But things change. Part of life, right?"

"Nura . . ."

I give her a hug. "It's fine, Khala. Really."

By the time I hurry back to my car, the sun is setting. I'm running late, but still within the respectable window.

Pulling out my keys, I pause. An unsettled feeling washes over me.

I'm being watched.

The sensation bears down on me with an intensity that feels as real as if someone were physically pressing their palms around my neck. Except there's no one here. No one mowing lawns. No children riding bicycles. The street is deserted.

It's nothing, I tell myself. Or maybe it's as simple as a neighbor looking out their kitchen window while they cook dinner. I must make an interesting sight in my sari and six-inch heels.

My phone buzzes with a text from Darcy.

Almost there. Running a little late!

Me too. On my way over now! I reply.

I adjust my sari. The car chirps when I click my key fob. That's when I see it.

The car.

It's parked around the bend of a cul-de-sac, four homes down. A gray Mustang. Pulled over next to the curb. There's a glint inside—a flash of movement. Someone's in there.

It could be a salesperson writing up a quote for a new roof. A child home from college, catching up on texts before heading inside. It could have nothing to do with me.

I know I'm jumpier than usual. Even the sound of the air conditioner sparking on in my house makes me flinch. Even though I've repaired the door, I still triple bolt it and check the locks multiple times throughout the night. I am the proverbial hammer who looks around and sees only nails.

But what if this time I'm right?

I stare at the parked car. There's movement again. Whoever is inside is watching me. A wave of fury swoops over me. I'm tired of this jump-woman crap. Enough. I march toward the parked car. If it's a kid texting, they'll be irritated and move on. And if it's my stalker—I think of that hooded man—well, he won't be my stalker anymore. My victim, maybe. They'll realize they poked the wrong bear. I unzip my purse. Grab the Mace tucked beneath my makeup bag. I rap my knuckles sharp against the driver's window. No movement. Then, slowly, the window lowers. My heart pounds, the stupidity of my actions fully hitting me. Before I can do anything, the window lowers completely. I stare at the unexpected person looking back at me.

"Genevieve?"

She eyes the Mace in my hand with a bemused expression. "You know that's the worst one on the market, right? Takes twenty seconds to kick in. I swear, you never consult me on these things." She takes a long sip from a Styrofoam soda cup. "It's hurtful, really."

"What are you doing here?"

"House hunting. What do you think I'm doing? I'm surveilling you." She rolls her eyes. "Car's in the shop. Like my rental?"

"Genevieve—"

"Nura, I'm keeping an eye out."

"Did you see anything suspicious?"

"It's been a dull evening."

"Are you planning to follow me to the mehndi as well?"

"You got it."

"You could have told me that you were going to be following me, Genevieve!"

"I told you that you needed coverage. So, I'm covering you."

I have competing impulses to hug her and strangle her.

"For someone so proud of their work-life boundaries, you have a funny way of showing it," I tell her.

"What can I say? I'm partial to you, Nura."

"Well, I'm partial to you too." I smile. "They've got restricted entry at that mehndi," I remind her. "I'd say it's one of the safest events I'll ever attend."

"Restricted doesn't mean impossible to get into," she says. "I'll chill in the parking lot and make sure things stay as boring as possible for you *and* the cosmetics heiress."

"I can't talk you out of it?" I appreciate her concern, but it's a Friday night. Knowing she's sitting out here is touching, but I also feel bad.

"Once you agree to a bodyguard, I'm gone." She pulls a long sip of soda from her straw, and the ice whistles. "Until then, consider me your shadow."

There's no arguing with her.

She turns on her car, the ignition rumbling. "After you."

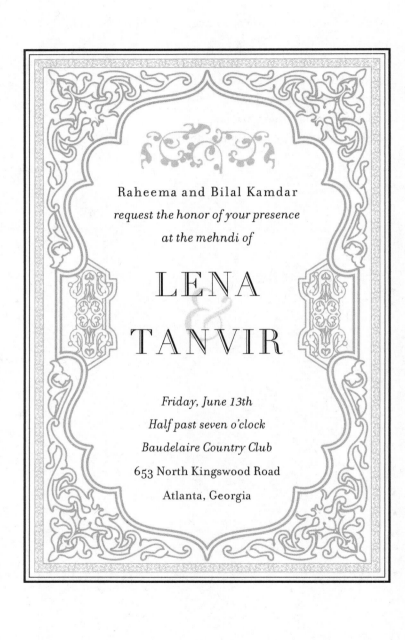

Raheema and Bilal Kamdar
request the honor of your presence
at the mehndi of

LENA
&
TANVIR

Friday, June 13th
Half past seven o'clock
Baudelaire Country Club
653 North Kingswood Road
Atlanta, Georgia

A banner adorned with marigolds welcomes me when I walk inside the swanky Baudelaire Country Club. I give my name and identification to the check-in clerk. Genevieve really doesn't need to be here. Unlike a hotel, where there could be a million different access points, there's only one way in tonight, and it's through metal detectors and a gate that's opened and closed by black-garbed guards who won't let you through without both photo identification *and* a signed nondisclosure agreement promising you won't share any media of the event online.

You really don't want to head home? I text Genevieve. It's as secure as can be here.

I'm all set, she replies. For all the security they have inside, they have no one out here, do they? Have fun. I'm catching up on podcasts.

My heart swells, touched by Genevieve's kindness. There's no point protesting. Once Genevieve makes up her mind, there's no changing it.

I hardly recognize the interior when I step into the main hall. Flowers in mehndi colors of red, yellow, and orange overflow on the stage, the tables, and the windows. A cushioned dais rests atop a stage adorned in yet more florals. The back windows overlook the golf course, which features exotic plants imported from around the world. The bride and groom probably already took their photos out there—a separate and pricey add-on to the wedding packages at this place—not that they'd have blinked at the expense. I know they've flown in Chef Zardar from Islamabad for this plated affair. Already, I can smell the buttery scent of naans going into the tandoori grills they had built on-site. This place is famous for not allowing outside chefs, but everyone has a price. I feel a wistful tug—I wish I'd let Azar come. Sure, it was a pity offer, but Mr. Foodie would have died over the eats here.

Darcy hurries toward me. Her blond hair falls soft against her shoulder. Her cheeks are flushed pink. "I am *so* sorry. I can't believe I'm this late. Traffic was a complete nightmare."

"Don't worry about it. I just got here too," I tell her. "Looks like it's a slow start to the festivities anyhow."

She adjusts the straps of her dress—then eyes me. "You look a bit flustered yourself."

"Had a bit of a scare earlier." I recount the run-in at Khala's home, and how Genevieve's parked outside the country club as we speak.

"Good on her," she says.

"Thanks for coming tonight," I tell her. "I know this is out of the way for you."

"It'll be nice to see Lena off." She looks around wistfully. "I forgot how beautiful this venue is. You know it's one hundred grand just to reserve the space? Not to mention the photos in the garden. The food. Décor."

"The Georgian Terrace will be just as wonderful," I assure her. "I personally like it better."

"We'll see if that's still on," she says with a sigh. "They announced another round of layoffs at Samir's work last week."

"Again?" I grimace.

"Just as we were getting ready to put down the second half of the deposit."

"Oh, Darcy, that's unbelievably stressful."

"I've crunched the numbers a million different ways, but if he loses his job, there aren't enough corners in the world I can cut to make it happen on my income. Samir suggested we push the wedding date out and regroup, but we already sent out save the date cards. The thought of postponing . . ." She bites her lip. "I told him, we'll just go simpler. Maybe we can shoot for the Springmont Club or something. Won't be as nice, but what can we do?"

"Hopefully it won't come to that." I pat her arm. "No matter what, though, the wedding isn't the most important thing, it's the marriage. Who you're marrying matters more than where you get married. You and Samir are riding high on that count."

"Well, that's definitely true." Glancing around, she sighs again. "There's no competing with weddings like these for mere mortals like us anyhow. Lena's coming in tonight on a gold-plated gondola carried by her cousins. Tanvir's arriving on a white horse."

"At least he gets an animal arrival at one of the events. I talked to the wedding planner yesterday to see if she'd had any luck on moving the needle, but she told me the venue isn't budging. Not that I blame them."

"Yikes." She winces. "How's he taking it?"

"I spoke to him this morning, and he's bummed, but he promised he's letting it go."

"Even without the elephant, you know this whole weeklong

event has got to cost somewhere in the seven figures. Samir's mom? She doesn't even want to throw us a basic mehndi. I begged her to reconsider, but no luck."

"You want a mehndi?"

"I know, I know. My sister said the same thing." She gives me a sheepish look. "But what girl doesn't want her wedding to go on and on and on for days?"

"Y'all do have a rehearsal dinner. So technically that's two days."

"Boring." She rolls her eyes. "Desi culture is the best for a reason."

As someone who works for our agency, she knows desi culture, but the parts she's complimenting right now are the parts everyone can see. The clothing. The decorations. The food and cultural rites of marriage. But desi culture goes deeper than that. It's not just the sapphire-encrusted necklaces or the Bollywood music the deejay is blasting from the corner of the room. It's caring for your elders, as I look out for my khala. It's the quiet considerations for those you love, for better *and* worse— sometimes even at the expense of oneself—that I associate most with my own heritage. But I can't blame Darcy for reducing it to what the eye can behold—what you do see *is* beautiful.

"It's clear his mother hates me," Darcy continues. "His older sister had all the works, and they covered every last cent. I know in-laws don't always love their daughters-in-law, but I've been trying *so* hard. Samir says they'll come around. . . . Here's hoping, I guess."

Poor Darcy. Intercultural marriages can be fraught, but knowing that doesn't mean it hurts any less.

"Even the grumpiest in-laws would come around to you." I put an arm around her. "Especially when they realize you're basically a desi girl underneath it all. And I can throw you a mehndi. I have that curated list of henna artists too. It won't be . . ." I wave a hand at the hall. "It won't be this, but it could be nice?"

Her eyes glisten. "Are you serious?"

"Let's call it maid of honor duties. My aunt's backyard would be the perfect venue, don't you think? We could put up a colorful tent and lights. It will look beautiful."

"Nura, you're the best." She gives me a hug.

An assortment of appetizers is placed on our table. Keema patties. Crispy samosas. Chicken kebab skewers.

I check my watch. "There is one part of desi culture you can't possibly love. We do not know how to start an event on time."

"Knowing Lena, this was always going to be a delayed affair," says Darcy. "But yes . . . it's getting late, isn't it?"

Judging from the restlessness among the guests, we're not the only ones wondering. I check the time and feel my anxiety rising, remembering the last wedding I attended where things began to run late and a disaster followed.

Scanning the space, I spot the bride's mother. Raheema is chatting animatedly with the caterer. *Lena's fine,* I tell myself. *All is well.*

I refresh my email. There's a message from Logan Wilson.

Hey, Nura. I'll be back in town tomorrow. Could I interest you in lunch? —Logan

"Unbelievable." I show Darcy the email.

"He's a dog with a bone, isn't he?" she says.

"I need to get him an electric collar so he'll stay far away from me. When does this become harassment? Are we already there?"

"He's just eager for his clickbait article."

"Except . . . he already has a story with Avani's wedding."

"I doubt she's cooperating."

"He doesn't need her to cooperate. Just presenting the facts about what happened, that a wedding I facilitated fell apart, would be enough to fuel gossip and speculation until the end of time. I can't imagine the impact for our agency." I purse my lips. "Maybe I *should* talk to him."

Darcy stares at me like I've sprouted antlers. "Hi, I'm Darcy, and what have you done with my friend Nura?"

"If he's going to publish a negative story, I should get the counternarrative out too."

"With Logan?"

"Maybe, I don't know. We just need our side of things out there."

"It *would* be nice to set the record straight. Remember the viral tabloid piece that said Piyar was a front for a high-powered escort service? We really should have gone after them."

"The curiosity from the press isn't going to let up. It's like Borzu said, Logan is a well-respected journalist. Any accusation he posts will be taken seriously."

"Want me to check if *The New York Times* is still interested in that puff piece?"

"That would be perfect."

A door swings open in the distance. The aroma of freshly baked bread wafts into the ballroom. Darcy tilts her head and eyes me.

"It must be strange to attend weddings without Azar," she says. "How are you feeling?"

"Happy to be here tonight with *you*."

"I checked out Zayna's profile this afternoon," Darcy says. "She posts nonstop, doesn't she?"

"Darcy!"

"Social media is the only acceptable form of stalking. I got curious after we ran into her." She hesitates. "You doing okay?"

"Why wouldn't I be?"

"You and Azar are close. . . ."

"Fine, I guess I'm nervous. Azar and me—we've known each other most of our lives. Even if Zayna genuinely *loved* me, how many people would be cool with our friendship?"

"She'll have to accept you come with the package."

"I don't think it works that way. It's early still, but they seem serious. I get the feeling our days as friends are numbered."

"I can't see Azar sacrificing his friendship with you for anyone. She'll get over whatever hang-up she has."

I think of our last wedding together. His fitted black sherwani. His dimpled smile. The shiver that ran through me when he playfully kissed my hand. If I were Zayna, I would not approve of me.

"Hope she's good enough for him," I say instead.

"We can look into that, can't we?"

"Good idea."

"Like you haven't already started?"

"I haven't!" I protest. "But okay, yes—I've been meaning to."

"A quick skeleton-in-the-closet scan is what a good friend would do, anyway."

Darcy's right. I'll make peace with this shift soon enough, but she *does* need to be good enough for Azar. That's non-negotiable. I clear my throat, eager to change the topic.

"How's the honeymoon planning going?" I immediately regret my question when I see her grimace.

"That's up in the air. I'm exploring a plan B. Something local and less pricey. There's a cute bed-and-breakfast in Savannah that I think could work. Low-key honeymoons are catching on these days. You know, for all their extravagance with the wedding, Lena and Tanvir are honeymooning at a resort off the coast of Charleston, South Carolina. It's two grand a night for the penthouse suite, but I was sure they'd end up in Bali for a month."

Lena and Tanvir. I glance around. People are checking their phones. The hushed murmurs are growing louder. I turn to Darcy. "I'm sure she's just gotten tied up in a dress snafu or something, but can you text Lena to make sure she's all right?"

"Sure." She pulls out her phone.

I tap my feet and try to wish away the whisper of dread crawling up my spine. That it's happening again. Someone slipped in. Left a note. Something's wrong.

"The text isn't going through." Darcy frowns. "Let me call her." She holds the phone to her ear. Shakes her head. "Straight to voicemail."

"I need to find Raheema."

I'm about to seek her out when I hear a commotion behind me. Out of the corner of my eye, I glimpse a glint of metal. Handcuffs. Police officers hurry inside. They brush past me.

Heart pounding, I trail behind them. Raheema and her husband are inside a room off to the side. They're holding hands. Raheema is trembling. There is no bride here. No groom.

I feel sick. Two weddings sabotaged in a matter of weeks. Whatever was done this time had been enough to prompt the parents to call the police. Raheema spots me. Tearfully, she waves me in.

"I don't understand." Her voice trembles. She clutches my arm. "How is this happening?"

I start to tell her that whatever note she found is likely forged, but she speaks first.

"Tanvir and Lena are missing."

THIRTEEN

It's not supposed to be like this.

"Ladies and gentlemen." The best man adjusts the microphone. The high-pitched feedback makes everyone wince. He clears his throat and tries again. "If we can have your attention, please."

At this late hour, we should be gearing up for the final mehndi rituals. The drink of milk the bride's sisters will offer the groom in exchange for money. Aunties should be lining up to feed them each a bite of sweet laddu.

Instead, Tanvir's father hovers next to the emcee. He buttons and unbuttons his sherwani vest. Despite the frigid air-conditioning blasting through the ballroom, his forehead gleams with perspiration. The police crowd before the stage like groupies waiting for the main performance.

"If I could just have a moment of your time," Tanvir's friend says. "We wanted to see if anyone has heard from Lena or Tanvir and—"

The groom's father snags the mic from him. When he speaks his voice is three octaves higher than I expected from the tall, imposing individual. "There's no need to worry," he says hurriedly. "But if you have any ideas where they might be, or if some sort of situation came up, we'd love to be apprised of it as soon as possible."

Guests break off into groups. Mumbling in hushed voices.

"Some sort of situation?" a woman near me asks. "What does that mean?"

"Feema told me they ran off to Vegas this morning," another woman standing next to us says as a growing crowd of ladies huddle closer, all dripping in gold.

"They're eloping?" gasps another. "What was this all for if they never planned on showing up?"

"We all know how dramatic Tanvir can be."

"How much do you wager that he's changed his mind?" someone else asks. "You know he was still moping over the elephant."

"Goodness. I hope the marriage is still on. Canceling could certainly complicate things," says another woman. "I don't know if you noticed, but Lena was looking a little . . . healthy at the bridal shower, if you know what I mean."

"I noticed that too!" someone else says.

I move away from them. Darcy hurries after me.

"Shouldn't we keep listening?" she asks. "Maybe they know something."

"They're pretending to be concerned, but they're really devouring gossip," I say bitterly. "This is more entertaining than the event was ever going to be. Any luck reaching Lena?"

"It's going straight to voicemail." Darcy bites her lip. "Radio silence isn't like her."

"Let's check in with Genevieve."

Moments later, we're squeezed into Genevieve's car in the parking lot. The laptop illuminates her worried face in the dark night. It's obvious by now that there is no mehndi taking place tonight—but every car is still parked exactly where it was.

"They didn't make it to the hall," Genevieve says as she types. "Not since I've been parked here, anyway. And look, she shared a post about getting her nails done this afternoon. She seems as happy as could be. Whatever went down, it was recent."

"*If* anything happened," Darcy interjects. "She might have gotten cold feet at the last second or something."

"Both of them?" I ask. "Tanvir's missing too. And if she was getting cold feet, she would've reached out. . . . She would have said something to us, right? Or at least her mother would have touched base! They shared all the highs and lows with wedding prep. Why would both of them have stopped now?"

Genevieve's phone dings. She reads the text. "Frank over at the control towers at Dekalb-Peachtree says the Kamdar private jets are still on the tarmac."

"Borzu said they didn't fly commercial either," says Darcy, looking at her phone.

"So they drove?" I ask. "Where?"

"It looks like their car's device location system was disabled," Genevieve says. "Ditto for their phone trackers. Borzu can't get any read at all."

"I-I don't understand. Why would they do that?" I ask.

"No idea. But even without the location tracker, if they're in the Atlanta area, their plates will get picked up at an intersection at some point," says Genevieve.

"Someone inside the mehndi hall was saying they heard rumors that she was thinking of eloping to Vegas," Darcy says.

"She's not eloping on her mehndi night," I say. "She picked out everything from the flowers to the napkins. There are millions of dollars on the line in endorsements and sponsorships."

We fall silent. I take in the lit-up venue. The lavish orange-and-red drapes hanging from the windows.

"Something's happened to them," I say quietly.

"She's the heir to a billion-dollar cosmetics empire. There's no telling who's got a vendetta against her so . . ." Genevieve's voice trails off.

"Or maybe the vendetta's against us," I say quietly.

Genevieve and Darcy don't reply. Which means they're thinking it too.

"I'm going to chat with the security team," Genevieve finally says. "I'll let you know if I get any insight."

Genevieve exits the car as Darcy pulls out her phone. She scrolls a bit, then grimaces.

"What is it?"

"TikTok's talking. The guests are sharing videos of the police storming in."

"Didn't they sign legally binding nondisclosure agreements?"

"How're they going to enforce all of them? Oh, wow." She cringes. "People are starting to list out theories about what happened."

"Like what?"

"Mostly what we've already overheard. This one's speculating that they ran off to Vegas." She points to her phone. "Oh, here's another one. It says they heard from someone who heard from someone else that they called it off last minute after a major elephant-related fight. And now this new one . . ." She reads the text flashing on the screen. Her lips press tight.

"What is it? Tell me."

She glances at me, her eyes bright against the glowing device. "Someone suggested that Tanvir might have done something to Lena. Wedding tensions boiling over."

"That's . . . that's ridiculous!" I sputter. "I just talked to him this morning."

"It's gaining hundreds of likes as we speak." She scans the

parking lot, her expression grim. "They'd kept the location of this venue private for tonight, but I bet the paparazzi will be here any minute."

The paparazzi. Followed by articles. Endless speculation. My head hurts.

"We'll know what's going on soon enough," I manage to say.

My phone rings, and my heart leaps with hope. It's Borzu.

"Got a tip on the police scanner," he says without fanfare. "Someone spotted a silver Aston Martin a few hours ago speeding down Interstate 85 near Buckhead."

"License plate?"

"No identifiers. Tanvir's not the only one in the city with a silver Aston Martin, but the timing is suspicious."

Borzu promises to keep me posted. We hang up as Genevieve slips back into the car. No updates. I tuck my phone into my clutch and look at the wedding hall. I need to check in on her parents.

It takes a few minutes, but eventually I find them in the back kitchen. I'd expected them to be surrounded by concerned relatives, but they are alone. The room is cold and empty. Trays of cooled tandoori chickens and racks of lamb rest in rows in the distance.

"Raheema," I say softly as I approach.

"Can you believe this?" Her voice comes out as a strangled cry.

I place my arm around her, comforting her as best I can.

"The police are only here because of who I am," says Lena's father. "They're convinced Lena and Tanvir ran off. It's complete hogwash."

"They may have spotted Tanvir's car. Hopefully we'll know what's going on soon."

At this, they look up at me.

"They found Tanvir's car? Where did you hear that?" asks Raheema.

"One of my associates got a tip about a silver Aston Martin spotted near Buckhead."

Raheema frowns. "When was this?"

Crap. The police didn't tell her. The sighting must have been unrelated. Or else unsubstantiated.

"It's probably nothing," I say. "I just want you to know we're looking into things on our end as well."

Raheema looks at me. Unspeaking. Then her eyes narrow. "If you're so good at looking into things, how did this happen? Tanvir has been getting more and more out of control with his demands these last few weeks. I'd about had it with him, and now this. . . . If he did something to her . . ." Her voice is low. Practically a growl.

"Raheema—"

"I trusted you." Her voice breaks. Her husband puts a hand on her shoulder, but Raheema lunges toward me. She presses a manicured finger against my collarbone; it pinches against my skin. "WHERE ARE THEY, NURA? WHERE IS MY LENA?"

Her cry is guttural. I shiver as her husband pulls her back. She pulses with rage. I get it. She's a mama bear searching for her cub. She will lash out at anyone. Still, it doesn't stop me from recoiling. For guilt to seep in all the same.

Tanvir didn't kidnap Lena. I know this as sure as I know my own name. But I think of the podcaster's menacing voice. The note at my doorstep. Gertie. What if what happened tonight has nothing to do with Lena and Tanvir? What if it has everything to do with me?

FOURTEEN

Forty-eight hours have passed. I have felt each and every one of those hours, minutes, and seconds as they ticked by. There are no new updates. No clue *whatsoever* about where Tanvir and Lena vanished to.

A part of me still clings to hope. They're in a cell signal dead zone. Or on a flight that Borzu somehow missed. With each passing hour, though, this wishful thinking becomes more and more fanciful.

Darcy nudges open my office door. "We're placing a group order. Chinese or Indian?"

"It's too early for dinner."

"Nura, it's nine o'clock at night."

I check my watch. She's right. This means we've been here for over fourteen hours at this point. Darcy's got faint circles under her eyes. She looks as exhausted as I feel.

"Go home," I tell her. "That goes for everyone. It's too late to still be here."

"Are *you* going home?"

"I can't."

"Then neither can we."

I bury my face in my hands. "I don't understand how there've been no sightings of them."

"No *credible* sightings."

That's true. Social media *has* turned up numerous sightings. They've been spotted in Belize. At a cantina in San Jose, California. Someone reported a man matching Tanvir's description who was seen digging a grave in the middle of an abandoned park near dawn this morning. The anonymously posted grainy footage garnered millions of views—but it turned out to be the local arborist, planting a crepe myrtle.

"How bad is the coverage lately?" I've been studiously avoiding seeking out the conspiracy theories for myself. If I start down this rabbit hole, I may never climb out.

"The prevailing theory is still the same, that there was trouble in paradise, he killed her, and now he's on the run," says Darcy. "But other conspiracies are gaining traction. There are some truly wild ones like how they tempted fate by throwing a wedding-related festivity on Friday the Thirteenth. Then there's growing speculation that her parents might have done it for the insurance money—apparently Karma Cosmetics had a rocky few months on the stock market leading up to the wedding. Someone also pointed out a few hours ago that Lena's former driver conveniently moved to Italy the day after she disappeared, and people are raising questions about the timing of that."

"So everyone is a suspect."

"Which means no one is. Not really."

"What about us?" I ask.

Darcy bites her lip. My heart sinks. It makes sense, though. If people think Lena's fiancé is behind this, they're going to blame the agency who set them up.

"Nothing online yet," she says. "But our inbox is . . ."

"A shitshow?"

"It's just trolls being trolls."

Of course our inbox is a hot mess. The Tanvir-related theories validate all the haters who flooded in after the *Vanity Fair* piece posted. This moment gives them a proper opportunity to gloat.

"Sherri said she'll get us something by morning," says Darcy.

"Good. We definitely need to put out a PR statement soon."

Because this time, the haters have the kindling they need to destroy everything my aunt and I worked so hard to build.

I draw in a deep breath and try to steady myself. Growing up, Khala always taught me the importance of inner stillness. In the early days when I still woke crying for my mother, she taught me how to meditate. To *breathe*. How to erase all thought and focus on my steady breath coming in and out. She told me to see my worries as though they were floating past me on clouds above or tumbling past me like sticks on a river while my true heart stayed centered. *Be present. Be here. Be with me,* she'd say as she would wrap me in her arms.

Now that I'm older, I understand Khala wanted to make sure I had tools to access peace in the chaos of life. Because no matter what the world throws at you, the earth continues to spin. One must keep moving forward. There is still work to do. And right now, my work is finding Lena and Tanvir, except—I brush back tears—there's nothing. Absolutely nothing I can do. The helplessness is killing me.

When Darcy leaves, I refresh my inbox. No updates. Tapping my legs, I look down at my phone. Then, as though my fingers have a mind of their own, I click Instagram. There's a new photo on Zayna's account. Or rather, *photos*. Featuring her and Azar. They're at a restaurant. At the movies. At . . . I pause. I look at this selfie of the two of them. His arm around her waist. They're both mid-laugh. She looks up at him as he's gazing down at her. I don't need to see the geotag to know they're at the botanical garden. The edge of the green-flowered Medusa off to the edge of the photo. A knife twists inside of me. This location has shown up in countless movies and television shows. It doesn't belong to us. Except it does.

That's *our* spot. It's like he's taking her to every place that's ever meant anything to both of us. Like he's erasing me from his narrative.

"Who's that?"

Genevieve. She's standing over my desk. Her hair's tied in a messier-than-usual topknot. I'm fairly certain she's in the same white T-shirt and jeans as yesterday.

I flip the phone facedown. "Oh, nothing. It was just Azar."

"I meant the woman."

"Her name is Zayna. She's Azar's girlfriend."

"Ah. So do we hate her?"

"It's more that I love him." I draw a sharp intake of breath. The sleep deprivation is getting to me, isn't it? Why am I even looking at her social media account at a time like this? "I didn't mean that— It's just . . ."

"Nura. Of course you love him." Her green eyes are filled with sympathy. "Doesn't require a PI to figure that out."

"He's happy," I say quickly. "Clearly, he's happy. So I'm happy for him. But . . ."

"You're only human?"

"Something like that."

"Been there," she says. "You know what might make you feel better? Food. We just placed a huge order from Zyka. Should be here in a few. I made sure to get two orders of their chili chicken."

"I'm not hungry."

"Not an option." She leans in. "How long can you stay holed up in this stuffy office? Come out and join us. You need to stretch. Drink some water. You've barely moved from this spot all day."

Grudgingly, I follow her into the main office. Borzu's on his computer. Darcy is sifting through file folders. The moon is round and bright through the window next to the wall clock. I can't remember the last time we've stayed here this late, but it looks like we're all settling in for a long night. My phone buzzes. A new email.

Hi, Nura,

    I had a chance to speak with Avani, and between her wedding fiasco and the Lena situation, there is a lot to unpack. Let me know when you can discuss.

Best,

Logan

"Well, now we know *someone* is drawing a connection." I sigh. "Logan wants to talk. He's putting the pieces together. And he managed to convince Avani to cooperate."

"Why hasn't he written anything yet?" Genevieve frowns. "It's been a while at this point. It's weird he hasn't."

"Logan Wilson is not a salacious journalist," Borzu says. "He's respected for a reason. The D'Angelo piece? He worked on that for a full year." He turns to me. "I know you didn't ask my opinion here, but I really think you should talk to him."

"You want to reward him for his harassment?" Darcy retorts.

"He's just trying to get the story!" Borzu exclaims. "Maybe we join forces and get to the bottom of it? He's good at what he does. I bet he can offer us a lot."

"What are you? His number-one fanboy?" Genevieve retorts.

"I don't think—"

They continue bickering, but my attention shifts to my phone. Nina is calling me. She never calls me.

"Is everything okay?" I ask once I answer.

"You need to come over. Now."

Her voice is tense. As though she's speaking through clenched teeth.

"Are you all right?"

"We'll talk when you get here."

"Is Khala—"

The call ends. My heart lodges in my throat. Another stroke? It has to be.

"I have to go," I tell the team. "Family stuff."

Genevieve grabs her keys. "I'll be right behind you."

"What? No."

"Your security detail starts in the morning," she says. "You need coverage in the meantime."

"Genevieve, you're working on no sleep as it is. And food is on its way." Before she can continue, I remind her, "I already shared my location tracker with all of you—you'll know where I am. I'll be back as soon as I can."

I squeal out of the parking lot. Khala's been racked with guilt about forgetting Lilah. Stress can trigger just about anything with her. Including strokes.

Please be all right, I silently pray as I pull into Khala's driveway, as I race up the steps. Breathing heavily, I fling open the front door and toss my purse on the nearby ottoman. Still gripping my keys, I hurry to Nina. She's in the family room with her arms crossed, her mouth pressed tight. Lilah hugs me, and I at last exhale when I spot Khala. She's over by the television. I can't make out her expression, but she's standing. She's okay.

"Lilah, can you go upstairs and brush your teeth? I'll be there in just a second," Nina tells her daughter.

Once the bathroom door swings shut upstairs, I turn to my cousin. "Nina, you made it sound like a life-or-death emergency. What happened?"

"What *happened*?" Nina repeats.

My head throbs from sleep deprivation, hunger, and confusion. I don't have time for her passive aggression.

"When were you going to tell me about the missing couple?" Khala asks.

Shit. Shit. Shit.

"Wh-who told you?"

"Are you not following the local news *at all*?" Nina asks. "This was airing when I called you."

She flips on the television in the family room and unpauses the frozen image. A reporter holding a microphone looks straight into the camera. She's in front of a sprawling home in what the lower third identifies as historic Brookhaven. My heart sinks. That's Lena's parents' home.

"While Officer Delray provided no comment, we can confirm from a neighbor that the abandoned vehicle found off the highway tonight did indeed belong to Lena Kamdar. There was, however, no sign of Lena or her fiancé, Tanvir Bashir. Based on evidence collected at the scene, inside sources can confirm that foul play is suspected."

Nina flips the television off. *Foul play is suspected.* I knew this. Of course I knew this. A billionaire influencer doesn't go missing on the eve of her wedding because she decided to go off the grid. Still, the confirmation leaves me woozy. I'm certain Tanvir didn't do it, but it's clear *something* has happened. They're in danger.

"How could you keep this from me?" Khala asks.

"I—I didn't want to add more to your plate."

"Is the Piyar agency not my business as well?" Her voice rises. "I am still a partner, am I not? I should not have to learn about this from the local news."

I sink into the sofa. The room is spinning. I don't have it in me to defend myself.

"Nura." Khala sits next to me while Nina hovers over us. "It's been clear to me that you have been preoccupied for some time. Do you think I do not notice the circles under your eyes? Your clothes are practically hanging off of you. I think it's time for you to finally tell me what is going on." She places her hands on mine. "Sweetheart, I need to know everything."

Maybe it's how she's looking at me. Like I'm seven years old again. Maybe it's because I've barely slept in forty-eight hours. Whatever it is, the words come tumbling out of me. I leave nothing out about the mehndi. Tanvir's father's high-pitched plea for aid. The gossip echoing off the walls.

"Nura." Nina covers her mouth with her hand. "This is serious."

"There's more."

I tell them about the note. The canceled wedding. The podcaster. All descending on me at once. And . . .

"Gertie's missing." My voice cracks. "The front door was open. . . . I don't know for certain if it's related. My front door *was* finicky. But we haven't found her yet. I'm so sorry, Khala. For not looking out for her the way she deserved."

When I finish speaking, I feel shaky. The room is silent. Khala is a ghostly shade of white. She grips the edge of the seat as though she might pass out. *What was I thinking?* She wasn't having a stroke before, but she might now. I start to minimize what I said, but what she says next erases those words from my mouth.

"It's happening again."

"Wh-what's happening again?" I stammer, unsettled by both of their expressions.

"Mom. No. Please," says Nina.

"You were right." Khala looks at her daughter. "We should have stopped this whole matchmaking business years ago. He is onto us."

"No one is onto anything," says Nina.

"What else could it be?" Tears slip down her cheeks. "This harassment is exactly the kind of thing he would do."

"Who is *he*?" I stare at both of them. "What are you talking about?"

"It's nothing. Mom's having a moment. You know stress does that to her."

She's right. Stress can cause Khala to relapse, summon memories from long ago. Whatever this conversation has stirred up, it's clearly traumatic. Before I can bring her water and reassure her, she looks at me and croaks, "I only ever wanted to protect you."

"You always *have* protected me, Khala."

"It seems I did not protect you well enough."

"Mom. Enough. He's dead," says Nina.

"Are we absolutely certain? Perhaps his family is behind this. They are not the sort to let things go." Her lower lip trembles. "They were biding their time, waiting to strike. Fiaz can be tricky."

Fiaz? I've never heard that name before. Have I?

"Who is Fiaz?" I ask.

"It—it's not important," Nina mumbles. She won't meet my eyes.

"Forgive me, Madiha." Tears stream down Khala's face. "I thought we were safe. I truly did."

"Khala, it's me," I say gently. "I'm Nura. Your niece."

"You are Madiha."

Nina takes Khala's hand. She tugs. "You need to lie down. This was a lot of information thrown at once." She glances toward me. "Why don't you go? We could all use some rest. We'll talk about this later."

I can't move. It's not what Nina said. It's the way she said it. How she won't meet my eyes. How badly she wants me to go.

"Who is Madiha?" I ask again.

"Madiha is your real name," Khala says.

"This isn't the time or the place for this, Mom."

"It needs to become the time and place," I say. "I'm not leaving until you tell me."

"You are right," says Khala. "It's long past time you learned the truth."

FIFTEEN

K hala begins to speak, and I don't move. I scarcely let out a breath.

"Our matchmaking began in Lahore years before my birth. Though back then, it was hardly a business. Matchmaking was simply what people did for one another," Khala says. "We kept an eye out for suitable matches for people in our lives, but my mother's uncanny ability to make auspicious ones drew attention quickly. I helped her as the work steadily grew, and when the time came that it grew to be too much for her, I took over."

I know all this. Our origin story is hallowed family lore. But I don't dare interrupt her.

"After Nina's father passed away, I threw myself even deeper into our work to escape my grief," she continues. "Business was thriving, we were fielding requests from people from all over Pakistan, and when your mother came of age, I was elated to find her a match."

My mother? I sit up straighter. This is new.

"One should never do matches for those we cannot be objective about," Khala says. "I could not be objective about my sister. The Usmani family came to us. They were seeking a match for their son. I had never met them before, but their reputation preceded them, and they were wealthier than I could comprehend. They had lavish homes on practically every continent. Private jets. I saw in them security for my sister."

My father came from money? I don't know much about him other than the hazy memories of what my mother had shared with me. His photo is still tucked in the top drawer of my dresser: a man with striking eyes, in jeans and a short-sleeved polo, leaning against a Corvette.

"It turns out that money is not enough to buy happiness," Khala says softly. "But money can certainly protect you from consequences. The Usmanis were part of the zamindar class. They owned practically a quarter of the farmlands of Punjab. They had their hands in everything from the government to the police. Billi shielded me at first. She made excuses for the broken arm, the sprained ankle. Her growing distance. It was once you came along that things changed.

"She finally came to me. She showed me her bruises. The cigarette burns. She asked me for help." Khala shivers. "You were not the son he had wanted, and she feared it was only a matter of time before his anger turned to you. Unfortunately, leaving is not simple when you are enmeshed with someone with limitless resources. I was the one who had made this mess. I was the one who had ignored the red flags. I needed to fix things. I sold everything I had. The cars. My house. We made a plan and waited until the right moment. When he was away on a business trip, a few weeks shy of your first birthday, we left for the United States."

The room is spinning. My head hurts. I'd known I was born in Pakistan. I was told that my father had died before we ever arrived on Western shores. From the look on Khala's face, it's clear this story is far from over.

"Your father, Fiaz, harassed our parents relentlessly, demanding to know our whereabouts. We lived in a one-bedroom apartment off Buford Highway, but we never told your grandparents where we had gone. To do so risked our safety. I tried as best as I could to stay under the radar, but our savings ran out quickly, and I could not provide for all of us on a receptionist's salary. I began matchmaking again. I visited mosques and mandirs. I put up flyers to advertise my services. My skills were even more in demand here than they had been back home. Your mother was livid. She did not care that I had new rules in place, procedures to prevent a situation like hers from happening again. She was afraid my work would make it easier for him to find us." Khala's voice quivers. "She no longer felt safe, so she moved you both to the other side of the continent. She kept her head down and did her best to go unnoticed. But—" Her voice breaks.

"It's not your fault, Mom," says Nina. "You're not to blame for what he did."

Khala looks at me. Her eyes water. "So many years had passed. I truly thought the threat was over. I began to let down my guard. But men like Fiaz know only revenge. He never gave up looking for your mother. With my name passing around people's tongues, it was only a matter of time before he found her."

Khala looks at her lap. Clearly struggling to say what comes next. My phone rings in my lap, but I barely notice it. I'm filled with an inexplicable dread. Like what she's about to say will serve as my dividing line. Before, when the world was a known quantity, and after, when the chessboard flipped on its head.

"He trailed your mother to her place of work one evening." Her voice is barely a whisper. "You were so young. Barely seven."

"Seven." Seven was when . . . *No.*

No.

No.

"He stalked her. Waited outside until her shift ended. He killed her, and when he saw the police cars approaching, he turned the gun on himself."

"She died in a car crash," I say numbly.

All these years I believed her car had skidded off the highway on a particularly wet night. All these years I believed my father had died of a brain aneurysm while she was pregnant with me.

"My name is . . . Madiha?" I ask shakily.

"It was. Nura was your middle name, and we changed it legally when we came to the United States to protect you," Khala says. "It means 'light,' and that is what you were to your mother during that very difficult time. To all of us."

"When were you going to tell me?"

"I should have told you sooner. It has haunted me for decades. But how to say the words?" asks Khala. "I kept telling myself, what good was there in saddling you with this?"

"It's my life." My voice rises. "I'm entitled to know about it."

"You were so young. It took so long for you to adjust and settle in," Khala says. "As time went on, I did not know how to bring myself to tell you."

"After everything else I've had to deal with, now this?" I look at my hands. I've been clutching my keys so tight they've formed indentations on my palms. It feels like a million pins are stabbing my insides. I graze my fingers over my silver bracelet. *This* was the reason my mother hated our work. Matchmaking had destroyed her life. She'd moved us to the other end of the continent to put as much distance between it and herself as she could. To keep us safe from a man who was hunting her. It hadn't been enough. Tears well up. I feel Khala's gaze on me. I move to speak, but nothing comes out. What can I say, anyway? My chest hurts. My stomach hurts. Everything hurts. I can't be here anymore. I can't sit here for a second longer.

"I . . . I have to go."

"Nura. Please wait," Khala says.

"Mom's right. You shouldn't drive like this," Nina says.

My lungs are burning. I have to get some air.

"I need space," I manage to say. "I need to . . . not be here."

"You are angry," Khala whispers. "I am so sorry, my child."

"I'm . . . I'm not . . ."

I want to deny it, but I *am* angry. I'm furious. I think back to the countless evenings sitting across from each other at the kitchen table, or at the agency when we worked side by side. She had a million opportunities to tell me the truth. She kept it to herself.

"I don't want to talk about this right now," I say. "I need . . . I need to be alone."

She moves to reply, but I brush past her. Into the foyer. Out the door. The cool night air presses against my face as I stumble onto the front porch. I let out a ragged breath. With trembling hands, I unlock my car, then pause. I forgot my purse. But going back into the house? I'd rather swallow broken glass.

The phone rings in my pocket. Borzu.

"I can't talk," I tell him.

"Wait! Don't hang up!"

"Borzu, I don't—"

"Listen!" His voice is frantic. "We know who it is. The person stalking you."

I wipe my eyes with the back of my hand. "Are you still at the office? I'll be right over."

I hear him typing. He goes silent. Then—"Nura, are you at your aunt's house?"

"Yes."

"Don't go outside. Stay where you are. Call the police. Now."

"I'm already outside. There's no one—" I hear the crunch of feet over gravel.

I turn.

"Hello, Nura."

SIXTEEN

A man. He's standing inches away from me. He's desi. From the glow of the streetlight in the distance I can make out close-cropped hair, a crisp white shirt tucked into khaki pants. My phone is still on. Borzu's shouting through it, but something inside me—the animal part of who I am—knows not to say a word right now.

The neighborhood is quiet. I'm not sure I've ever properly appreciated how far apart the homes here are. Azar's old house across the street stands a good acre away, and judging by the darkened windows, no one is home. I glance at Khala's house.

"I wouldn't," he cautions. "Not if you want the people in that home to be safe."

"You." That same deep masculine voice. The hint of amusement beneath the surface. A chill goes through me. "You made the recordings."

"I was hoping you'd heard them." He breaks into a grin. "Narcissists like yourself surely have an alert set up, right?"

My Mace. I move to grab it, then remember I left my purse in the house.

"My cat—" I break off. "What did you do to her?"

"Your cat is fine. I'm not a monster, Nura. I figured taking her might get your attention."

"What do you *want*?"

"I want what you took from me."

Took from him? "Did you apply for our matchmaking services? I'm sorry if we didn't take you on as a client, but we can work something out. We can talk about it."

"Me as *your* client?" The amused expression is gone. His eyes narrow. "Fuck no. Why would I want that? My dad's guzzled the Kool-Aid, thinks you're some kind of miracle worker. I know bullshit when I see it."

Is Borzu hearing all this? Are the police on their way?

"You took her from me," he continues. "Brainwashed her into falling in love with someone else with your fucked-up arranged marriage trap."

"Avani?" He already broke up their wedding. What will it take for him to move on? "Wait"—understanding dawns on me—"are you . . . are you talking about Lena?"

"Bingo."

I rack my brain. Did Lena have a scary ex? How did I miss this? I take in his narrowed eyes. "Wh-where is she? What have you done to her and Tanvir?"

"Wouldn't *you* like to know? It took me years, but I was getting *so* close." He takes a step closer toward me. "We were finally friends. She was finally starting to get it. That we were meant to be together. I'd worked up the nerve to ask her out. Got us reservations for a romantic dinner. That's when she dropped the bomb on me. She told me she was working with you. Said you were going to find her 'the one.' I warned her it was cultish bullshit. That you're a snake oil salesman. I said she should look at the people who were already in her life. I was too late. She got mad at me for wanting to *help* her. Told me to leave her alone. If it wasn't for your meddling, she would have been mine." He glares at me. "And then you have the nerve to try to set *me* up? That's a bridge too far."

"I haven't tried to set you up!"

"Uh-huh."

"I haven't," I insist. "I don't know who you are!"

"My dad thought he could run my life. Try to get me matched up behind my back. Nice fucking try. Bad enough you ruined my chances with Lena. Then you tried to fuck *me* over? No way. You're not going to get a chance to hurt anyone else ever again."

Matched up behind my back. I move to protest, and then I grow still.

Oh.

I take in this man's set jaw. His glowering expression. So similar to the man I spoke to just over a month ago. The one with the graying goatee. I remember how he leaned across his desk. How he glared at me and demanded I set up his son behind his back. Basit Latif.

"If your father is Basit Latif, he did reach out to us," I tell him. "But I told him no. I never signed you on as a client."

He doesn't reply. It's as though he can't hear me. As though my words are mist in the air. He's clearly out of his mind. There's no point in reasoning with him, but I think of Lena and Tanvir. I have to get through to him. I have to try.

"How is hurting Lena going to make her see things your way?" I ask him.

"Ever heard of staging an intervention? I tried with the podcast. I thought for sure the fallout with Avani and Dev would've brought her back to her senses, but by then she was in too deep with you. My emails bounced back. She *blocked* my number." He moves even closer. We're practically nose to nose.

I fight the urge to shrink away. To move back. There's no telling what he'll do, but smelling my fear will only embolden him. "I thought if I could get some time alone with her to explain, I could make her see we're meant to be."

Lights turn on in Khala's house. Her front door swings open.

"Auntie!" Lilah hops onto the front porch. "You forgot your purse!" She holds up my leather bag.

"Go inside, Lilah!" My knees go wobbly. "Now!"

The man pulls something from his pocket. My blood goes cold. A gun. He holds it low. "Get in the car. It's you or her."

Nina joins Lilah on the porch. "Nura, come back. Let's talk." She pauses as she sees the man. Confusion crosses her face.

In a split second, I feel the cold metal press sharply against my midsection.

"I'm fine, Nina!" I call out. "Nothing to worry about. Just . . . catching up with a neighbor."

Please don't come closer. Please close the door.

She frowns. Wordlessly, she ushers Lilah inside. The door shuts. A sob escapes my throat.

"Doubt she bought that piss-poor performance. She's probably calling the police," he mutters. "Get in the car. If you care what happens to them, you'll do as I say."

"Listen, I get it," I tell him. "You're furious. But I can't make Lena fall in love with you. Hurting me isn't going to get you what you want."

"It's probably too late for Lena. That's my tragedy to own. I'll make my peace with it."

"What does that mean?" My voice rises. "Have you hurt them? Are they all right?"

"Stop talking!" he barks. "In the car. Now. I'm going to stop *you* from hurting anyone else ever again."

I need to hold him here a little longer. There's no telling what will happen once we're in that enclosed space together. He's clearly capable of anything. Surely the police are on their way. They'll be here any second. The porch light turns on. My mouth goes dry. If they come out again, he'll kill them. Tears fall freely down my face. I open the car door.

"Attagirl. In we go."

A car screeches in the distance. A red Jetta. Darcy's Jetta. She bursts out of the driver's side. Races toward us.

"Back away, asshole!" she screams.

"Darcy!" I cry out. "No!"

"Are you fucking kidding me right now?" The man's face reddens. He turns from me. Moves toward her. "I am not in the mood for this shit."

He lifts his gun. Aims his weapon at Darcy. There's a cracking sound, like thunder.

Dots cloud my vision.

No.

Not Darcy.

No.

Before I can move, the man jerks backward. His eyes widen. Like a puppet without its strings, he slumps to the ground. Blood blooms across his shirt. He sputters, trying to speak, and then he's silent. His mouth forming a perfect O.

Darcy. She's lit up beneath the glow of the lamppost. The silver of her gun glints against the streetlight. She's trembling head to toe, then collapses into herself, sinking to the ground as blue-and-white lights flash in the horizon.

Everything sweeps by in a blur from there. Lights flicker on in nearby homes. A voice on a loudspeaker from a police car orders Darcy to raise her hands in the air. Officers race out of their cars. In a matter of seconds, she's cuffed.

"Wait!" I scream. "She saved my life!"

The cops surround the man's lifeless body. Neighbors assemble in the distance, wearing bathrobes and watching with bafflement the police activity in this sleepy neighborhood.

They're pulling her into the back of a cruiser. My breathing grows shallow. The police don't know the whole story. They didn't see what almost happened. That he was about to shoot her. That she's the reason I'm still alive. I move toward the police car. There's a squeeze on my shoulder. My khala. She wraps her arms around me.

I need to go to Darcy, I want to say. The words feel stuck in my throat. Nothing comes out. The police car pulls away. She's gone.

"Let's get you inside. You need to drink some water," Khala says. "And you need to change your clothes."

I look down at my outfit. Blood. There's blood splattered across my blouse. My pants. His blood.

"Come inside, sweetheart," she whispers. "The police need to speak with you."

I don't want to go inside. I want to be anywhere but here. But it's as though I'm a child again. I let her guide me up the front stairs. The police are speaking to me in hushed voices. I try to follow along, but it's hard to focus when what I want more than anything right now is to fade into oblivion.

But I have to talk to the officers. Clear Darcy's name. We have to find the missing couple. Though he never answered my question. Did he spare Lena's and Tanvir's lives? Or, when he realized it was futile to try to win her back, did they meet the fate that I was about to meet myself?

SEVENTEEN

Gertie lets out a mournful meow and leaps into my arms as soon as I unlatch her crate the next morning. We're still within the confines of the fluorescent-lit police station, but as she nestles against me and purrs, my jaw unclenches and the world is suddenly just the smallest bit brighter. I've always seen Gertie as Khala's pet, but pressing her close to me, I understand: She's mine too.

The officer at the front desk hands me papers to sign and smiles at the two of us. "In case it helps you feel better, I heard she was looked after. Had a litter box, food bowl, and everything."

That does make me feel somewhat better, but—"Darcy saved my life," I tell him. "She doesn't deserve to be behind bars. Who can I talk to about this?"

"She's giving us her statement and going over the timeline. No charges have been filed against her."

"Lena and Tanvir." I'm almost afraid to ask. "Are they—"

"It's an ongoing investigation," the officer begins. But then, taking in my expression, he lowers his voice. "Look, they're unharmed. The guy's phone activity led us straight to one of those fancy lakeside cabin-mansion combos out in Woodstock—same place we found your cat. Property belongs to the suspect's father. We found the guy's car parked around the corner from where he confronted you. His trunk had ropes, zip ties, drugs—it's an open-and-shut case, really. Your friend'll be going home soon."

I let out a trembly breath. Lena and Tanvir are safe. Darcy will be released. My stalker is dead. It's over. I wait for relief to envelop me, but instead I feel like I've slipped into an ice bath.

The bell chimes overhead when I step into the office the next morning.

"Nura!" Genevieve jumps up from her desk. Hurries toward me. "How are you even here?"

"You need a month off after everything that happened," says Borzu.

"I'm only here—literally standing here—because you saved my life." I choke up. "If you all hadn't been working on this late into the night, figuring out who it was . . ."

"Darcy figured it out," Borzu says. "She went through Lena's file. Even your old spiral notebooks, page by page. She found a throwaway line about a man named Farhan who'd gotten obsessed with her. I did a search in our company-wide emails and found his name in your inbox."

"*Mine?*"

"Basit Latif mentioned his son's name in your initial email correspondence. That's when everything started to fit. It took a minute to triangulate his whereabouts, but when we realized he was in Atlanta, we knew we had a problem."

The front door chimes again. Darcy. She's dressed impeccably as always in a solid shift dress. She barely makes it inside before we tackle her into a group hug.

"I'm okay." She hugs us back. "Really."

We spoke on the phone after she was released from the police station, but this is our first time seeing each other face-to-face. I try to speak, but tears spill instead. What can I say to the person who saved my life? No words will do.

"Thanks, Darcy," I finally manage to say.

"The way that girl ran out the door once Borzu identified the location!" Genevieve lets out a low whistle. "She had major 'mother lifting a car to protect her baby' energy."

"I just . . . I can't believe it really happened," Darcy says. "That image of him with the gun pointed at you, it's burned into my brain."

"It's over now. Thanks to you. I can't believe you're in the office today," I tell her. "Go home and get some rest. Honestly, you hereby have my permission to quit here and now and still get a paycheck from me for the rest of your life."

"I can't stay home. I just keep replaying the night over and over in my head. I'd rather be here and get my mind off of it if I can. For a little while at least," Darcy says. "I have a meeting with my lawyer in a few hours. Until then, I want to busy myself as much as possible."

"Lawyer?" Genevieve frowns.

"Nura got me all set up." Darcy looks at me tearfully. "Thanks again."

"Of course," I tell her. "The agency has your back one hundred percent."

"Why do you need a lawyer?" Genevieve asks. "There is no prosecutor in the world who would bring a case against you."

"Genevieve's right," I say. "It's just a matter of dotting the i's and crossing the t's. This will be in your rearview mirror in no time."

"I hope you're right," Darcy says. "I can't believe I *killed* someone."

"It was self-defense! And Nura defense. I'm sure Nura's aunt's security cameras captured at least some of the exchange," says Borzu. "You've got nothing to worry about."

"See, this is exactly why I wanted to come in. I was coming up with all the worst-case scenarios. I feel a little more centered now."

I understand how Darcy's feeling. It's good to be with people, and maybe work will clear *all* our heads. Except it turns out that none of us can work today. With the wall-to-wall press coverage about Lena and Tanvir's rescue, we stay gathered in the conference room, sharing updates back and forth.

"Looks like there's a new video from Lena," says Borzu. He mirrors his phone to the screen. "It was posted a few minutes ago."

There's Lena on the television. Her first public statement. Her face is devoid of makeup. Her eyes are red and puffy. Her fiancé sits by her side.

"These have been the most terrifying few days of my life," she says, her voice welling with emotion. "We were tied up. Blindfolded. We didn't know where we were. If anyone could hear our screams. I didn't know if we'd make it out alive. I was making my peace with the end."

"It really put everything into perspective for me. About what really matters." Tanvir looks tenderly at Lena. "I admit it. I lost my way leading up to the wedding, but who cares about a *wedding*? Only one thing matters, which is being with you, Lena, for the rest of my life."

Tears stream down her face, but she's smiling. "We're stronger than ever now, and we're only just beginning."

He kisses her.

I wipe away my own tears. I spoke to them this morning. They were shaky but in good spirits. Still, seeing the visual of them together now and watching hearts fill the screen, it really and truly hits me: They're together. They're safe.

"Check out the views," Darcy marvels. "It's gone from a thousand to half a million since we started watching. Maybe our inbox will finally get under control now."

Borzu looks at his phone. His expression shifts. "The police are holding a press conference."

Switching over to the local news, we watch officers gathered at a platform. A man in a blue uniform stands at the center and speaks to a crowd via a dozen mics affixed to the podium. We listen with bated breath: As expected, the suspect has been identified. Farhan Latif, son of a Michigan state senator, kidnapped the heiress of a cosmetics empire along with her fiancé on the eve of their wedding.

"So it begins," mutters Genevieve. "It'll be a 24/7 circus from here on out."

She's right. This is tabloid gold. This is the stuff of a soapy Netflix miniseries.

"How soon before news outlets are reporting that we took a call with Farhan's father?" I murmur.

"Why would that matter?" Borzu says. "We kicked him to the curb when he gave us bad vibes. Farhan was obsessed with Lena way before we got into the picture. A video went up a few hours ago. One of Farhan's old college classmates was talking about how far back his obsession goes. This doesn't tie back to the agency."

"Except for the fact that *I'm* the one who killed him," Darcy says softly.

"Oh, Darcy." I look at her. "They didn't mention anything about that."

"It's only a matter of time. Don't get me wrong, I'd do it again. In a heartbeat. But the thought of it getting out, people talking about it . . . looking at me, knowing I'm a killer." She shudders. "I don't know if I can take it."

"You're a hero for what you did, Darcy. If word gets out, people will throw a ticker-tape parade in your honor," says Genevieve. "You did what you had to do. Remember, no matter what happens, we've got you."

"Whatever comes, it's like Genevieve said, we'll weather this together." I give her a hug. I'm worried about potential fallout too, but she saved my life. I will never be able to repay her for her bravery, but I'll do whatever I can to ease her worries. She has enough trauma to deal with—taking a life, even under the circumstances she was forced to do so, has to exact a cost.

Back in my office, I close the door and settle down at my desk. Pull out my tablet. Click back onto the private browser I've had up since this morning. The one with the open tab and the quarter-column article that took hours of searching to unearth. I've read it so many times it's ingrained into my brain at this point. *Two Fatalities in South Mission.* A murder-suicide. Dispassionately described as "a domestic dispute between a Pakistani woman and her estranged husband in San Francisco's crime-prone Mission District."

A domestic dispute. Tears prick my eyes. They didn't even say my mother's name. They just flattened her into another statistic. Calling the area "crime-prone," like what happened was her fault, since she was in a dangerous part of the city. And what did being Pakistani have to do with any of it?

I look at her photo, the one I'd saved to my phone years ago. She's smiling into the camera. She has on a yellow blouse; her dark hair is pulled back. Bangs frame her eyes, which look so similar to my own. She's younger than I am now. I'll never know what she went through. The particulars of the abuse she suffered. I've helped multiple clients over the years, from a variety of different faiths and backgrounds, who have overcome abusive relationships. I supported them. I held their hands when they wept. All that time I had no idea my own mother had experienced the same thing. She'd endured unspeakable abuse until I arrived. From then on, she did everything she could to protect me. To keep me from knowing such horror.

I click on the other open tab. After hours of searching, I found the social media profiles of some of Fiaz Usmani's family. Nephews. Nieces. They all have the same full mouth as my own. An elderly woman sits in a wheelchair in one of the photos, holding two great-grandchildren in her arms. Is she his mother? I grip the tablet tighter. Does she feel shame for looking the other way? For the monster she created?

I know Khala feels bad for keeping the truth hidden from me. She looked haunted when she told me about my past. But I'm too raw right now to unpack everything. And I can't help but wonder: Would my mother have kept all of this from me like Khala had? I was barely older than Lilah is now when she died, too young to process any of this, but when I was old enough, would she have given me the ugly truth? I'll never know. This man took her away from me before I'd ever find out. He upended my life without a second thought. Meanwhile, his relatives smile and pose for selfies. They pretend it never happened.

My phone buzzes. I check it even though I know who it will be—Azar and Khala have been checking in nonstop. Khala's called five times today. I texted her back that I'm well and I'll be in touch when I'm ready. I've sent her videos and photos of Gertie. I told her I love her, but I'm not ready yet. I need time to process everything.

But when I take a quick look, the incoming text message is not from Khala.

> Logan here. Hope you're faring okay. I received critical in-formation we need to discuss. This is a complex story with lots of moving parts, and I can't do it justice without your perspective on everything. I hope you will reconsider.

I grit my teeth and toss the phone facedown on my desk. I'm not sure how he got my number, but it's hard not to read between the lines of his text. A story is coming out soon. I can be involved in the story or simply the object of it. I massage my temples. I do not have it in me to take on one more thing, least of all this.

My door creaks open, and Darcy slips inside.

"I come bearing coffee." She pushes a latte forth.

"I should be getting *you* coffee."

She shakes her head. "I just want to pretend nothing changed."

But things *have* changed. I look at Darcy's forlorn expression. Farhan was unhinged. He was poised to shoot her. He would have if she hadn't stopped him. But that doesn't change the reality that taking a life is no small matter.

"Have you had a chance to see Dr. Higdon?" I ask her gently. "It might be time to get a regular schedule started."

"He's squeezing me in tomorrow morning," she says. "He thinks we should meet twice a week for the foreseeable future, but I don't know how much talking helps anything. I've talked to the police so much, my voice is going to give, and they still keep coming up with more questions. Like I'm going to remember something that will make any of this any less fucked up? I just want to knock myself out and forget any of it ever happened." She shivers. "The sooner this all is behind me, the better."

"I get it. I wish I could erase it all from my mind's eye as well."

She looks at me worriedly. "How are *you*?"

"Still shell-shocked. I keep thinking I'll go for a run after I get home from work. I know it's safe now. He's gone. But I can't bring myself to do it. I feel exposed even thinking about it."

"My body hasn't gotten the memo it's over either. I spilled my tea this morning when the UPS guy rang the doorbell to deliver a package. That was when I knew I had to come in to work."

"This whole thing is going to be a marathon, not a sprint. We need to figure out how to not think about it 24/7 or we'll slowly go insane."

She purses her lips. Then brightens just the littlest bit.

"Uh-oh," I say. She picks up her phone and types. I know that look. "Darcy, you're not signing us up for a meditation retreat or something, are you?"

"No meditating, but I do think we should get our minds off things. Even if it's only for a little while."

"What do you have in mind? I don't think I'm up for axe-throwing."

"Me either. I was thinking of something a little more low-key. Like a double date?" She points to her phone. "There's an opening for seven o'clock this evening at Meta Sushi. You and I have been meaning to go there forever."

"This is the exact worst time to try to set me up, Darcy."

"Nura! I didn't mean literally. I texted Azar and Samir for a casual get-together. Samir's in."

I fidget. It was my idea for us to try to get our minds off of things, but I'm not sure I'm up for fine dining this soon.

Her phone chimes. She glances at it, then me.

"That's Azar. He's in too. If you're not comfortable, we don't have to. I guess I just thought it might be nice to be among friends. Celebrate that we're alive? Besides, you and Samir haven't had a chance to really get to know each other. The engagement party was swamped with people. Maybe this could be a small way to feel normal for a little while. What do you think?"

She gives me her most winning smile. Even though she doesn't need to. I'm not sure I'm in the mood to be out in the world at large, but that doesn't matter. Darcy needs a distraction, so of course I'm in. This woman saved my life. I'll do whatever she asks. Thanks to her, the danger is over. I wish my brain could communicate this to my body, which still feels tense as a live wire. Waiting for what comes next.

EIGHTEEN

Twinkle lights frame the golden Meta Sushi sign. We are sitting on the patio overlooking the Chattahoochee River. There's a veritable feast spread out before us. Spicy tuna and two rainbow rolls. Twelve different pieces of nigiri. Edamame. Dumplings. All placed at the center of the table and served family style. Looking around, I can almost pretend this is an ordinary night out. *Which it is,* I remind myself. The danger is behind us. How many times will I need to say this to myself before my body actually believes me?

"I don't know why we haven't done this sooner," Darcy says. "I feel like I'm bringing Samir over to meet his in-laws. Nura is like a sister to me at this point."

"I'm still processing everything that happened." Azar's voice catches. "Thank you, Darcy. I can't thank you enough."

"Me either." I look at her. "You're a hero."

Darcy winces. "Come on. No more of that. I'm serious. You would've done the same for me, Nura."

"What's next for the rescued couple?" Samir asks. He leans back, one arm resting on Darcy's chair. He's still got on his work clothes. Gray slacks. A navy-blue tie. A starched white button-down with the sleeves rolled up to his elbows.

"I spoke to Lena again a little while ago," I say. "The public response has been overwhelming. Oprah's in talks with Lena's management team to do a one-on-one sit-down with them about the whole ordeal. First things first, though, they're getting married."

"The wedding venue is offering a redo of the nuptials. Baudelaire Country Club is going to host a new mehndi celebration too, on the house," says Darcy. "That photographer Jade offered to do their photos for the nuptials. Karma's stock is skyrocketing."

"And bonus," I add, "Tanvir's getting his elephant for the wedding after all."

"After everything they've been through, I'm glad things are looking up for them," says Azar.

"How is wedding prep going for the two of *you*?" I ask the couple. At this, they simultaneously break into a smile.

"Samir survived the latest round of cuts," Darcy says. "And guess what? He surprised me a few hours ago and put down the rest of the deposit for the Georgian Terrace! Looks like we'll be getting married there after all."

"Darcy, that's fantastic!" I exclaim.

"I told Samir he didn't need to do that. What if his work blindsides us again with another round of layoffs?"

"The Georgian Terrace was your dream from the start, Darcy," Samir says. "Why not make this dream come true?"

"Hmm, maybe because debts don't pay down themselves?" Darcy elbows him teasingly.

"You're not in this alone anymore, remember?" he says. "You deserve the perfect day you've always dreamed of. If this ordeal has any lesson for us, it's that life is unexpected. May as well lean in to the moments that matter while we can."

Over dessert, Azar asks Samir for stock market advice while

Darcy fills me in on the menu options they're whittling down. As we talk beneath the twinkling lights, the rush of the Chattahoochee rumbling in the distance, my shoulders start to soften. This is what normal feels like. An ordinary meal with my friends, suddenly so precious. It's over. I'm safe.

"It's been nice to chat," Samir says as the bill arrives. He grabs it and hands the server his credit card before any of us can protest. "Maid of honor is no small task. I hear you're throwing her a mehndi too?"

"A bridal shower–mehndi combo. I thought it might be fun."

"How did I find a girl more into desi culture than I am?" Samir groans.

"Considering you're not into it at all," Darcy says, poking him, "the odds were high."

"I'm into the culture! It's just our never-ending weddings," he protests. "The whole rigamarole of dholkis, sangeets, bangle ceremonies, and all the rest of it—it's exhausting."

"How can you turn down an opportunity for a proper South Asian wedding? You take all the cultural things for granted," she says. "I have a *real* appreciation for desi culture."

"No one's debating that." Samir grins and pulls her close. He glances at us. "Did you know that she even tried to convince me to ride to the wedding hall on a horse? A *horse*."

"I want it to be perfect, that's all. Hopefully your mother will see that eventually," Darcy says. "I'm not the Indian bride she was hoping for, but I'm doing my best."

"She'll love you. Give her time." He kisses her.

"No one needs time to love Darcy," I protest.

"No argument from me there," Samir says. "It surprised my mother, is all. She was over the moon when I told her I'd signed up for the Piyar app."

"Then dumbstruck when you brought *me* home," Darcy adds.

"Love finds who it will," I say. "You're a great match, and I should know. Your mother will realize it soon enough."

They gaze at each other. Their love surrounds them like a warm halo. Looking at them, I can see why some people do go through the effort. Putting themselves out there repeatedly. Braving terrible date after terrible date in hopes of finding the one who makes them smile like Samir smiles at Darcy. I can see the allure of wanting to come home to someone other than an aging feline. I guess I can see why someone might try.

"'I have a real appreciation of desi culture,'" Azar says, mimicking Darcy. "More like a real *appropriation*."

"Azar!" I toss a pillow at him. We said our goodbyes over an hour ago. Now I'm at Azar's place. "She saved my life!"

"So I can't call her out? How is that fair?" He pauses. "Actually, that's completely fair. Duly noted. No more picking on Darcy."

"She's really nice. You just have to get to know her better."

"She *is* nice, but she can be a lot, don't you think? A horse for the wedding? Really?"

"Fine, a horse is a bit much." I laugh. "She's just really immersed in the culture, with all the weddings she's helped throw. Most of our clients are desi."

"I know." He stops and considers. "I guess what gets to me is she can put it all on when she wants to. The clothes and jewelry are fun, but she can also take it all off. Brush out that blond hair and she's back to being cozy in her privilege. She gets to have it both ways."

"I think you have to know Darcy to understand. When she's

in on something, she goes all in. We started chatting at the coffee shop because I was obsessed with her foam latte creations. I'd watch her while I waited for my order. Every day a new design. Hummingbirds. Tulips. Roses. When I finally asked her about it, she told me if you're going to do something, you may as well give it your all. She even invited me to come by after the shop closed to teach me how to make them myself."

"That explains the latte machine gathering dust in your kitchen pantry."

"Yep. She had a rough life growing up. Her dad fled the scene in her toddlerhood, and her mom's a poster child for how not to parent. Darcy basically raised herself. I think 'going all in' is how she's learned to cope."

"Well, great. Now I feel bad."

"I get it. If it were anyone else, I'd definitely side-eye it, but it's . . . it's just Darcy."

I slip off my heels and curl up on the sofa, grabbing the cashmere throw I'd gotten him as a housewarming gift years ago and wrapping it around myself as he opens and closes cabinets in the kitchen. In contrast to my century-old historic home in Morningside, Azar's got a three-story stucco townhome in the trendiest part of Brookhaven. Compared to my ancient fireplace and original nineteenth-century wooden floors, his home is a portrait of sleek contemporary cool. Black dinner table and chairs. Dark frames with black-and-white art on the walls. A white sofa. White bed. The red teakettle on the stove—which I gave him for his last birthday—a welcome spot of color. Looking around, I don't see any sign of Zayna. No sweater left over from a visit. No slippers tucked on the shoe rack. Not yet at least.

"Do you ever really use that teakettle?" I ask.

"Of course not. I only pop it up when I know you're coming."

"You knew I was coming over?"

"I was covering my bases."

"I'm glad Darcy insisted on the outing," I tell him.

"I was surprised you were up for it," he says.

"I wasn't. But it was good to get to know Samir. And to get out of my own head. Our next outing should be with Zayna. We keep meaning to get together for a hangout."

"Hmm? Oh, sure. Chai?" he asks, opening the cupboard next to the stove.

"Yes, please."

He pulls out a box of tea leaves, fills up the kettle with water, and places it on the stove. I glimpse his laundry room through the open door.

"No. Way." I get up and walk over and press the door wider. The basket on the washer is stacked with neatly ironed and folded clothes.

"You iron your scrubs now?" I trace a hand over his minty-green work outfits.

"What else am I supposed to do?" he calls from the kitchen. "Toss them in a heap?"

"Yes. That's exactly what you're supposed to do! I think you're getting worse."

"I'd argue better," he protests.

"Hmm. Maybe I'm jealous. You're so organized."

"Just built that way."

The space smells like cinnamon and cloves when he flicks off the stove. I head back to the couch as he brings over the steaming cups and sits next to me on the sofa. Reaching over, he grabs the remote and flips on the television.

"Hold up!" I protest as he clicks the History Channel app. "I haven't even started the latest season of *Wild* yet. You're already on episode six."

"You didn't miss much," he replies. "No one's tapped out of the competition yet. They're all starving. Lots of rabbits getting out of snares. It turns out mushroom soup can make you sick. There, now you're all caught up."

"Azar! Those are called spoilers." I take a sip of tea. "Hey. Good chai."

"I added star anise, how you like it."

"It's way too late for caffeine. But somehow chai is exactly what I need right now." I settle against the couch.

My mother drank chai at night.

The memory comes to me unbidden. The two of us sitting at the two-person table wedged in the corner of the kitchen overlooking Dolores Park. She took her tea with one spoon of sugar. A dash of milk. She'd nod along, smiling, her head leaning against the window, her hair falling just past her shoulders, as I prattled on and on about the minutiae of my day. She'd stop me to interject questions now and then. In all my memories of her, she was always smiling. I was too young to have understood how much she'd been carrying.

"Where'd you go just now?" Azar asks.

"I'm still here. Just tired. It's been a long day."

I look down at my cup. Steam rises, warming my face.

"You looked a bit distant through dinner," he says. "I get it. Do you want to talk about what happened?"

"I want to forget that whole moment on the lawn." I shiver. "When I saw Lilah with my purse standing on the front porch and ready to rush over to me, I didn't know what I was going to do. What would have happened if things didn't line up the way they did?"

"But things did line up the way they were meant to," he says. "That's what matters, doesn't it?"

I trace a finger around the rim of the teacup. He rests his own beverage on the coffee table.

"Is there something else?"

"Isn't that enough?" I force a laugh.

He doesn't smile back. His eyes are filled with concern.

How does he know? How can he always tell? It's always been this way.

"I swear you should've skipped med school and joined me at the agency. We could use a clairvoyant."

"Only when it comes to you, Nur."

I swallow. If I change the subject and move back to critiquing everyone's homemade structures on the show, he'll move on too. He's not one to keep poking. But slowly, I tell him about that evening with my khala. Why I'm newly a stranger inside my own skin. I'd only meant to outline the broad strokes of what I learned. But as I start telling him about it all, everything tumbles out of me. Fiaz. And Madiha. Every sordid detail.

When I'm finished, I feel shaky. Azar rises and leaves the room. He scoots closer when he returns. Hands me a tissue. Only then do I realize I'm crying.

"I'm so sorry." His arm that had been draped across the sofa behind me moves to my shoulders. I draw closer to him. "That's an enormous amount of information to take in."

"It's making me question . . . everything. About my family and who I am. What about me is real and what's not."

"Whatever your name was—whatever your origin story—you're still you, Nur."

"I don't know what to think anymore. I just . . . it's hard to wrap my head around it. All those years. Khala had a million opportunities to tell me the truth."

"I'm guessing she didn't know how."

"That's what she said, but as hard as it might have been, at some point I was owed an explanation."

"You're right, Nur. She should have told you long ago."

We sit quietly for a short while. I am grateful to him for this silence.

"You know what I think? You need a break," he finally says. "Tell the team to hold down the fort. You're trying to keep on keeping on like nothing happened, but no one can handle everything you've been going through and be fine. You need time to rest and recover."

"I can't just take time off whenever I want. I have a client coming by tomorrow for an intake meeting. My inbox is a disaster."

"You can always reschedule the client meeting. And inboxes are always a disaster. Ignore it."

"Sometimes I feel like you don't know me at all," I tease him.

"I do know you. That's exactly why I'm saying this. You're tired. I can see it on your face. You need to take a full week off at the very least."

"I can't take that much time off. I have a wedding this Saturday."

"Skip it."

"No way." I shake my head. "There are at least four potential clients I promised to meet with there."

"Your job can't take precedence over *you*."

"My job isn't like yours. This agency, it's a part of me. It doesn't take precedence over my life. It *is* my life." I give him my most winning smile. "But if you came with me to the wedding, it'd definitely feel less like work. For old times' sake?"

His smile fades. Right. Zayna. What was I thinking? Our

dinner tonight had been so relaxing and warm, I got a bit too comfortable.

"Forget I said anything," I say quickly. "I'm a big girl. I can handle it."

The television drones low in the background. After a few moments, he turns to me. "Actually, count me in."

"It's probably best you don't," I say. "I'm pretty sure Zayna hates me, and this won't endear me to her."

"She doesn't hate you," he says. "And . . . I don't love the idea of you going there alone."

"Farhan's gone," I tell him. "You don't need to babysit me."

"It's babysitting to eat samosas and chicken tikka?"

"This one's a Greek and German wedding. No samosas, I'm afraid. They *will* have a chocolate fountain made with Porcelana cocoa, though."

"Then I have to go, don't I?"

"Zayna really won't mind?"

"She'll understand."

But will she? Because sitting as close as we are, his breath warm against my skin . . . if Zayna knew what I was thinking right now . . .

"You know what?" I tell him. "I'll take the rest of the week off until the wedding. And if you change your mind about going with me, or Zayna would rather you not, I can do it on my own."

He looks at me intently. "I'll be there, Nur."

NINETEEN

I can honestly say now that one cannot underestimate the life-changing magic of eight uninterrupted hours of sleep. It turned out Azar was right. A few days off lounging at home with Gertie, and I feel better already. I'm still triple bolting my doors, but I'm only checking them a few times each night instead of compulsively every hour.

I felt so much better that, after weeks, I finally laced up my sneakers and went for a jog this morning. No AirPods yet—baby steps on the road to less paranoia—but running down my tree-lined sidewalks, past the pizzeria and the toddler playground, swerving around mothers with strollers and ambling window shoppers, it was the first time in a long time I felt normal.

I've just finished showering and blow-drying my hair when my phone buzzes on the bathroom counter. An alarm reminding me to get ready for the wedding. Not that I needed it. The downtime was good—necessary—but there's only so much downtime a type A person can put up with before they start considering how to dust the back of the refrigerator.

I slip on my dress. A floor-length chiffon that cinches at the waist. I slip off my usual silver bracelets, opting for a tennis bracelet and matching diamond earrings. Pulling up the address, I see it's a barn wedding just over an hour outside of Atlanta. I forward the information on to Azar. He'll join me after he gets off work. I press send as a phone call comes through. It's Khala. Again. I hit decline. Again.

Please, beta, she texts. I just want to hear your voice.

I'm fine, I reply. I love you. I need time.

The rational part of me knows it's unfair to be distant. Having to talk to me about the past, about my mother's murder, must have dredged up painful memories for her. I'm sure she's blamed herself all these years for what happened. I don't. She loved my mother—I know this without any doubt in my mind. She didn't mean to put her in harm's way. No one knows they're about to make a deadly decision—only in hindsight does everything become clear and obvious. Khala thought she was helping my mother find the perfect match. Providing her younger sister with financial security from a well-established family with a good reputation. This is how arranged marriages were done back then. People didn't dig deeper.

Our agency rules take on new meaning for me, though. Khala's strict edict about not advertising. Not matching those we are close to. How the smallest white lie about one's past is a deal-breaker. Why she won't tolerate anyone who asks about income brackets. She'd wanted to make sure what happened to my mother never happened again. The rules were her penance.

I look at the phone and hesitate. Maybe I should call her. It's the right thing to do. *After the wedding,* I tell myself. *I'll call her, and we'll have the conversation we need to have.*

I swing by the office before I head to the wedding. Darcy's hunched over at her desk when I open the door. She startles at the sound of the chime overhead.

"What are you doing here on a Saturday?" I ask her.

"Says the lady who's also here."

"I admit it, I have a problem. I appreciate you holding down the fort, but after everything you've been through, you should be taking it easy."

"Work's been exactly what the doctor ordered. A few more minutes and I'm out of here," she assures me. "I'm heading to Samir's folks' in a few for dinner."

"That sounds great. Are things any better with them?"

"Actually, yes. Maybe it's finally hitting them now that we've secured our deposits that this wedding is happening. I feel like they're starting to thaw toward me. Samir thinks so too."

"Good! It was going to happen sooner or later."

I grab the notebook I need from my desk. The one filled with half-legible scrawls about the potential clients I'm meeting tonight. When I'm back in the main office, Darcy's pensively studying the computer screen.

"Uh-oh. More hate mail?" I ask.

"Not hate mail."

"Darcy . . ."

"Promise you won't freak out?"

"That only makes me freak out more." I stride toward her and look over her shoulder.

"I'm keeping track of online chatter. Someone posted on a subreddit devoted to Lena and Tanvir. They're talking about Avani's wedding implosion," Darcy says.

Shit. Shit. Shit.

I read through the thread.

BANDITXYZ345: Look, I know you're all going to call me a conspiracy theorist or whatever, but I don't think the whole "Farhan being the kidnapper" is the whole story. My dad is friends with his father, and I heard Farhan was using Piyar to get matched up himself. Did Nura set up Lena and Farhan first, before she met Tanvir?

STARLIGHT4U: Avani Patel is my cousin. My aunt shelled out serious cash for the Piyar agency to match her daughter up, and the wedding blew up the night before. Turned out the guy the agency said was all vetted and perfect was actually a criminal! My mom was going to introduce me to Nura that night. I dodged a bullet.

There it is: My worst fears brought to life on a website.

"Don't panic," Darcy says quickly. She points to the screen. "It's not all bad. These people stuck up for us."

JINMARDO7658: This agency's been around for decades. You're talking about two weddings that went south out of hundreds that went off without a hitch. They're not God.

KNIGHTLYRU: Lena said this guy was obsessed with her since college, but sure, keep reaching.

"It's only this one post," Darcy says into the silence. "It's been up for three days and it's barely gotten any traction."

For now. It's only a matter of time before others connect the dots. Like Logan. He must have come across this thread. He's getting closer and closer to a story that will sink my agency into the ground. Farhan had been dead set on destroying my reputation; it looks like his work continues beyond the grave.

"I know it's impossible not to worry," says Darcy. "But try to put it out of your mind as much as you can. I'll get the PR team in the loop before I head out for dinner. Nothing else we can do right now. Go to the wedding, have fun. Send Azar my love."

"How are you so amazing?" I ask her.

"It's why you pay me the big bucks." She winks.

"No, it's why you're my friend." I give her a hug.

PLEASE JOIN US IN
CELEBRATING THE UNION OF

Tabitha Georgiou

AND

Timothy Wolf

SATURDAY, JUNE 21ST

HALF PAST SEVEN O'CLOCK

SANDISTA ORCHARDS

ELEGY, GEORGIA

TWENTY

Light-filled lanterns shine among the trees surrounding the property when I at last make it through the winding roads and arrive at the farmhouse wedding venue. I take in the sloping hills and the hint of the Blue Ridge Mountains in the distance.

The barn is less a rustic structure to house animals than a full-fledged wedding venue with the accoutrements of a barn. The roof is painted dark in the illusion of rustic shingles. A vintage weather vane with a rooster sits on top. An artistic metal structure of a tractor is perched by the white fabric tent for dinner. From my car, I hear a pianist playing in the distance. Other attendees pull in and make their way to the festivities. Which I should be doing too. I'm reapplying my lipstick when I hear a knock on my car window. I flinch. But it's Azar. Of course. When will my nerves finally steady themselves?

"You look beautiful," he says when I step out.

"As do you," I reply. "Tuxedos suit you."

"Cell service was spotty most of the drive. This place is in the middle of nowhere. Now I'm doubly glad I came."

"So you *did* come to babysit me."

"I'm just saying . . ."

"Azar." I press my palms against his chest. "I. Do. Not. Need. Looking. After."

He places his hands over mine. "You can't blame me for caring."

A jolt of electricity runs through me at his touch. I feel a strange sensation, as though the background is blurring, as though it's only the two of us here. As though he feels it too. *It's the setting,* I remind myself. The twinkle lights in the trees. The music floating through the air. But with his hands over mine, I feel unable to look away.

"Who knew rural Georgia held such charms?" he says when we make our way to the wedding tent. The sun is beginning its descent. The mountains are tinged with lavender and pink.

"It's as rural as you can get without leaving the metro Atlanta area. Did you see the apple orchard next to the property?"

"Shall we go apple picking?"

"I don't think we're dressed for the occasion." I tug his bow tie.

A waiter swings by, proffering smoked trout on toothpicks. I take one and nod approvingly.

"Not sure if it's because I ran today or what, but I'm starving. This could probably taste like three-day-old mackerel and I'd love it."

"Did I hear correctly? You went on a run?" he asks.

"I'm not sure I appreciate the insinuation! I ran a half-marathon last year."

"I know. I was there. You finished top ten."

"Hopefully now that everything is behind me, I can finally get back to my old routine."

Another server brings by what he describes as grilled rosemary chicken on mini skewers.

"Not bad," Azar says as he takes another one.

"Did you say 'not bad' to what was probably a twenty-dollar bite of poultry?"

"I call it like I see it," he protests. "Money can buy expensive food, but it doesn't mean it's exquisite."

I move to reply, when I see him glance down. His phone is buzzing. He picks it up and reads the number. His face pinches.

"Everything all right?"

"I have to take this call. One second." He strides toward the parking lot.

I look at the growing number of guests mingling on the lawn and check the time. My heart skips a beat. The festivities are running a few minutes behind.

It's normal, I remind myself. Timely weddings that go off without a hitch are the exception, not the norm. *She's getting ready. She's not in danger. Farhan is dead.*

And yet . . .

I walk the perimeter until I spot a door partly opened on the side of the farmhouse. Tentatively, I pull it wider. There's Tabitha, the bride. A hairstylist is putting the last touches of baby's breath in her hair. There are no creepy letters on her desk. No strangers lurking by the doorway. *She's fine. She's safe.* Of course she is.

Tabitha spots me at the edge of the door and brightens.

"Nura!" She gestures for me to come inside. "I'm so glad you're here."

"You look like you stepped out of a fairy tale." Her shimmering gown flows like liquid. "This is a gorgeous venue. I'm so happy for you both."

"Thank you for helping me find my Timothy."

"It's a pleasure to match people as perfect for each other as you are."

"Just a heads-up, there are at least five more people here who are probably going to tackle you and beg you to take them on," she says. "Sorry in advance?"

I laugh and give her a hug. I give her space to get ready and prepare for her big day. Back outside in the main grassy event space, I glance in Azar's direction. He's still on the call, off in the distance by the artistically rendered tractor. I pull out my phone to check messages—then I click Zayna's profile. I look at the newest photo, which is not a selfie. Instead, it's a leather suitcase on a bed with striped sheets. Inside, I glimpse folded jeans and a floral makeup bag. The caption: Checking out Helen Resort and Spa with a special someone this weekend.

A special someone. My chest constricts.

"Sorry about that." Azar approaches me.

"Everything okay?" I ask.

"Yeah." His expression is strained. "Shall we get to our seats? Looks like they're getting ready to begin."

"Azar. Who was on the phone?"

"Oh, that was Zayna." He shrugs but doesn't offer more.

I fold my arms and look at him until he gives in.

"It's nothing. We're going to Helen tomorrow to do some hiking and check out that waterfall. She got off her shift early, so she rang me to see . . ."

She called like a girlfriend does. To see if he was home. If she can come over to his place so they can head out in the morning together. For the romantic weekend getaway she was so excited about that she had to post it online for the world to see.

The warmth and lightness inside of me flickers off. This is why he was of two minds about coming to this wedding. He knew he had another obligation. He's here out of pity. I'm a nagging kid sister who needs looking after.

"Does she know you're here? With me?"

"It's no big deal."

"That doesn't answer my question."

He sticks his hands in his pockets. Doesn't reply.

"If she didn't like me before, she's going to hate me now."

"She'll come around."

She'll come around. Not a denial. She *does* hate me.

"And if she doesn't come around? Then what?" I ask. "Things are serious between the two of you. If she doesn't approve of us, what happens next?"

"What do you mean?" Azar's eyes flash. "You and me. We're friends, right? But I need more. And I finally found someone I connect with. Zayna . . . she's great. At the end of the day, you and I will always be friends, but there's more to life. At least, for me there is, but I guess you wouldn't understand that not everyone is like you, obsessed with work to the point where I have to come along to weddings to spend any reliable time with you. Not everyone is happy to be alone for the rest of their life."

I can't breathe. It's like I've been slapped. He knows how important my job is to me. I thought he understood. And happy to be alone? How can he not see that I had found someone too—but that someone wasn't interested in me? Violins play Mendelssohn's "Wedding March." I shakily glance at the crowd settling in. I need to find my seat. I'm here to work. I need to get my game face on. But how?

"Wait," he says. "That came out wrong. I—"

"I think it came out exactly. right." The music picks up in volume. "I have to go."

"Nur. Listen—"

"Just leave, Azar. I'm serious. Go to Zayna, have a great trip together, and leave me alone. I have work to do."

Before he can reply, I turn. I walk past the glittering trees to the ribboned white seats facing the altar. I sit in the back row.

Tears prick my eyes. I'm not going to cry. I can't cry. Not here. Not now. If he leaves, good. I'm glad. It's not like I'm waiting for him to tap my shoulder. To slide into the seat next to me. To take my hand in an implicit apology . . .

The minutes tick by. He doesn't come.

The bride walks down the aisle toward her starry-eyed soon-to-be husband. I think back to the other day at Azar's place—how he'd held me when I cried. And this evening, when I'd gotten out of the car. The way he'd taken me in. His hands over mine. His eyes gazing into my own. In that moment, I could have sworn something was shifting between us. I was wrong. It's like Khala says: We can't trust ourselves to be objective about those we care for.

I scan the crowd, wondering if anyone saw our argument. Azar was here to be my cover—the matchmaker with her dashing partner—but if a potential client was watching, they wouldn't have witnessed two people in love; they'd have been witnessing the end.

Deep breath. In. Out. It's game time. I cannot look like a frazzled mess. I focus on the nuptials, which *are* beautiful. Even more beautiful given that the last wedding related event I attended ended in disaster. I take in the personalized vows exchanged over a violin quartet. The flower girls hold pink and violet flowers to match the deepening colors of the sky.

After, I grab a seat under the sprawling white tent, strategically choosing a spot near the gas heaters going at full blast. It's June, but there's an undeniable chill in the air.

"Hey, Nura," a man's voice says.

I look up, my smile automatically in place to introduce myself to the potential new client. But it's not a new client. It's Logan Wilson.

"Nice wedding." He sits down at the empty seat next to mine. Casually. Calmly. "I got turned around on the drive over and nearly wound up in the middle of an apple orchard. I didn't even know you could *grow* apples this far south."

He's got a leg crossed over his knee. He's talking to me as though he belongs here.

"What are you doing here?" Disbelief is rapidly displaced by anger.

"I know. This is a bit unorthodox. But I figured now was as good a time as any for us to chat."

"Who told you where I was?"

"That's not important."

"I'd say it's extremely important."

"I have my sources, but"—his expression grows somber— "we really do need to talk, Nura. For your sake as much as mine."

"How very altruistic of you." I grip my clutch so tight my knuckles go white. How long has he been here? Watching me? Did he wait until Azar was safely gone before pouncing? *Did he witness our fight?* I look around, feeling exposed. Most people are still lingering by the cocktail tables. Servers are setting up dinner. No one else is near us. "I've already been through enough drama to last me several lifetimes," I say through gritted teeth. "I don't need any more stalking."

"Stalking?" he repeats. "I've been called a lot of things, but stalker's a first."

"I saw you getting lunch at the chaat house," I tell him. "You were two doors down from where I was. Are you trying to tell me that was just a coincidence?"

"Oh." He startles. "Well, sort of. I didn't know you were there, but yes, I was talking to people in the area who are in the marriage space—for background."

"So you admit it."

"I admit to being a journalist. Not a stalker," he replies. "Your story keeps getting bigger and bigger. I was of two minds coming out here to meet with you. My editor keeps telling me to do a write-around, but I need your perspective to do this story justice. When I read your email, I figured you were up for talking. I thought this was simpler, so you didn't have to set aside a separate time to speak, since you'd mentioned how busy you are."

"My email?" I repeat. "Does gaslighting pay off in your line of work?"

The anger almost drains out of my system. Azar was right. It was too soon to get back in the game. I don't have the band-width to deal with Logan on top of everything else.

"Wait!" He hurries after me as I march out of the tent. Toward the parking lot. "I'm not trying to play games here. I did get an email from you. Earlier today."

I swivel toward him. "I'm not rewarding your harassment."

Logan pulls out his phone. He hands me the device.

My stomach lurches. There *is* an email with my name in his inbox.

The subject heading: *You win.*

With a trembling hand, I click the email.

While my first and most ardent wish would have been for you to leave me alone, it is clear that will not be happening. I'll consider your offer to cooperate if we can arrange for your questions to arrive over email. My life is extremely busy and I do not have the time nor space to set aside to meet you.

"I take it you didn't send this?" he says into the silence.

"No. I don't use Yahoo Mail."

"Ah. Well, that explains a lot." He clears his throat. "Shit. This is . . . this is wild."

He keeps talking, but blood throbs in my ears. *It's over. It's supposed to be over.* Farhan is dead. Who is sending emails impersonating me? Could it be Basit, in a sick twist of vengeance? Or does someone just want to watch me squirm? And if Logan fell for it, how many others have gotten emails they believe to be from me?

"This will make for some fun clicks when your piece posts, won't it?"

"Nura." He looks me square in the eyes. "I'm not interested in gotcha journalism. I *also* happen to find it highly disturbing that someone impersonated you. I'm keeping up with the online chatter," he continues, "and I have a police source who's told me you were involved on the night of Farhan's death. I also know that it was an associate of yours who killed him. I'm not trying to be salacious, but it's clear there's a story with a capital S here. Wouldn't it be helpful to have a journalist on your side? To get the story down right?"

"You mean you."

"I won't be the only one making the connections; it's only a matter of time before all of this is public information. I'm here because I want to help you. Really." He glances around and then at me. "To be frank, I'm concerned. Whoever sent me that email is trying to con me too."

"Whoever it is, their sights are set on me, don't worry. I—I have to go."

"Nura. Please. We need to talk. I have—"

"Please." I hold up a hand. My voice cracks. "Not now."

I walk away. He does not follow.

Something is wrong, I text Borzu once I'm safely inside my car. *Are you home? I can come to you.*

I turn on the car and try to keep my hands steady. I thought I was safe. I thought the threat of danger was behind me. Now the small sense of security I'd allowed myself to feel is gone. There's no way I can go back to my place tonight. Not after seeing this.

The engine rumbles to life. I pull out of the parking lot. The two-lane road is deserted. There is no city light pollution. No streetlamps and no stars. The moon is shrouded by clouds. I flip on my high beams.

My conversation with Logan roils inside of me. Someone at the police station leaked the details about Farhan's death to him. It was only a matter of time, I know that. It's like he said, this information will all go public eventually. But it's happening sooner than I expected. Or at least sooner than I feel ready for. My stomach hurts thinking about Darcy. When she finds out the press is sniffing around, it will turn her world upside down, but I can't keep it from her. I'll call her from Borzu's place. She needs to hear this from me.

A whirring sound buzzes in the car. I graze my fingers over the dashboard, but before I can locate the source of the sound, a sudden stream of wiper fluid floods the windshield, blurring my vision.

What the hell?

I grip the steering wheel. How did I hit the fluid? I press the wipers but nothing happens. Instead, another stream attacks the windshield.

This can't be happening. It's pitch black outside and I'm in the middle of nowhere. Again, I slam the levers to activate the wipers. Nothing. *It's fine,* I try to tell myself as panic builds. *Cars can glitch. I'll pull over. Troubleshoot.* Peering through the glass, I try to make out a safe spot to stop through the blurred screen. Suddenly, my dashboard lights up. A woman's operatic falsetto blasts through the speakers.

My ears ring. My very smart car decides to completely fall apart now, on a country road in the middle of nowhere? Through the streaming liquid blasting the windshield, I make out a spot to park a few paces ahead. The hill starts sloping downward. I slam on the brakes. Nothing happens. There's no resistance. It's as though there are no brakes at all.

Tears stream down my face. My teeth chatter. My entire body is shaking. How is this happening?

Abruptly, the music stops. Haunting silence rings in my ears. The car bounces harder and harder over bumps in the road, gathering more speed as it careens downhill. The landscape shifts around me.

Lights flash on the other side of the road—a car coming at me. The odometer won't stop climbing. And now I'm beelining toward the oncoming car. I jerk the wheel away. My car swerves. Lurches toward what appears to be a glowing reflection on an iron gate, getting brighter and brighter.

Oh sh—

TWENTY-ONE

Fluorescent lights blast onto my face. I blink, groggily opening my eyes wider. The world is bright and spinning. . . .

I focus. *I'm alive.* I raise my hand. Weird white bracelets on my wrist. I'm in a fabric gown. There's a crinkling sensation beneath me as I move.

I struggle to sit up but my ribs feel like they're pressing into my organs. The pain takes my breath away.

A chair scrapes against the floor. Someone squeezes my hand. "You are okay," Khala whispers. "You are okay."

The hospital door swings open. A man in a doctor's coat walks inside. "Glad to see you're up."

"Where am I?"

Khala's eyes stay on me. "You are at Decatur Medical, beta."

"How . . . how long have I been out? Gertie," I gasp.

"Don't worry about Gertie. Darcy is taking care of her," Khala says. "Right now, you need to rest."

"What happened?" My head throbs like a thousand nails are pressing through my skull.

"You were in a car accident," says the doctor. "All things considered, you're fine. You have a few bruises and a cracked rib. A mild concussion. It could have been much worse."

The wedding. Logan. The spoofed email. The million different emotions that had been running through me come flooding back.

"I was leaving early from a wedding," I tell them. "My car started going haywire." I explain how the wiper fluid sprayed. The music on full blast. My brakes, suddenly useless. "It was like my car got . . . hacked? There was nothing I could do. I swerved to avoid an oncoming car. Hit a fence. The rest is a complete blank."

The doctor jots something down on his tablet.

"The car is totaled, isn't it?" I murmur.

"Don't worry about your vehicle. You are okay, that is what matters," Khala says. "But . . ." She looks at the doctor.

My heart skitters. "Just say it."

"Your toxicology report came back," he says. "They found high levels of oxycodone in your system."

"The painkiller?" I've never taken prescription painkillers in my life. "I didn't take any oxycodone."

"Any ideas how it showed up in your system?" the doctor asks.

"I don't know!" A stab of irritation passes through me. Are they looking at me this somberly because they think they've stumbled onto an addiction?

Before I can say more, the hospital door swings open. Azar sweeps inside. His hair is sticking out every which way. He's breathing heavily. Perspiration dots his forehead. He rushes to my bedside.

"Azar," the doctor says. "You're not on call this weekend."

"Your khala's messages," he says breathlessly. "They all came in at once when I got to the . . . There was no signal. Shit. Nura. What happened? Are you okay?"

"Your colleague here is asking if I have an opioid addiction.

Apparently my blood work shows that my body was full of drugs."

"Drugs?" Azar looks at the doctor. "How did you find drugs in her system?"

"Shannon ran the report," the doctor says. "I'll have her bring over the full breakdown."

"Maybe I was roofied." I think of Logan. It seems impossible, but this entire situation makes no sense.

"The labs came back negative for Rohypnol," the doctor says.

"What about gamma hydroxybutyrate?" Azar asks. "We don't routinely test for it, but it's a growing threat."

"GHB? You think?"

"It would have the same effect as Rohypnol. We need to test ASAP, though. It leaves the system quickly."

"I'll put an order in." The doctor makes a note on his tablet. "The more we can rule out, the better."

"Rule it all out," I say. "I didn't take anything!"

"Ms. Khan, they had to treat you for an overdose," the doctor says. "Your injuries aren't too bad, but the levels of drugs in your system . . . had a Good Samaritan not pulled over and called an ambulance, you would not have survived."

An overdose? I lean back on the raised bed trying to make sense of the doctor's words. Did I take a sip of anything while Logan was at my table? I can't recall, but that doesn't mean it didn't happen. But I didn't feel drugged while driving. Did I? Tears prick my eyes. What else happened? Why can't I remember?

The doctor chats with Azar briefly before he excuses himself. The door closes behind him. I try to still my breathing. Both Khala and Azar watch me worriedly.

"Azar."

The memory returns in a sudden burst. We had an argument. A horrible fight before the crash.

"Your trip . . ."

"I'm so sorry, Nur." His voice breaks. "I shouldn't have left."

"Was the car behaving strangely earlier?" Khala asks. "When you were driving to the wedding, was it acting up?"

"It was working completely fine," I say as a nurse comes in. She draws blood from my left arm.

I try to remember the last bits of the evening. Logan showed me the spoofed email. Someone was posing as me. It's connected to whatever happened. It has to be. I need to reach out to Logan. I need to see that email. When the nurse leaves, I turn to Khala.

"Where's my phone?" I ask her. "Did they get it out of the car?"

Khala hands me my purse from the counter. I retrieve my device. The screen is cracked, but it works. I type in my passcode. There's a sharp rapping at the hospital room door.

"It better not be the police again," Khala says.

Azar's expression darkens as he goes to answer the door. I hear a muffled conversation. Stilted. Angry. He steps back. Two police officers enter the room. Officer Kirkpatrick, I read on his lapel. The other officer is a woman, her blond hair tied back in a ponytail. Officer Delray.

"Glad to see you're better," Officer Kirkpatrick says.

"This is not a good time," Azar says.

"It's fine, Azar," I tell him. I understand his protectiveness. I *am* tired—the ache in my ribs is growing sharper. But the sooner I answer their questions, the sooner they can figure out what is going on. Who is behind this.

"We understand you've had quite an ordeal," Delray says.

"I was drugged. Can't figure out how quite yet." I wonder if Logan poisoned an appetizer. I have no idea how drugging someone works, but it doesn't sound outside the realm of possibilities. "And someone did something to my car, which caused it to crash."

The officers exchange glances. "We understand you had a high amount of oxy in your system," Kirkpatrick says.

"I don't take any pain medicine other than the occasional Advil, much less oxycodone."

"There are street names for oxy as well," he says. "Roxy? Perc? OC?" He rattles off a few more. "Do any of those sound familiar?"

I look at them, unable to speak. I thought they were here to get answers. To help me. Their questions and demeanor imply otherwise. "I did not ingest any illegal substance."

They do not reply.

"Not sure if you've had a chance to check out my car," I continue. It appears I have to do their work for them. "There must be some evidence that it was tampered with. Someone did this to me. The drugging. The crash. All of it."

They still don't speak. It's a tactic I'm familiar with. I do the same during my intake sessions with clients when I need them to tell me things they'd prefer not to share, like sensitive family information or indiscretions they're not proud of. The longer I let the awkward silence linger, the more likely they'll rush to fill the void with the information I need. That's what they're doing to me.

Fine. I don't need them. I'm not a damsel in distress. I have my own team. We'll get to the bottom of this one way or another.

"Ms. Khan," says Kirkpatrick. "We *are* looking into your accident, but we're here for a slightly different query. It's about

Lena Kamdar and Tanvir Bashir. We were hoping you could tell us where you were the afternoon of June thirteenth."

"Hold up," Azar interjects. "As I told you at the door, she's been in a traumatic accident. She is still recovering. The last thing she needs is you interrogating her."

"Why *are* you interrogating me?" I ask slowly.

Kirkpatrick pulls out his notepad. "We're trying to piece together the day they went missing so we can have the most comprehensive portrait we can. You worked directly with Lena and Tanvir, didn't you?"

"I set them up through my matchmaking agency," I tell him. "But I wasn't with them the day they went missing. If I'd known anything useful, I'd have reported it."

"You were following along quite closely, though," he says. "We heard you were listening on a police scanner."

"I have private investigators on staff. We were concerned about the disappearance and wanted to help."

"I understand," Delray says. "That's what *we're* trying to do. Get a full timeline of the day."

I suppress an eye roll, but if they need this information to move along, there's no harm in telling them where I was. "I was probably at home getting ready for the event." I check my agenda on my phone. "And then around six o'clock I was at my aunt's home, getting jewelry for the evening."

"Do you have any way for us to verify that?"

"I can verify it," Khala says sharply.

"My phone would also confirm where I was."

"Can we see it?" Kirkpatrick asks quickly. Too quickly.

"And the oxycodone," Delray asks. "Where did you procure it?"

"I told you already." I grit my teeth. "I *don't* take oxy. What conclusion are you trying to reach here?"

Delray glances at Kirkpatrick. "The reason we are inquiring is that the couple was forced into the back of their own vehicle at gunpoint. They were ordered to take oxycodone."

Blood rushes to my head. They had the same drugs in their system as I did?

"But . . . Farhan did it. . . . He kidnapped them."

"We are trying to determine if he was a solo actor or if he had assistance."

The way they look at me . . .

"Wait. Are you implying *I* assisted him?"

They do not reply.

"Do you hear yourselves?" Azar glares at the officers. "She's going to overtake two people? She doesn't even own a gun."

"We didn't say she did anything."

"That's enough now. Time for you to go," Azar tells them.

"Before we leave, we had one last question," Delray says.

She reaches into a bag and draws out a silver bracelet etched with flowers.

My bracelet.

"Does this look familiar to you?" Delray asks.

"Wh-where did you get that?" I feel woozy. I move to reach for it, but Delray takes a step back and shakes her head. "We're holding on to this. It's evidence."

"Evidence of *what*?" Panic bubbles inside of me. That's my mother's bracelet. They can't just have it.

"Ms. Khan, we discovered this not far from where Lena and Tanvir were held. Lena's mother recognized it as yours," says Delray. "We simply want to clear things up."

I know our relationship is a business one. But for her mother to have cast suspicion my way is gutting.

"This doesn't make sense." My voice breaks. "What is going on?"

I try to sit up. The purse falls from my lap and tumbles to the checkerboard floor. My keys, stray receipts, everything falls out. Including a pill bottle. White tablets tinged with blue fan out on the vinyl floor.

"How did those get in there?" Kirkpatrick says wryly.

"They're not mine." I want my voice to come out strong, authoritative, but it's a whisper. A whimper.

"You wouldn't mind if we checked—" Kirkpatrick kneels down, but Khala juts in front of them.

"She would certainly mind."

"Now, hold up one second," he begins.

"Absolutely not," she snaps. "Your accusations are outright defamatory, and they end right now."

"We're just trying to get to the bottom of whatever is going on. We're on the same side," Kirkpatrick says.

"Does she have to answer any more questions from you?"

He sighs. "She does not."

"You are on a fishing expedition, and I suggest you cast your lures elsewhere."

"Ma'am," Officer Kirkpatrick begins. "I could just—"

"My name is Shameem Mirza," she says firmly. The way she looks at those officers. Her back straight. Her eyes shining. Tears spring to my eyes. That's her. The woman I knew so well all those years, there she is.

"You both are invited to leave." She points to the door. "She will not be speaking to either of you again without a lawyer present."

I wait until they're gone before I sink into the bed.

"Oh, my sweet Nura." Khala grips my hand. "Don't worry. You will be just fine in no time . . ."

She keeps talking, but it's hard to focus on her words. I want to thank Khala. To talk to both her and Azar in order to make sense of this madness. But the two officers have taken all my energy. As they exit the room, the doctor reenters. Words float in and out. *GHB . . . three times the prescribed levels . . .* I can't hold on to any of this as exhaustion roots within me and sleep takes over.

TWENTY-TWO

"Lay low," says Amara. "Until I can find you a real lawyer."

"You *are* a real lawyer," I say. Amara is, in fact, a former classmate who went on to law school and holds the record for the second-longest dating streak with Azar. Looking around her office on the forty-second floor of Franck and Carter, the legal treatises stacked behind her, the enormous oak table, and her high-back leather chair, I shoot her a side-eye. "If you're not a real lawyer, who is?"

"I'm a real *estate* lawyer. Getting you the lease on the corner of Skylance and Block was easy peasy, but I'm out of my depth here. You need a criminal attorney—I know, I know," she says upon seeing my stricken expression at the word *criminal*. "But considering you already got yourself a bodyguard, you may as well get the right counsel for the other type of protection you need."

Fiona Levi, bodyguard to the stars, *is* standing outside this very door right now, thanks to Genevieve pulling a few strings. Fiona keeps watch at all times. She trails behind my car in her Lincoln everywhere I go. Fiona—and Gus, who trades shifts with her—has a list of my trusted circle, and other than them, she's on guard for anyone who so much as looks my way. It's

beyond strange to be followed like this, but I'm relieved knowing someone is keeping a watchful eye out. No more half
measures; my harrowing ordeal has ensured I take this as seriously as the situation calls for. I even checked into a hotel last
night.

"I can't believe you're dealing with so much," Amara says.

"Me either. How is this my life?" I tell her. "On top of it all,
I also have to worry if the police will arrest me. The way they
interrogated me at the hospital, I felt like their prime suspect."

I can't even blame them. The bracelet the officer had shown
me had fooled me too. But once I was home, to my relief, I
found my mother's jewelry exactly where I'd left it.

"It's why you need to be sure you're properly lawyered up
ASAP," says Amara. "But don't freak out. If they had enough to
arrest you, they'd have arrested you. Have they asked you to
come into the station since the hospital confrontation?"

I shake my head.

"There you go," she says. "And they did find GHB in your
system, didn't they? You obviously didn't inject yourself with
that, right? GHB can cause memory loss. Whoever gave it to
you wanted to knock you out and make sure you wouldn't remember."

But will this be enough for them to back off? They may be
more careful with flinging accusations, but that's not the same
as moving on. They're probably digging as we speak, just digging more quietly. And they're digging because someone wants
them to. Whoever did this knew the type of bracelet I had and
slipped medication into my purse. They orchestrated my accident. And hurting me wasn't the only objective. They're trying
to get me to go down for what happened to Lena and Tanvir.

"Any guesses on what happened with the car crash?" she asks.

"Borzu says the car was remotely attacked. Modern cars are

basically giant smartphones," I tell her. "There have been reports of windshield-wiper hacks to prank people, ditto for blasting music. . . . Hackers can even mess with brakes remotely."

"Are you still keeping tabs on Logan? I looked him up—it's hard to imagine he's behind it, but people can have sides to them we'll never fully understand."

"He's in New York at the moment."

"Not that those pills are yours," Amara says, "but even if they were, you wouldn't be the only one in our fine city with a bottle of oxy on their person. You have an alibi for the day Lena and Tanvir were kidnapped. Your face is on your aunt's security camera at the exact same time they were taken."

I look out the window. From this vantage point, the trees dotting the concrete walkways below look like stalks of broccoli. "It's killing me that whoever is behind this is out there somewhere, watching this circus unfold."

"It's enraging. I wish I could help you more directly, but luckily, I can do the next best thing and get you some amazing recommendations. The lawyer I connected Darcy with is top-notch. And, hey, I know you got your kick-ass team for investigating, but we have great private investigators we contract with too. If you want more eyes on this, or anything at all, don't hesitate to ask. I'll help you however I can."

"It helps to talk everything through with you," I tell her. "I appreciate you taking an hour out of your billable day for me."

"Anytime. Let's hope they catch the fucker behind this as soon as possible."

Darcy and Genevieve are glued to Borzu's desktop when I get to the office later that day. This is becoming an all-too-familiar sight.

"Any updates?" I ask.

They swivel toward me—bleary-eyed as though they've done nothing but stare at the screen until I arrived. Which, perhaps, is true.

"Nura, thank God you're okay." Darcy wraps me in a tight embrace. I wince. My ribs are still incredibly tender. The discharging doctor offered me pain medication, but after the accusations hurled my way by the police officers, I don't even want to touch an Advil.

"Cracked rib. Mild concussion," I tell them. "The car is totaled. But it could have been much worse. Thank you for cat sitting while I was in the hospital, Darcy. And thanks for sorting out the bodyguard, Genevieve."

"You were long overdue for some personal security," says Genevieve. "I should've gotten on that way sooner."

"We thought the threat was over," I tell her.

"Well, now you have a second set of eyes. And they're the best of the best."

Genevieve glances at Fiona, who's standing outside the office door, leaning against the gray brick wall, her cat-eye sunglasses concealing her watchful gaze.

"Did the police have any insights?" Borzu asks.

"At best, they think I'm an addict who veered off the road. At worst, they think I was in cahoots with Farhan."

"Could Farhan's father be behind all of this?" Darcy asks. "He's got limitless resources. He could easily have people do his bidding for him from afar."

"I doubt it," Borzu says. "I haven't seen any movement to indicate anything's awry. He's not exactly smart about encryption with the things he gets up to. If he was behind this, I'd know."

"Logan feels more likely to be the culprit than Basit. He turned up at the *wedding*," I tell them. "Funny how trouble follows him. He was at Avani's wedding when the faked papers were slipped into her dressing room. He was in town when someone stole Gertie. Now he's at a wedding where my car was tampered with?"

"There's no such thing as coincidences," Darcy says grimly.

"But his phone pinged him at the wedding at the time of the accident," says Borzu.

"What difference does that make? He could've hacked in remotely from the wedding if he wanted to. Or paid someone to sabotage Nura, no?" Darcy asks.

"Sure, but what's his motive?" Borzu asks. "He thought you were up for a conversation and came over to interview you. He just wanted to cover the story right. He's a persistent journalist, but it doesn't make sense for him to try to hurt anyone."

"Maybe he put things in motion to create the story of a lifetime," Darcy says.

"He has all he needs to go viral," Borzu points out. "He's been three steps ahead of everyone this whole time."

Borzu's right. Despite all the information he has at his fingertips to write an explosive hit piece, he hasn't.

"When the public finds out about the police inquiry into my whereabouts, and my car accident . . ." I shudder, imagining the press that will descend upon us. "I might have to permanently move into the Lowen."

"How long are you staying there?" Genevieve asks.

"I'm not sure."

"Those are some fancy digs," Darcy says. "I pictured you as more of a historic B&B type of girl."

"They had the best security of all the hotels I looked into.

They've got discreet metal detectors at the entrance and armed security by the front desk. Between my own security detail and the hotel's, I actually managed to sleep properly last night."

"Sooner or later, whoever is doing this will slip up," Genevieve says. "And we'll be there to catch him when he does."

I think of my conversation with Khala. Fiaz is dead, but he has a family.

"I have a few more names to look into," I tell her. I jot down the Usmani family relatives I found on social media. The ones with features hauntingly similar to my own. I hope she won't inquire further, and to my relief, she simply takes the paper from me and nods.

"How's that online message board?" I ask. With everything that's happened, it's slipped my mind until now. "Are there any more replies?"

Darcy's eyes dart to Genevieve and then Borzu. "There's been no movement on the subreddit."

"But?" I prompt.

"There *is* weirdness afoot," Borzu admits. "People are trying to review-bomb our testimonial page. They're not going to get anywhere with that since I approve whatever is posted, but it's wild. See for yourself." He types on his computer, then nods to the screen.

I'd give negative stars if I could! They took my money and fled. Save yourself the headache and get away from these con artists while you still can. —*Simran*

Worst agency and worst customer service. I was better off sticking to Bumble. At least it's free and not a fraud! —*J. Schaeffer*

SCAM ALERT You know the story about the emperor who has no clothes? That's the Piyar agency. Save your money and yourself! —*Jenny Ho*

My mouth feels dry. It's not the reviews themselves. Review bombing happens—we got plenty after the *Vanity Fair* piece called us a throwback to arranged marriages. We normally pay it no mind. The ultrawealthy aren't checking my Google reviews before signing me on. They're relying on word of mouth, their friends and family members, those who can vouch for me personally and show them the tangible net positive my services added to their lives. But the review bombings of the past were disjointed, nonsensical rants. All of these people came straight to our own website to trash us.

"Why do they all say we took them on as clients?" I ask.

"I checked their names against our agency database," Darcy says. "They're not in the system. Not even from when your aunt was solo at the agency."

"I'm guessing your name found its way into a toxic corner of the internet," Borzu says. "Trolls love doing coordinated attacks, which explains why they're so similar with their accusations that we're scammers and why they all went to the same spot to leave their reviews. Don't worry, I'll get to the bottom of it."

"Borzu's got this," Genevieve tells me. "But we do have some pressing things to talk about. Like your phone."

"What about my phone?" I curl my fingers protectively over it.

"Whoever is behind the car crash might have been tracking you that way."

"I thought the phone was cleared of trackers."

"It was, but nothing's foolproof," says Borzu. "Someone may

have Trojan horsed it or something. Better to be safe than sorry."

"So I ditch my phone?" I laugh a little and pretend my anxiety isn't ramping up at the mere thought of putting it aside. My phone is an appendage at this point. "Can't you wipe it clean? Add some extra layer of protection or something?"

"We need to be extra cautious. You don't have to get rid of it. Just keep it at your home; you're not there right now anyhow. For going out and about, use a burner. At least until we know what's going on. That way, whoever is doing this can't detect your movements—if that's what's going on."

Borzu pulls open the cabinet above his desk and grabs a flip phone encased in plastic and tosses it to me.

In my office, I settle into my chair and wrestle with the packaging. I let out a yelp as my fingernail chips. Cursing, I grab a pair of scissors and tear through the plastic. I look down at the black flip phone. This is my life now. I am someone's prey—weaving and bobbing, trying to survive.

Darcy steps inside my office to go over my agenda for the day. My iPhone buzzes. My heart leaps into my throat. I quickly grab the device, hoping it's Azar. But it's not. It's a text from a client. He's asking to reschedule our meeting that was set for next week.

"We've kept your schedule pretty light," Darcy tells me as she scans her tablet. "But you do have two weddings coming up. Do you want to still attend?"

"We'll need to cancel," I tell her. "Can we send them some fine chocolate and our regrets?"

"You got it." She scrolls her device. "Shahin's wedding was up next."

"The one on Jekyll Island?" I feel a pinch of disappointment. I'd been looking forward to that one. Azar was going to go with me. I'd booked us adjoining rooms.

Other than the occasional text message check-in, we haven't spoken since my discharge from the hospital. I wonder if he rescheduled his romantic getaway. Maybe that's where he is right now.

"I'll send Shahin your regrets," Darcy says.

"I'll call her myself," I tell her.

"You sure?" Darcy asks. "She's going to be pissed."

"She is. That's why I think it's best if she hears it from me."

When I call her an hour later, Shahin picks up on the third ring.

"How are wedding preparations going?" I ask.

"Well, thank you."

There's a moment of silence. I realize she's not going to elaborate.

"I wanted to let you know that unfortunately I won't be able to make it to the wedding. I've been in a car accident—I'm fine!—but there are a lot of loose ends I have to deal with. I'm sorry. I was really looking forward to being there."

"Thanks for letting me know."

That's it? I'd prepared myself for her trademark dramatic gasp. A plea for me to attend at all costs. Before I can tell her she can pass along my contact information to her friends, she speaks again.

"You caught me at a bad time. We will miss you at the wedding. Be well."

The call ends. I stare at my phone. Before I can put it down, it rings again. It's Erica—otherwise known around the office as Yoga Lady. We chatted last week. She took my advice to get a life coach and had just given her two weeks' notice at her consulting firm, where she was perennially unhappy. I have a list of matches for our next meeting, but maybe she has follow-up questions. This is usually the point in the timeline when people grow antsy.

"I'm afraid I don't have an update since last time we spoke," I tell her once we've dispelled with the usual formalities. "But I'll have a robust list of eligible bachelorettes for you when it's time for our call next week."

"That's . . . that's not why I'm calling." There's a stretch of silence. "This isn't going to work out," she finally says. "I can't do this anymore."

For a moment I think she's having second thoughts about quitting her job.

"I appreciate everything you've done," she continues. "The life coach was a blessing. You helped me figure out so much."

But.

"I've decided to take a break from matchmaking."

You were begging me to speed up the process last week.

"I'd love to know what happened," I manage to say. "If there's been some sort of misunderstanding, we can talk through it, clear up any concerns you might have."

"It's nothing like that. I want to take a different tack, is all."

She's firing me. Kindly. Politely. Firing me.

I think of the faked email. From me to Logan.

"Did you get any kind of out-of-character communication from me?" I ask. "I've had someone impersonating me. It's nothing we don't have a handle on, but—"

"Why would someone— No. Nothing like that. I know I already put down a deposit for the next part of the process. Keep it."

There's no hesitation in her voice. No room for counterargument.

"This is . . . coming out of nowhere," I manage to say. "Are you sure you can't share why you feel the need to take such a drastic action? I'd welcome whatever feedback you might have."

"I'm just not interested anymore."

There are a million scenarios I'm always braced for. Anxious clients who want to meet The One on the first go. Who want more options and make it faster please. But a polite woman who simply wants to move on? This is a first. And I can tell from her tone that she won't be dissuaded. She's made up her mind.

The call ends. I stare at my phone. It's finally happened, I realize. Chatter about me has moved from the hypothetical and whispers on a random message board to the mainstream. With trembling hands, I pull up the search engine on my computer. Did Logan hit publish on his article? Am I the main character of the day? Are people blaming me for what happened to Lena? I type in my name. I type in Lena. Tanvir. Nothing new is out there. The old subreddit remains static. There is no article.

But my clients have gotten the memo. The handful of online comments from a cousin of Avani's and a friend of Basit's calling me a bad matchmaker, they probably barely scratch the surface of what's happening behind the scenes. The rich are their own culture, and news travels like wildfire within it. They are likely beating my reputation into the ground behind closed doors at this very moment. People at this stratum of wealth won't publicly shame me—doing so would only make them look bad for working with me in the first place.

But I get it now. My reputation is shot. And in my line of work, reputation is everything.

I'm done.

TWENTY-THREE

've turned the air-conditioning in the room down to sixty-three degrees. There's nothing like being at a hotel in freezing temps to have an excuse to tuck into the warmth of the covers and do absolutely nothing but watch trash TV and try my best to get my mind off everything else going on. But it's impossible to turn my mind off right now. A million worries loop endlessly. It's like I'm short-circuiting. There's only so much a brain and a body can take.

I eye my running shoes, set by the door. The Lowen has a state-of-the-art gym, and now that I have protection, I can safely "run it out" on a treadmill. A run will do me good. Except, right—I wince as I stand up, quickly remembering my ribs aren't exactly ready for that kind of physical exertion. Instead, I grab my laptop charging on the counter and burrow back into bed. My inbox greets me with more grim news. Randa wants to pause on moving forward. Sebastian is inquiring about my refund policy. Four clients wanting to part ways in as many hours—this is the tremor behind a dam about to burst.

I'm done. I have to look away. There's only so much of this I can take. I'm about to shut my laptop when it begins chirping. An incoming video call. Beenish.

"Et tu, Beenish?" My heart sinks. I answer the call. I'm not going to beg and plead. If she's made up her mind, there's not much I can do about it. Though it doesn't mean it won't hurt like hell.

The video starts blurry but slowly comes into focus. Beenish is outdoors. Thick palm leaves flutter behind her. The sky in the backdrop is bright and blue. Birdsong sounds in the distance. She's squinting at me through her phone.

"Can you hear me?" she asks.

"Beenish, before you say anything," I begin, "I want to tell you—"

"No! Me first!" she interjects. "Nura Khan, I just called to say I love you."

I blink at the unexpected proclamation.

"Guess where I am right now?" she sings out. "I'm on my tenth date with Nayab." She's grinning ear to ear. "We're off the coast of Florida. It's so pretty out here! And we get to have some real downtime, you know? Just the two of us."

"Did I hear that right? You've been on ten dates with Nayab in the span of three weeks?"

"Yep." She beams. "I'll be honest, I was a touch irritated in the beginning when you made me do all the coaching sessions. I wanted to get on with things, you know? But I get it now. My work with Dr. Higdon was transformative. He helped me see that I did love Austin, but that the relationship was past its expiration date. It's like you said, he became more of a habit I needed to learn how to kick. Considering we'd been together for nearly a decade, it was a really ingrained habit. But now, with therapy, and the acupuncturist for my nerves, it's all clicking. I feel like a different person. I feel more like *me*. And I definitely was in the exact right headspace to meet Nayab. He's . . . Nura, he's a dream come true."

"Darcy thought you'd both be a great fit. I'll be sure to let her know!"

"She was one hundred percent right! I know you probably want me to talk to other people, but there's really no need. I think this might be it."

We could be done with the conversation here. I could reiterate how happy I am for her and be grateful that I'm not getting fired. But sooner or later she'll catch wind of the swirling rumors. I'd rather she hear about them from me.

"Beenish, this is the best kind of update. I can't tell you how you've just made my day. While I have you here, I did want to talk to you about something serious." I hesitate. I just need to say it. "There are rumors going around about me. About mistakes people think that I've made as a matchmaker."

"Oh, that?" She waves a hand. "I heard all about that ridiculous nonsense."

"You—you did?"

"Don't worry. I shut it down immediately."

"Wow." Tears fill my eyes. "Thanks, Beenish."

"Anyone who believes the haters is missing out. I know how amazing you are. Your agency is the best thing that ever happened to me."

When we're done talking, I lean back against the pillows. A wave of relief rushes over me. Beenish heard the rumors but didn't turn on me. One client who trusts her own judgment over rumors won't be enough to save my business, but I'm going to savor this moment.

I close my laptop and set it on the nightstand next to me. My stomach rumbles. I realize with a start that I haven't eaten all day. Before I can grab the hotel phone to order room ser-vice, there's a knock on the door. Reluctantly, I extricate myself from the warm cocoon of my bed and pad to the door.

It's Azar—one of the people on my very short list who needs no vetting by Fiona to come through. Except we haven't been talking. He's holding two bags with LEE'S PHO stamped along the sides.

"Auntie told me where you're staying," he says. "Figured I'd bring you some comfort food? I can . . . I can leave it with you."

He's looking at me with baleful eyes. Food. His love lan-guage. His apology.

"Come in." I open the door wider.

Back in my room, Azar glances around. "Is the air condi-tioner on the fritz?"

"I like a chilly hotel room."

"Then the pho is even better timed."

"You didn't have to bring dinner."

"Your stomach begs to differ. I can hear it all the way from here."

"Damn traitorous belly."

It's so easy to slip into our usual routine. I want to resist. The argument is still fresh in my mind. But it's Azar. And as he sets the bags on the round table by the window overlooking the glittering Atlanta skyline, I understand now that we won't be forever, but I'll have him in my life as long as I can.

When he unlatches the first container, the lemony scent fills up the room.

"Nice digs," he comments.

"I've been saving all these years for a rainy day," I tell him. "And right now it's pouring."

"I still can't believe you have a personal security team. I'm glad you have it, but it's chilling to remember why."

"When living in strange times, do strange things?"

He sets down a gym bag he had draped over his shoulder. Unzipping it, he pulls out ceramic bowls. Two soup spoons.

"You have a microwave, right?"

"Did you really stop by your house to get silverware and bowls?"

"How else are we going to eat this properly?" he asks.

"You're as bad as my aunt."

"Or as good?" He grins.

He prepares the soup as I sit down at the table. When I take a sip of the brothy concoction, it fills me with warmth.

"How *are* you and your aunt these days?" he asks.

"I keep meaning to call her and have a proper conversation about everything, but life has been a bit much lately." I gesture to the hotel.

"That would be an understatement. This is a great hotel, though."

"It's worth every penny. I even splurged on a spa pedicure yesterday, though I should probably be more careful now, as I'll soon be penni*less*." I fill him in on the Great Client Exodus.

"Nur. That's awful."

"I don't think it's fully hit me yet. Everything my grandmother began, that Khala built . . . it might end with me."

"It won't. Beenish stuck by you, right? She won't be the only one."

"I wish I had your confidence."

We finish our meal in comfortable silence. The constant buzz of thoughts settles the slightest bit with him sitting across from me. It's among the top things I love about Azar's company. Our conversations always nourish me, but our silence together can be equally fulfilling.

"So how long are you staying at Casa Lowen?" he asks when we finish up.

"Not sure. Another week? Forever?"

"I suggest tonight be your last night."

"Time for me to put on my big-girl pants and deal?"

"Time for you to come to my place."

"I can't impose on you like that."

"It's not imposing if you're invited."

"How long does that go on?" I ask. "Am I just supposed to move in forever?"

"Sure. Stay indefinitely."

"The guy who irons his scrubs and arranges his shirts by color and size wants me invading his space?"

"Actually . . ." He tilts his head and looks at me. "I do."

My heart skips a beat.

"I'm sure Zayna would love that."

"Yeah, well." He looks away. "We're over."

I straighten. "What happened?"

"It . . . it wasn't working out."

"You looked about as serious as I've ever seen you with any-one." *Oh.* He really liked her. And their relationship was ruined because of me. "Is it because of your trip to Helen getting canceled? Khala shouldn't have called you. I can explain it to Zayna."

"It's fine. Really." He looks at his empty soup bowl. If it's fine, why does he look heartbroken? My own heart hurts to see him this way. Whatever went down between them, it's still raw. I won't press.

"How about dessert?" I ask, hoping to change the conversation.

"I knew I forgot something." He gives me a sheepish look.

"Room service to the rescue."

Twenty-five minutes later, I grab the two bowls of brownies and vanilla ice cream from the door. Azar lifts the remote from the nightstand.

"Can't let *anyone* else be in charge of the remote, can you?"

"It's the one measure of control in my life," Azar says.

"Have at it."

He turns on the television and flips the channels.

"Not sure I remember watching live TV," I say.

"It's a surreal experience."

"Hold up." I shoot out my hand and grab his arm. "That's our show. *Wild.* Go back a channel."

"I thought you didn't like to watch episodes out of order?"

"Comfort brownies require comfort viewing." I get on the bed and scoot over to give him space to sit facing the television.

"Fair enough." He settles on the edge.

"I hate it, but I rarely have time to watch a show all the way through anymore," I admit.

"The last time I watched an entire season of *Wild* straight through was in college. I wonder if they still have the same survival-pack options they can bring along to help them."

"You know they all pretend they didn't choose the beef jerky, but tell me how Jax survived six weeks on bark soup alone?"

"Some of them are real lightweights."

I look at my bowl of ice cream and brownies. "We wouldn't last a day out there."

"Not true," he protests. "We've camped before."

"Are you referring to the tent we staked out in your back-yard? When we were ten?"

"It was still camping."

"We ran straight back into the house when that owl began hooting."

"That owl was spooky!"

The hum of the air conditioner stills. I shift. This moment, both of us sitting on the bed, the television on in the background, talking about the most random things—all of this is bringing me back to a day I try so hard to forget.

"Penny for your thoughts?" he asks.

I shrug as casually as possible. "I was thinking of college. We took it for granted, didn't we? Hanging out like this."

"We really did."

"This was our ritual. Grab a bite and head back to the dorms to watch this show every Thursday at nine o'clock."

"We stayed true to that, all the way to the very last night."

I tense. Did he really bring it up?

"Still remember that, huh?" I say lightly.

"Of course I do, Nur."

I want to make a joke. Shift the conversation, anything to distract him from that moment, but he speaks again.

"I think about that night all the time."

"I'm mortified." I groan.

"Why?"

"Really?" My cheeks burn. "I nearly destroyed our friendship."

"Our friendship isn't that flimsy, Nur. I know we were a little loopy from being so sleep-deprived. It was finals week. It happens."

Let it go. He's given me my out. I can agree and say that's all it was. The show is back from commercials. We can go back to watching. Eat our desserts. But he watches me so intently, I can't stop myself.

"I didn't want to kiss you because I was sleep-deprived. I wanted to kiss you because I *wanted* to kiss you," I tell him. "I wanted to kiss you because you were leaving. Because I didn't know if I'd ever see you again, because . . ." My voice trails off.

He doesn't say anything for a moment. Then—

"I wanted to kiss you too."

Am I . . . Am I hearing him correctly?

"But . . . you jerked back, Azar. The look on your face . . ."

"I freaked out, Nur. What do you do when the moment you've been hoping for your whole life finally happens?"

I stare at him. Unable to speak. Unable to move.

"I panicked. And then before I could gather myself and tell you how I felt, you started laughing. Told me it was a mistake. You looked mortified. You begged me to forget it. I accepted it. I made my peace with it, but—" His eyes lock into mine. "But that doesn't mean I've gotten past it."

"Azar—"

"Why do you think it never ends up working out for me?" he asks. "Why am I a perpetual bachelor? Why did things fizzle with Zayna?" He searches my face. "I tried. I tried harder with her than I had anyone else, but it didn't work. Because she's not you. No one else is you. Why did I leave New York as soon as I could? That day I showed up at your place to tell you I was back in town . . . I swore to myself I'd work up the nerve and tell you how I felt. But then you made it clear you didn't feel the same. Again, I accepted it. I figured even if it can't be the way I'd want it to be in an ideal world, I wanted to be near you. However I could be in your life, I'd take it. I love you. And it's time I finally told you instead of being so afraid I'd lose you if I said anything. In the hospital the other day, when I knew I really did almost lose you . . . my whole life flashed before my eyes. Nur, I love you. I do."

He sits so close. I take in the wavy hair across his forehead.

His heart-shaped mouth. His breath against my skin—sweet and warm.

"How do you feel?" he asks. "All these years later?"

"Azar." My voice breaks. "How could you not know how I feel? I love you too. Always have. I can't remember a moment that I didn't."

He moves closer to me. So close there's hardly any space between us. He cups my face gently with his hands. "Can I kiss you, Nur?"

"You're about ten years too late, so yes, I think—"

He kisses me. My breath hitches, and then I kiss him back. Harder. I taste the chocolate against his tongue. His arms wrap tight around my waist. I sink back onto the bed, his mouth still pressed against mine. I run my fingers through his hair, wrap my arms around him, drawing him closer. He kisses my neck. His mouth trails my collarbone. Tears spring to my eyes. Ten years. We lost a decade over a misunderstanding. But slowly, all thoughts vanish. There is only this moment. Azar and me, together.

TWENTY-FOUR

Someone out here in the world, at this very moment, is trying to frame me for things I haven't done. Right now, I am walking to the parking deck of the Midtown Lowen hotel with a bodyguard. I have been fired by not one, but four clients.

And I have never been happier than I am in this exact moment.

Keys in hand, I'm walking—no, floating—to my rental.

Order some room service for breakfast, I text Azar from my ancient flip phone. Their waffles are the best.

I'm sticking it back in my purse when I hear a voice call out my name. "Hey, Nura! Wait up!"

Logan Wilson. He emerges from a stairwell. He's in blue jeans. A dress shirt. He's heading straight toward me.

"Back off!" Fiona shouts at him.

He looks at her, confused, and then at me. He continues walking in my direction.

In an instant, Fiona tackles him to the ground. I can't help but stare at her in awe. The speed with which she moved—she's a force. I shift my attention back to Logan. What is he doing here? And more troubling: How did he find me?

"Easy! I just had meniscus surgery!" he cries out, his cheek pressed against the dark asphalt of the parking lot. "I mean no harm, I swear!"

"Do you know him?" Fiona asks me, her knee pressed into his back.

"Unfortunately. What are you doing here, Logan? I'd love to hear the story this time."

"May I get up?"

I nod to Fiona, who reluctantly releases him. He winces as he stands up.

"Shall we mark this down as yet another coincidence?" I ask as she pats him down.

"Not a coincidence."

"Go on."

He glances at Fiona, who rests one hand on her holster.

"Could we sit down at a café? I'd love to have a proper conversation."

"Are you kidding me? I'm not going anywhere with you," I tell him. "As soon as you finish talking, I'm going to the courthouse to get a restraining order. Who told you I was here?"

"I can't reveal my sources," he says. "But I'm here because I want to help. Like I've told you before, I have information to share with you. Things you really need to see. I mean it, Nura."

He moves a hand to his back pants pocket. Glancing at Fiona, he quickly adds, "I'm just getting my phone, I swear."

He holds the device toward me. Not an email this time. A text.

For the millionth time, I'm not sitting down for a chat with you. I'm not getting on a call. If you want to interview me, it'll have to be like this. I know what you want. It's about John, Jenny, or Simran. Right? Here's what I have to say:

Yes, things got out of hand. I have a lot of clients. It can be
hard to keep track. Mistakes happen. I'm only human.

"From the look on your face, I'm guessing you didn't send
this text," he says into the silence.

Jenny. Simran. Those are the same names as the trolls who
were trying to smear me on my own website.

"How do I know you didn't invent this text yourself to convince me to talk to you?" Even though this feels almost per-
functory. He's not lying. I know it deep in my bones. He's
telling the absolute truth.

"I guess you don't. You have to take my word for it. The thing
is, though, I've spoken with each of these people. They all confirmed they worked with you."

"They may not be lying," I say. "Sometimes people are under
the impression that I'm personally matching every single ap-
plicant who uses our app, but we have too many users to be
personally familiar with each and every person."

"They said they were with your VIP services."

"That's impossible. I know every personalized client. We've
also run these names in our database. They're not in our system."

"They've got the receipts, Nura."

"Show me."

"I'm still working on getting everything organized, but I've
got a running tab with screenshots they shared of texts and
emails." He pulls his phone back, taps into a folder, then hands
it to me.

My brain can't process what I am seeing.

There are pages and pages of texts. Emails. Voicemail tran-
scriptions.

Hey, Nura! Hope this email finds you well. I was waiting to hear back about next steps. I tried the agency number but it just goes to voicemail? I hope you're okay? Anyway, please get back to me. . . .

. . . Nura. WTF?! We spoke nearly every day when you wanted my money, but now you're nowhere to be found. . . .

. . . If you could find the time to cash my payment, I think you could find the time to deign to reply to at least one of my emails? . . .

. . . I know life can get busy, but it's been a month?! I'd appreciate it if you could confirm you received this email. . . .

It's like an infinite scroll of complaints. Clients I've never heard of, asking for updates on their cases. Requesting meetings. Accusing me of taking their money and running. But their accusations don't shake me quite as deeply as seeing what are presumably my responses.

Jenny, you need to be patient. I have a long list of clients and I work with them in the order that they signed up.

Don't make me regret taking you on, John. If you don't like how I do things, you're welcome to look for your soulmate elsewhere.

Dear Simran, as I have explained to you many times before already, I'm diving deep to get a list of partners set up for you, but these things take time. I have a few exceptional people in mind that I think might just be perfect for you, but if you keep harassing me, I can't work with you anymore. More soon. Best, Nura

Best, Nura. My pulse pounds in my throat.

"I've never worked with these people," I manage to say. "These replies here, they aren't from me. I didn't write these."

He looks quietly at me for a second. Then he says, "I believe you."

"I don't understand. . . ." My voice shakes. "Why is this happening? Who is doing this?"

"That's what I want to know too." He takes a step closer to me. "Let's set up a real meeting, Nura. I'll show you everything I have. I have a lot more information on my computer. Things I've printed out. Let's figure out what's going on. Together."

"I've pushed you away so many times at this point. Why do you want to help me?"

"Nura! Because this is seriously fucked up. I do features. Profiles. I wanted to do a profile on you. Clearly, I've stumbled into something way deeper. Someone really wants me to bring you down. I want to know who. And why they're using me as a pawn. I'm not publishing a word until I can figure out what bigger play is going on here." He hesitates. "Also, not to overstep here, but I'd be remiss if I didn't tell you to be careful."

"I'd say I'm being as careful as I can." I nod toward Fiona.

He gives her a nervous smile, then looks back at me. "Even still. I'd make sure no one's tracking your whereabouts."

"I'm obviously getting tracked. You're here, aren't you?"

He points to the Subaru rental I'm standing next to. "Is this your car?"

"My employee Borzu checked it," I tell him. "Before I left work yesterday, he inspected the whole vehicle and made sure it was clean."

He walks up to the car, leans down, cranes his neck, and pulls out a dark circular object. He holds it out to me. "Haven't seen a real-live tracker in some time," he says.

"But he checked the car yesterday evening," I say numbly as he hands it to me.

Borzu?

No. No. Borzu can't be behind this.

And yet—there's a tracker there. How did a tracking device get attached after he'd cleared the Subaru as safe? Had I even checked under the car after he looked? I wouldn't have. I trust him.

"I don't have a motive for you, but it's obvious that someone wants to see you go down," says Logan. "They've made me a part of this story too now. Until I know what they're after, I'm doing my best to hold off and stay quiet. I don't like being someone's puppet. I want to find out what's going on and what their angle is."

"It'll be a great story," I say bitterly.

"It could be. But right now, I need to know what the hell is going on for my own sake. And don't take this the wrong way, but considering the sensitive information I'm receiving, my money's on the fact that it's someone close to you."

I hate how easily the words leave his mouth. As though he's telling me the sky is blue. Except, he's right.

But it makes no sense. Why would Borzu do this? My trusted circle is small because I'm careful whom I let inside. Even if hacking into a car and trailing my location are things Borzu could do in his sleep, it still doesn't explain *why*.

I think back to his expensive coffee maker. The brand-new car with the glass ceiling. The cinder block shelves long gone, replaced by contemporary bookcases.

Is he skimming off the agency? Even contemplating this is too much to bear.

"Can I think about it?" I finally say.

"Of course."

He heads toward the distant stairwell and disappears into the darkness.

I flick off the tracker's blinking light. Tossing it to the ground, I crush it with the back of my heel. As I look around, hundreds of office buildings and hotel windows stare back at me. Logan said aloud what I've been too afraid to allow space for in my heart—but now it's all I can think about: Whoever is after me, they aren't somewhere out there in the world at large. It's someone here. Someone local. Someone I know.

⌐ ✦ ⌐ ✦ ⌐

TWENTY-FIVE

The scenery rushes by in a blur as I speed toward the agency. Fiona's black Lincoln is behind me, keeping pace. Hitting a red light, I reluctantly press the brakes. I anxiously tap my fingers against the steering wheel. Logan's words won't stop ringing in my ears: *My money's on the fact that it's someone close to you.*

He's wrong. He has to be. It can't be true. There's no way it is.

But it doesn't hurt to rule everything out, does it?

While the light shines red above, I grab my phone from the passenger seat and text Amara.

Any chance I can take you up on the contact information for an independent investigator?

Her response comes immediately: Check your inbox in five—will send you a PDF with our vetted options.

I push away the guilt curdling inside me. I'm only doing this to clear things up for myself. This way I can put Logan's pushy presumptions out of my mind once and for all. I'll have proof positive nothing is amiss.

My phone buzzes as the light turns green. It's Nina: Can you come over when you have time? Mom's okay now. But swing by when you can.

My heart flutters. I make a sharp U-turn and head down the street toward Khala's home. Nina said she's okay *now*. Which means she wasn't okay before.

I check my smartwatch and push down the lump rising in my throat—this gadget is basically useless now that I don't have my phone on me, but I still wear it every day, checking my steps each evening. I haven't seen Khala since I was at the hospital. We've not had a real conversation in ages. I keep meaning to, but I haven't been ready. I figured we'd unpack everything later when life was less fraught, except we don't always get to choose our timing, do we? Sometimes life swoops in and makes our choices for us. Sometimes we can push things off for so long that the perfect moment doesn't arrive, and it's too late. The knot of resentment that I've been carrying loosens. Now all I feel are the pinpricks of tears behind my eyes.

Even if Khala is all right today, I'm going to get more and more messages like these as the years go by. Dr. Pang said that her memory won't go out all at once, like a light turning off, but more like a flicker—bits at a time—until things eventually accelerate. What if the first memories that flicker for Khala are the ones of me?

I pull into the driveway. Fiona and I walk up the steps to Khala's front door. All I have to do is turn my key into the lock and step inside, but I'm frozen at the prospect. Afraid of what awaits me on the other side.

Summoning up my nerve, I knock on the door. I hear small footsteps, and then the door swings open.

"Auntie!" Lilah exclaims. She gives me a hug.

"Hey, you!" I kneel down to give her a hug and push away the image of her on the front porch last time I was here.

"Who's that?" She peers over my shoulder.

"That's Fiona." I point to her. "She's helping me out."

The security guard pulls off her sunglasses and gives Lilah a wave, her otherwise businesslike expression switching seamlessly to perky kindergarten teacher.

"Guess what? I got a stuffed Eevee! Want to see it? It's as big as me!" Lilah tells me excitedly about the newest addition to her Pokémon collection. "Mama got it for me because I know all my sight words."

"That's great! I would've thought you'd pick Charmander."

"They were all sold out." Her expression falls. "Mama says we'll check again next time."

"Where *is* your mom?" I ask her.

"On the phone with the doctor." Lilah points to the stairs leading to the second floor. "Nani's in bed because she broke her leg."

"She what?!"

I rush toward my aunt's bedroom. Khala is indeed in bed. A black boot encases her right foot and runs up to her knee. I hurry to her side.

"Nura." She turns off the television. Her eyes light up. The joy is so clear on her face it makes me ache.

"How did this happen?"

"This?" she chuckles. "It looks far more serious than it is. I tripped walking to the kitchen last night. Wish it was a more dramatic story. I thought it was a sprained ankle, but turns out it's a light fracture. I will be back to normal in no time."

"You should have told me right away."

Though we both know why she didn't. She's downplaying her pain. Her frustration. Because this is her way. To try to make the path easier for me. To ensure the motherless girl who showed up unexpectedly at her doorstep all those years ago doesn't have to take on any more heartaches than she's already endured. This is all she's ever tried to do—make things easier for me. Raising her young niece had never been in the plan. She was an empty nester at last, her daughter grown and off to college, when I arrived. But she'd never made me feel like a burden. She only showed me love.

"Nina is making a big fuss, but I am all right. Really," she insists. "Tell me, though, how are *you*?"

"I'm . . ." I want to tell her I'm okay. The need to say it is overwhelming. But—Khala was at my bedside when the cops questioned me. She more than handled it. She didn't fall apart. And what affects me affects them too. I need to let my family know what's happening. Even if I'd feel better if they didn't. No more secrets.

"Things aren't great," I tell her.

The door creaks. Nina pokes her head in.

"Mom, I'm going to head to the— Oh." She pauses when she sees me. "Nura. Hey. I'll leave you two to talk."

"Stay," I tell her. "There's news I need to tell you both."

She sits at the edge of Khala's bed. They watch me expectantly.

With a deep breath I dive in. I tell them everything. I hold nothing back. When I finish, they watch me with haunted expressions.

"I've got round-the-clock security," I tell them. "Fiona's outside right now. I'm safe. But I'm going to look into getting coverage for all of you, just in case."

Khala still doesn't speak. Maybe honesty was not warranted in this instance. If her stress levels shoot up—

"It sounds as though you are doing everything right," Khala says. "You have security cameras at home as well as the office.

Your team is monitoring everything. Let's pray we find the person behind this as soon as possible."

"Ameen," says Nina.

I look into Khala's warm eyes. I think of the words she said to me as a child when I was lost in my grief: *Be present. Be here. Be with me.* I squeeze her hands. All those years ago, she was teaching me how to savor this temporary time with her. It hits me as though anew: I am going to lose her. Whether through her degenerative condition or the passage of time. No matter how much I want to, there are some things I can't fix. But while she's here, I'll try to not only be there *for* her, but be with her too. And maybe, at least for now, she can handle more than I've given her credit for. Secrets never strengthen, they only calcify.

When I step back into the foyer, Nina follows me.

"When will she get out of the boot?" I ask her.

"She can't bear any weight on it for at least eight weeks," she says. "Then there's some fun physical therapy to follow."

"I wish I'd known."

"It was a long morning at the ER, there was nothing you could've done, but you're right, I should have told you right away. I just didn't want you to think I was expecting you to drop everything. You have every right to be angry after everything that happened."

"Nina." I quell my familiar frustration. "I want you to expect things from me. I would drop everything for her because I want to. She's your mother, but she's also important to me. Yes, I know I was upset, but that doesn't change that we're family."

"I know," she says. "You're right."

"She really fell right here in the house?"

"Tripped over the rug on her way to get water," Nina says. "I was asleep, and she didn't even call out. I found her in the morning. She's got a spiral fibula fracture. The bone is broken in three different spots."

Lightly fractured. Right. "We should get her one of those buttons you can press if you're in danger."

"The 'help, I've fallen and can't get up' thing?" She grins. "I think she'd rather fall and stay on the floor."

"We'll have to get it attached to her against her will, then."

"Have you met my mother?"

"We can be persuasive if we set our minds to it."

"You mean gang up on her? I like the sound of that."

"Yeah." I smile a little.

We look at Lilah coloring at the coffee table. "I'll look into an after-school helper," I tell Nina. "Things got sidetracked at work, but I'll get on that ASAP. You're going to need support."

"I've been making it work."

I hesitate, remembering the last time I made this offer, but say it anyway. "I can watch her too. I want to be a bigger part of Lilah's life."

"Careful what you offer," she warns. "You free tomorrow?"

"I can be. We assemble a mean puzzle together."

Her smile falters.

"Wait, is there really something going on tomorrow?"

"It's no big deal." She shrugs. "I have a networking event at the High Museum. The executive director invited me to attend. There's a vacant part-time docent position. Not as exciting as curating a collection, but it means more time with Lilah and looking after Khala. Mom was initially going to watch her, but . . ."

"In what world is this a networking event? This is a job interview. Yours for the taking, I bet."

"I don't know about all that," she says. "I doubt Portland will even recommend me given how abruptly I bailed."

"Those were extenuating circumstances. I'll be here to watch Lilah. I'd be happy to. Azar and I can tag-team it."

"If we're finally being real with each other—Azar and you? Total mystery."

"Well," I reply. "Maybe not so mysterious anymore?"

"Do you mean what I think you mean?" She breaks into a grin. "About fucking time." Her smile wavers. She looks at her hands. "I'm sorry, Nura. For everything. For how you found out about the past. That wasn't right. I've been on her to tell you for years."

"Why didn't *you* tell me?"

"I should have," she says. "It's crossed my mind a million times. How do you break something like that to someone, though? How do you upend someone's life? I didn't want to be the one responsible for saying what can't be unsaid. Doesn't make it okay. I'm sorry. And even sorrier you found out the way you did."

"It explains why you were so against the work we do."

"I was angry for many years about how everything unfolded, how she slipped right back into a job that caused our family so much trauma."

"All this time, I thought the reason for your digs at our work—at me—was that you were jealous," I tell her. "I'm feeling pretty stupid right around now."

She regards me silently, then says, "You weren't wrong. I have been jealous. When I was growing up, Mom was getting the agency off the ground. We didn't even move into this house until I was a junior in high school. You and I had different childhoods. We were raised by different women. I resented the job; I hated how much it took her away from me. Now that I'm a mom, I get it. The choices she had to make weren't simple. In the early years, my mom was carrying all of us alone. I didn't love it, but now I get that she did what she needed to do to keep us afloat. She was doing her best. I'm happy for you, Nura. I'm glad you got the best of her. And somehow you can manage to spend five minutes with her without wanting to strangle her. Who wouldn't be jealous?"

"I want to be more involved. With Lilah, with everything going on around here," I tell her. "I know I messed up last time you leaned on me, but I can do better."

"It wasn't your fault. Lilah's bullheaded."

"Don't know where she gets *that* from." I raise an eyebrow, and Nina laughs.

"I'll watch her tomorrow," I tell her. "Thanks for trusting me."

I think of my conversation with Logan. His emails. His insistence that he wants to help. It's possible he's pulling one over on me. But I can go into a conversation with him with my eyes wide open. Maybe he can help me figure out what is going on. I certainly can't fix this on my own. Maybe he gets the story of his life, and maybe I can finally find out who is after me.

TWENTY-SIX

The morning sun filters into my kitchen from the skylights above. When I first came back to the house yesterday afternoon, I had every intention of packing up a handful of things and checking out of the hotel to head to Azar's place, but once I actually stepped into my foyer, Gertie greeting me, I felt a rush of homesickness for my cozy cottage. Luckily, Azar is easily dissuaded. He brought over a duffel bag last night and set it by the door. It's there now.

The phone rings. Nina.

"Yes, we're still on for this afternoon, and yes, I'll be there right on time, and *yes*, I'm sure," I say immediately upon answering.

"Am I that predictable?"

"Little bit."

"I guess I have a bit of a hard time relying on people."

"I had no idea," I tease her. It's not even noon yet. "I'm swinging by the agency to grab a few things, but I'll be at your place by four o'clock with time to spare. Promise."

"It's just a networking event," she says. "If you're busy, I could skip it."

"It's an unofficial job interview."

She groans. "I'm trying not to think of it like that, or I might have a full-on panic attack."

"Please. They'd be lucky to have you. Things are slow at the office today anyway. Darcy's out for wedding fittings, and Genevieve took a sick day. My schedule is clear. I've got an alarm reminder on my phone so I won't lose track of time. Plus, guess who's getting the award for Number One Auntie this year? I swung by the store last night, and they restocked the stuffed Charmander. I grabbed the second-to-last one they had."

"You got Lilah the Charmander? She is going to—"

There's a squeal on Nina's end of the line.

"Chill, Lilah. Sorry, Nura," she says as the squeals continue unabated in the background. "Lilah's got ears like a puppy. I think you're definitely far and away Auntie of the Year. Azar still coming over to tag-team with you?"

"He'll join us once he's off work. We're going to head to the Stone Bowl House for Korean food. I haven't tried it yet, but the foodie swears we'll all love it."

"Foodie spots are wasted on a four-year-old," Nina says. "She'll be equally happy eating a box of mac and cheese."

"Azar's response to this would be that we need to refine her palate."

"Don't refine it too much," she warns. "She's picky enough as is."

I hang up and fill my water bottle. I pull back my hair and eye my smartphone perennially charging on the counter.

"I miss you," I say half-jokingly to the glowing device. I've heard some people get so used to dumbphones, they never want to go back. For me, absence only makes the heart grow fonder.

A call comes in on my flip phone. Genevieve.

"I have an update on the Usmani investigation," she says.

"You're supposed to be off today," I remind her.

"A cold doesn't mean I can't fit in time for a little research. Turns out they're a pretty huge family, and they live all over the world. It's a feat to track them all down, but I'm working on accounting for everyone."

"Thanks, Genevieve."

"The good news is, so far I haven't found anyone local," she says. "And the States-based folks seem pretty intent on living a Kardashian-adjacent lifestyle, but nothing nefarious. I'll keep you posted if I learn anything more."

"I really appreciate this."

"Happy to help."

I drop my phone in my purse. Earlier today I spoke with the PI that Amara referred me to. He's still looking into Borzu, but so far there's been nothing remarkable to note. Borzu frequents three locations almost exclusively: home, his mother's place, the agency. Nothing unusual. Nothing suspicious.

I thanked the investigator. I told him it was a relief. Borzu was my trusted employee. He had no reason to deceive me. But, eyeing the broken tracker in my purse, I wish I could feel relief.

I park at the agency parking lot. I'm so distracted, I barely notice Fiona keeping pace with my brisk walk until I reach the agency's glass entrance door. Borzu's inside. He's at his computer.

Amara's PI said nothing suspicious had turned up so far, but . . .

I turn to Fiona. "I know you like to stay outside to survey the perimeter, but do you mind hanging out inside the agency with me today?"

"My pleasure," she replies.

Borzu startles when the bell chimes overhead.

"Nura. What are you doing here?"

Borzu's clean. He's done nothing wrong.

But then why does he look like a deer in headlights?

"Did I interrupt you?" I ask.

"No, of course not. I . . . I was catching up on work. I thought you were babysitting today."

"That's not until a bit later."

He's dyed his hair blue to match his long-sleeved cerulean-colored shirt. I notice for the first time the Movado watch on his wrist. Gucci sunglasses rest by his computer. None of this necessarily means anything. Sure, it's a new habit, but he's paid well enough to afford all of these luxuries without blinking. I've worked with him for years. He's never given me a minute of doubt.

And yet—my car was hacked. My location was tracked. The PI said nothing seems amiss, but Borzu is a master at surveillance, which means he'd be a pro at getting around attempts to surveil him.

I need to find out for myself.

I place the device on his desk. Fix my gaze on him.

"Where'd you get this?" He frowns at the tracker.

"Take a wild guess."

He lifts it and turns it over. Looks up at me incredulously. "Was it on your car?"

"I found it there yesterday morning."

"Are you serious? Why didn't you tell me sooner?" He examines it more closely, then wrinkles his nose. "This is such a basic one."

"As basic as it might be, it worked."

He squints at something on the device, then types on his computer.

"It's from Amazon." He points to the identical item online. "It's at least five years old. There's no way someone bought it from a brick-and-mortar." He scratches his head. "I don't get it. Why would anyone go through the hassle of getting this one? There's way more sophisticated stuff on the market for only a little more money."

I look at his perplexed expression. My heart hammers in my chest. I need to say it. Address it full on. It's the only way to truly know.

"Borzu, what's with all the lifestyle changes? The expensive watch. The fancy coffee machine and new furniture in your condo. The Tesla. What's going on?"

His relaxed demeanor vanishes. He studies his lap. "Yeah. So. There's, um, a few things we need to talk about. I keep meaning to. It's just . . . with everything going on, the timing's never been right."

"Now's as good a time as any."

"I made an app."

I blink at the unexpected explanation.

"It's a satellite tracker," he continues. "Gets way better reliability than anything currently on the market for when you're out of cell tower range. I put it up as a soft launch a year ago just to see what would happen, and it really took off with hiking and outdoorsy types. It ended up gaining a niche popularity that got lots of Silicon Valley types interested. There was a bit of a bidding war to acquire the application. I got bought out a few months ago, and, well . . ." He gestures at his sunglasses. "My mom said I gotta do something with the windfall."

"I don't understand. Why didn't you just tell me?"

"Because it's a violation of the noncompete in my employee agreement?" He looks at me sheepishly. "I wasn't even thinking it would go anywhere. It was a free app mostly for my own amusement, but once it snowballed, I couldn't figure out how to tell you."

"The noncompete was to avoid conflict with the Piyar app. This was never a conflict. . . ." *Oh.* I look at him. "Are you quitting?"

"Leaving the agency? No way." He shakes his head. "I love this job. You all are like family to me. I hate that I've been distracted, though. I . . . I feel awful that I haven't been giving it my all."

"Borzu, you've been here at all hours helping."

"I could have done more. If I had my head fully in the game, I'd probably have figured out who is behind this already. It's not like it's some ghost lurking in the bushes—it's a person. With a trackable amount of information."

A car alarm beeps in the distance as Borzu keeps talking. My chest constricts. Borzu *had* been keeping something from me, but nothing bad. How did Logan get into my head and make me doubt the people I trust most?

"I'm sorry, Borzu," I tell him. "For asking you all these questions. I appreciate everything you do. You had every right to keep this to yourself."

"I'm the one who's sorry. For not telling you everything."

"You have nothing to apologize for."

He won't meet my eye. "Not about the app. There's, um, something else I need to tell you. I don't know how to say it."

Before he can continue, the doorbell chimes.

The front door swings open.

A man walks in.

Logan Wilson.

TWENTY-SEVEN

Logan's eyes scan the space curiously, then shift to alarm when they land on mine.

"Nura." He takes a step back.

In three quick strides, Fiona's between us. Her hand rests on her holster.

"Whoa." Logan raises his hands. "I didn't mean to startle you. I swear, I mean no harm."

"He's here to see you, Borzu?" I ask.

"It's . . . it's not what you think."

"That's not an answer," I say, my eyes trained on Borzu. Logan clears his throat, but I ignore him. "You knew I was babysitting today, so you figured the agency was as good a spot to meet with him as any, and . . . oh. You." My stomach turns, the puzzle pieces fitting together. "You're the anonymous source. You sent Logan to the wedding."

"I fucked up, okay?" Borzu rubs his head. "Logan called the agency. You were out of the office that week. He wanted a comment. The piece was going to print ASAP. He had multiple sources on the record saying you'd made critical blunders as a matchmaker. When he told me you were up for talking but didn't have time, I figured that wedding in the mountains was as decent a place to have the conversation as any."

"You took him at his word? You could have confirmed with me first!"

"I know. You're right. But it was time sensitive, and your phone kept going to voicemail. He was going to do a write-around. I couldn't let him. This is *Rolling Stone* we're talking about! If people thought we ruined our clients' lives and didn't properly vet applicants—that makes all of us look horrible. And it would be the end of the agency. I meant to tell you after. But then the accident . . . the bodyguards . . . things have been out of control." He hangs his head. "It's no excuse. I just . . . I wanted to clear the agency and your name from whoever is out to destroy both."

"And Logan is here today because . . . ?"

"I need more information than I can dredge up on my own," Borzu says. "Logan's got a treasure trove of receipts and interviews. Screenshots of conversations he says prove his case. I was hoping he would share some in exchange for me working with him."

"Borzu said he's hacking into the spoofed email account today," Logan says.

Borzu nods. His shoulders are hunched. He may have been misguided in his actions, but his intentions were good—I can see it written all over his face. I'm less than thrilled that he was Logan's anonymous source, and we will need to discuss this in depth later, but he wanted to help our agency. To help me.

"Is there anything else I should know?" I ask him. "No more secrets, please."

"Nothing else, I swear. Well, okay"—he stops himself—"if

we're completely coming clean, I was the one who finished the last slice of carrot cake from Darcy's birthday last year."

"Ah. At least that mystery's solved."

Cake notwithstanding, as frustrated as I am that he chose to do what he did in the manner that he did, there are more urgent matters to address.

I look at Logan. I can choose to continue to distrust him. I can kick him out of the office right now. But . . . Borzu thought he needed Logan's help. He trusts him. I'm going to take a leap of faith and trust him too.

"What are we waiting for? Let's hack that email," I say.

Forty-five minutes later, we're in.

"Looks like this account was made solely to spoof you," Borzu says. "That's not exactly a shocker. There's also nothing in here except the message to Logan."

"So they're not contacting anyone else and impersonating me?" I ask.

"Not from this account," says Borzu. "We should be able to see where the email came from. I'll look into that after I rescan our servers."

"You think our servers got compromised?" I ask him.

"Probably not. I just want to rule every single thing out. I did a sweep last week, but a deeper scrape for everything, including our remote team, could only help."

Ah. He wants to make sure the person behind this isn't someone who works for us. He, too, is beginning to wonder.

"I feel like there's something obvious we're missing," he continues. "It's been messing with my head. I got here at eight o'clock this morning and did a once-over on the entire office. I went through every single one of our cabinets and checked under the desks looking for bugs. I can't figure out how we're constantly running into dead ends." He turns to Logan. "Did you bring the files?"

"I'm a man of my word." Logan unzips his messenger bag. "Received the last one this morning."

Borzu's eyes widen. "So you weren't bluffing."

"I never bluff, Borzu." Logan pulls out a manila folder.

"What's that?" I ask.

"These are the receipts," he says. "The signed matchmaking contracts from the people who say you worked with them."

"Well, they're not going to be my contracts . . ." But my voice dies in my throat when he hands them to me. They are matchmaking agreements. *Our* matchmaking agreements. There's the same henna graphic along the margins. The same Helvetica font.

And my signature.

There's the familiar curve of the N. The swoosh of the K in Khan. With a gun to my head, I wouldn't be able to tell it apart from my own actual signature.

"These are fake," I say shakily. "I never worked with these people. How did someone get access to our contract template?" I ask Borzu. "Did a hacker get into our cloud files?"

"There are time stamps on each file to indicate when documents are accessed. When they're downloaded. It marks who downloaded them and where they were downloaded. There's been no unusual movement."

"*Someone* got to them," I say. "They must have managed to get past the security blocks somehow."

"Or did they get their hands on an existing contract from an actual client?" Logan asks. "Someone you've worked with in the past?"

It's possible. How do I begin to narrow that down? I study the names. John Schaeffer. Jenny Ho. Simran Kaur. These were the same names of the trolls who'd tried to post to our agency website. The same names Logan had shared with me.

Wait. I look at the names again.

Kaur.

A wisp of a memory flutters.

"Borzu," I say slowly. "Can you pull up the file with our denial letters?"

He clicks open the folder. There are likely thousands of rejection letters in here. Leaning over, I type *Kaur* into the search bar.

There she is.

"Simran Kaur—she was a potential client," I say. "I remember now. She called constantly and wanted matches in a certain income bracket. We declined her application."

"So that explains her wanting to smear us," says Borzu.

"I don't understand," says Logan.

"She didn't get what she wanted," I say. "So she decided to get even with us by tarnishing the agency's reputation."

Taking in Logan's skeptical expression, Borzu explains, "People don't take kindly to rejection. That's why our online reviews are a mess."

I type in *Jenny Ho*. Then *John Schaeffer*. Sure enough, they're in the database too. Why didn't they show up when we searched before?

"There you go," Borzu says. "Looks like these folks joined forces in an attempt to bring the agency down."

"I really don't think that's what they're after," Logan insists.

"They all have the same motive. I don't know how they coordinated their efforts, but we can figure that out soon enough," says Borzu.

I bite my lip. I wouldn't put it past anyone to join forces to mess with my business or smear me personally, but could they have been so angry I refused to match them that they'd try to kill me? I trace my hand over the agreement. Studying it. Then I lean closer.

"Wait," I say. "This . . . this isn't our current agreement. I mean, it is, but this double comma here on the first line—we caught this typo after we printed out a box full of them. Back before Borzu switched us to electronic files only."

I point to the first sentence.

This agreement is between Piyar matchmaking agency and _____ on the date of _____ ___,, 20___.

"I saw the two commas as soon as I unpacked the boxes from the print shop," I say. "I was kicking myself. Darcy made fun of me for asking her to shred them over one small error."

Darcy.

"Do you think she forgot to shred them?" Borzu asks.

Blood pounds in my ears. That's it. It's the only explanation. It *is* the reception desk—up front and accessible to anyone who steps inside. Maybe she'd left a few stray templates on her desk. Maybe someone came by and saw one. Snatched it. That *has* to be it. Because if that's not what happened . . .

Stop, I tell myself. *Don't go down that road. She would never . . .*

But I have to know.

I hurry to her desk. Yank open the drawers. Each one contains neatly organized rows of thank-you cards and wedding invitations. There's nothing there. Of course not. There wouldn't have been.

"I went through everything here already," says Borzu. "Even

that nightmare of a closet by the bathroom. I would've noticed a box full of blank contracts."

My eyes land on the planter in the corner of the office. The overgrown fern that Darcy gifted the agency years ago. It's set atop a tall stand draped in creamy damask satin. Except it's not a stand. It's a filing cabinet. A holdover from Khala's agency days, when filing cabinets lined the entire wall of our former cramped basement office. I'd kept this one for sentimental reasons. I'd forgotten all about it.

I hurry over. Pulling back the satin, I give each metal handle a firm yank. They're locked. Every single drawer. Were they locked before? I don't know what I expect to find in here, but I know I need to get into this filing cabinet. Now.

"I need a key." My voice wavers. "Where am I going to find a key for this ancient thing?"

"I can get you in there without one," Fiona says. She grabs a paper clip from Borzu's desk and unwinds it with one long twist, not so much as scraping her red fingernails. "These are old-school—doesn't take much to get them to open."

In a few swipes and turns, the cabinet unclicks.

I press the first handle. The drawer is empty. Save some scrap paper and an old thumbtack, the second one is vacant too. I hear Borzu's voice faintly in the background as I go through the other drawers. Third. Fourth.

"I can't believe we didn't get rid of this dinosaur yet," he says. "I'll take it to the dump on Monday."

I open the last drawer. My heart catches in my throat.

This can't be real. I'm seeing things. I must be.

There are files in here. Rows and rows of neatly organized folders. Numbly, I pull out the first manila folder. Flipping it open, my breath hitches.

Blank matchmaking agreements. Our agreements. I zero in on the first sentence. There it is. The double comma.

The other folders contain more contracts, but these ones aren't blank. They're filled out and fully executed agreements purportedly signed by me for clients I've never worked with.

I stare at the name on the next file. Jenny Ho.

Here's John Schaeffer's file, and Simran Kaur's.

Every last one, without exception, is signed with my name.

The next name makes my blood go cold.

Basit Latif.

"How?" I croak. "How is *he* in here?"

I turn the pages of the agreement. I stare at the very last page. This one does not contain my signature.

It's Darcy's.

My heart thumps wildly in my chest. The room is shifting around me.

No. No. No.

Not Darcy. The person who knows where I am when no one in all the world does. The person with keys to my safety-deposit box. The keys to my own home.

"Darcy is taking on clients behind my back? Sh-she wouldn't do this." I look at Borzu's pale face. "There's got to be a logical reason for this. You kept your involvement with Logan from me, didn't you? You had a reasonable explanation. Maybe she has one too."

Borzu moves to speak, but nothing comes out. What can he say? There's her name. It's her signature. There's no explaining this away.

Breathe. But nothing enters my system. The room spins on its axis. Beads of perspiration dot my forehead. I lean against the wall.

"Darcy would never . . ."

Except she did. I'm staring at the proof in my hands. Numbness spreads through my limbs. It's as though my body is protecting my mind from what it can't process.

A phone alarm sounds. My alarm. A reminder that I'm due at Nina's. My agenda from a life that suddenly seems like it was ages ago. But Nina's depending on me. I can't let her down.

"I . . . have to go."

"Nura, you can't be serious," Borzu says.

"Borzu's right," Logan says. "You can't leave right now."

But this doesn't make sense. It can't be true.

"I have to babysit my niece," I say shakily. "Nina's counting on me. I'll . . . I'll call you after."

"I can't access Darcy's location." Borzu's typing on his phone. "You need to stay put. We have to figure out what the hell is going on."

"I have Fiona. I'm safe. Change the locks to the agency. ASAP. We need to secure this place until we can talk to Darcy and give her a chance to explain." My voice breaks. "There has to be a way for this to make sense."

Before he can reply, I'm out.

I get in my car and turn on the engine. My phone buzzes. It's a text from Nina.

Sorry again for ruining the Charmander surprise. Just so you know, she's already stationed by the window waiting for you. Prepare to be ambushed!

The stuffed toy. I cringe—I forgot it at my house. I check the time. I can still rush home and grab it and make it to Khala's with a few minutes to spare.

I lower my car window. "Change of plans," I tell Fiona, who

is pulled up in her car next to me. "I'm going to go home to grab a quick thing, but it should only delay us a minute."

"I'll be right behind you, but are you sure you're good to drive?" Fiona asks worriedly. "I can take you home. You can get your car later."

"I'm fine," I tell her.

Even though I'm not fine at all.

I'll probably never be fine again.

TWENTY-EIGHT

I hurry home and shove the door closed behind me. With trembling hands, I clasp and latch the dead bolts.

I know Fiona is outside. I know I'm safe.

But nothing feels safe. Least of all the thoughts running on a loop in my mind. I catch a glimpse of myself in the foyer mirror. My cheeks are blotchy, my eyes bloodshot.

Leaning against the wall, I let out a ragged breath. I press my palms together to steady myself, but within the safety of my home, Gertie circling my legs, the numbness from today's revelation is wearing off. A sob escapes. The reality of my situation presses down like bricks.

I need to grab the stuffed toy for Lilah. I need to get going. I have to help Nina. She's counting on me, and I don't want to let my cousin down. . . . But who am I kidding? I can't be a good caretaker for anyone in this condition. I want to unsee everything from the office, but Darcy's signature flashes through my mind on repeat. Tears prick my eyes. The weight of this betrayal is threatening to crush me.

I've just picked up my burner to call Nina when I hear a creak against the wooden floor behind me.

Then a voice.

"Put down the phone, Nura."

TWENTY-NINE

Darcy is in the back hallway by the kitchen. My hallway.

She's wearing jeans. A dark hooded sweatshirt. Her hair is pulled into a bun. Stray strands frame her face. She's not wearing any makeup. Her face is ghostly pale. I scarcely recognize her.

"You know," she says softly. "Don't you?"

"Darcy . . . I—I'm sure there's been some kind of misunderstanding here."

She looks at the front door. "Is Fiona out there? She is, isn't she?" Before I can reply, she walks across the kitchen and snatches my phone out of my hands. She types something, hits send, and tucks the phone in her back pocket. Letting out a long exhale, she looks at me. Her eyes glisten. "I'm so sorry about this, Nura. I didn't mean for any of it to happen. You have to believe that."

"Of course," I say quickly. "There's got to be some kind of explanation."

"I was almost in the clear. I swung by the office this morning, and when I saw Borzu through the window running around like a chicken with his head cut off, I just *knew*—" She breaks off. "Borzu had to go and ruin everything. It's like I hurry and tie up one loose end, and another one pops up. It's fine." She wrings her hands. "It'll be okay. I'll deal with him later. One thing at a time. One thing at a time."

"He misunderstood. He must have," I say. "You and I have known each other for five years."

"*Six* years. I guess you didn't really notice me that first year, did you?" She smiles at me sadly. "I was just the barista filling your orders."

"What? No! Of course I noticed you. We chatted all the time, remember? You showed me how to make the perfect latte. We were friends."

"*I* noticed you long before you noticed me. You, your life, it was all so . . . perfect." A tear slides down her face. "I couldn't take my eyes off of your perfectly manicured nails, your Louis Vuitton bag. Every outfit you wore was a name brand I could only dream of. It was like you had the whole world figured out, you know? Like I didn't feel bad enough being a law school dropout with crushing debt. God, I wanted to be you."

My chest hurts. My head hurts. Everything hurts. This can't be happening. Darcy was my first hire. She was so warm. So helpful. So easy to talk to.

To trust.

My hands tremble. I try to steady them, but it's no use. I can't seem to stop them.

"Why, Darcy?" I manage to ask. "Taking on clients that we declined . . . working with people behind my back . . ."

"I had no other choice. You have to understand that," she pleads. "I wouldn't have done this if I didn't absolutely have to. My debts, they were like a mountain growing taller and taller every day. It was crushing me."

"You could've asked me for help. If you were going through such extreme hard times, we could have figured a way out."

At this, she laughs and shakes her head. "Do you hear yourself, Nura? As nice as you can be, at the end of the day, your clothes and shiny diamonds are like blinders for you, aren't they? The rest of the world doesn't grow up in a wealthy relative's house and inherit a golden business to go with it. Regular people have to work hard for every little thing, and it's still never enough. We owe money forever unless we take matters into our own hands. Which is what I did. All those clients you turned down, for what? A white lie about the grades they said they got in college? A minor infraction with the cops? Or because they deigned to ask you the wrong question? No one can live up to your impossible standards. You were so picky. I tried to talk to you about it for years, but once someone was out of your favor, you refused to give them a second chance. So I took on some of those people. Helped them. And they paid me enough to actually make a dent on what I owed. It was a win-win. It's not like you wanted to work with those clients, anyway."

"You took on *Basit*?"

"Yeah, so . . . Basit was a tough one." She looks contrite. "He wanted nothing to do with you, but once I talked him down, he was up for working with me. So I dealt with him directly. It was kind of freeing not to have to pretend to be you for a change. Of course, then Farhan came along and ruined everything, though the payments *did* free me of Andrei once and for all."

"Andrei? Y-your ex?"

"More like a loan shark with benefits. Though the benefits wore off years ago." Her expression darkens. "He'd started amping up his threats. Found my new place. He was going to hurt me, ruin my chance of happiness with Samir. But it's handled now." She looks at me and shakes her head. "Seriously,

Nura. I get that Basit was pushy and rude, but he offered to *double* your fee. Did you even think about it? Nope—you were offended. You didn't even consider how that kind of money could change a person's life. Of course, *now* I know it was a mistake. There was no fixing Farhan. He was fixated on you from the jump. I tried to get him to see reason, but then he started getting pissed at *me* for talking him out of his insane ideas." She shivers. "It was a complete nightmare. He wanted to prove to Lena that you were a fraud. You have no idea what he actually wanted to do to Avani and Dev to prove his point before I intervened. I tried to keep him from going off the deep end as best I could."

"The mug shot," I say slowly. "The threatening note left at the agency. That was *you*?"

"I'm so sorry about that." She wipes away tears. "He made me do it. Somehow he figured out that I was going rogue by representing him. Threatened to expose me to you if I didn't play ball. I couldn't let that happen, not when I was so close to finally being free."

I remember the shock that coursed through me at seeing the forged court documents that Avani's mother had crumpled and tossed at me. The late night at Borzu's trying to figure out who could have done this. A wave of nausea passes over me.

"He kept spiraling," Darcy continues, her words coming fast. "He was convinced I could make Lena fall in love with him. I never thought he'd actually go so far as to kidnap them. I tried to talk him out of it. I went to the cabin to beg him to let them go. He wouldn't listen. It was like talking to a rock. I realized he was actually going to kill Tanvir that night. . . . I had to stop him. Neutralize him. But I needed to buy some more time, so I offered up your location as a compromise."

"*You* were the one who told him I was at my aunt's?"

"I wasn't going to let him do anything to you, Nura. I had it all figured out. He'd race over to your aunt's. Then I'd do what needed to be done. Thank God, it all went according to plan."

"Darcy . . ."

"I stopped him, didn't I?" Her eyes are bright. "He didn't kill Tanvir. He didn't hurt you. And look at Lena, she's got more brand endorsement sponsorships than ever. A million new followers. I bet she'll have a book and movie deal in no time too. This whole kidnapping thing ended up being a net positive for her in the end."

She says this all so sincerely. As though this is a normal workday and she's leaning against my office door with a tablet in hand, updating me about the day's business. Darcy was my friend. I was going to be the maid of honor at her wedding.

A chill goes through me. She didn't need to tell me all this. Why is she confessing everything now? She needs this moment for some reason.

My mouth grows dry. I take in her tear-streaked expression. She's here to finish what she started, isn't she?

I glance around. My purse is on the counter. Where did I put my keys? I look at the curtained window. Fiona doesn't even know someone's in here with me. Who knows how Darcy sidestepped my security cameras and how long she's been hiding in my home, waiting for me?

Darcy follows my gaze. "I'm sorry, Nura, but that's not how this story ends."

My voice comes out a choked sob. "Darcy. Please."

"This is hard for me too," she says earnestly. "You have no idea. If there was any other option, I would do it in a heartbeat. I've gone over it a million different times, but there's only one way out for me. And, Nura, I'm going to need you to play ball, okay? If you don't follow along . . ." She hesitates. "There are going to be consequences you won't like."

"Consequences?" Who is this woman standing across the room from me right now? How can any of this be real? "Darcy, what are you talking about?"

She closes her eyes, and then: "Look, I'm sorry, okay? But I hired someone. They're waiting by your aunt's house right now, and they're armed."

"Whatever you're planning, you don't want to do it."

"Of course I don't want to do this! Can't you see how hard this is for me?" She shakes her head. "But sometimes we have to do hard things, right? I'm not bluffing about this, Nura—if you don't do what I say, your family dies. That's a promise."

My family *dies*? Jesus. "Who *are* you?" Hot tears trail down my cheeks. "What do you want me to do?"

She looks visibly relieved.

"This part's easy, I promise." Darcy unzips her purse. She pulls out a translucent bottle. Ten white pills tinged with blue clatter onto the kitchen table. "You won't be in pain. I read up on it to make sure. It'll be like drifting off to sleep." She gestures toward the cabinet above the sink. "Now, why don't you go ahead and get yourself a glass of water?"

These pills. The same ones that fell from my purse at the hospital.

"The car accident," I say softly. "How?"

"Do you really want to know? It'll only hurt your feelings." She looks at my stricken expression. "It was simpler than it seems. The dark web and a few thousand dollars. Honestly, the plan was for it to all be over that day. The police weren't getting off my back ever since that night I shot Farhan. They're *still* on my case. It's ridiculous. He was at your house with a gun. I guess I kind of messed up, though. I accidentally called Farhan from my regular phone. It was just the one time. Barely a few minutes, but they're fixated on that. I knew they'd back off if they found a different suspect, and you're the most logical one. If you were gone, that would be the end of it. But someone drove by that night and ruined everything. I never ran so fast in my life. Thank God it was a moonless night."

"You were there? Y-you drugged me?"

"I was trailing the road to see where you landed. . . . I did get scared you might sideswipe *me* too. You were out cold when I reached you; it would have been perfect. I'd even tucked the pills into your purse. Clean and simple and done." She sighs. "I should've gotten a bigger syringe. It obviously wasn't enough."

"Now you want me to take these drugs."

"It ties in perfectly to the blood work that came up after the car crash," she says. "You didn't *mean* to die. It will look like an accident. An overdose."

"Darcy—"

"Nura." She folds her arms. "We're friends, so I'm trying to be as nice as I can about all this, given our history, but if you don't do what I say, the people standing by your aunt's house *will* kill your family. I'm not bluffing. If you care about them, you need to move quick."

Lilah's bouncing curls flash through my mind's eye. I shudder. Darcy could be lying. I would never have thought she'd be willing to hurt my family. But I don't know her very well, do I? I can't risk anything happening to them. I walk to the kitchen cabinet. Pull out a clear cup. I press my hands against the cool metal faucet and turn it on. Water splashes off the edges of the glass. My burner phone rings. Again. And again. Darcy yanks it out of her pants pocket.

"Nina? What does *she* want?" She powers it off and wipes it clean with a tea towel.

"Have you thought this through?" I try again. "Don't you think the police will be suspicious when they find out you were here when I died?"

"Have I thought this all through?" She laughs a little. "I came early to cat sit and took a nap upstairs. I came down after I woke up and found you lying on the sofa," she says. "I thought you were sleeping. Didn't want to wake you, so I waited a bit—but then I saw the pill bottle on the table." Her eyes widen. "At least your family will be alive to mourn you, so there is that."

My heart pounds against my rib cage. I have to get out of here. There's got to be something I can do . . .

She gives me a sympathetic look. "You still think there's a way out, don't you? I see how your eyes dart around. To that pen on the counter. Your keys. You're desperate. For something, anything, that might deliver freedom. Denial is normal. One of the five stages of grief or something, right? But time is of the essence here, so I'm afraid we're going to need to go ahead and skip to acceptance. Because sooner or later, you're going to have to wrap your head around the fact that tonight, Nura Khan, you will die."

"Look—"

"Say one more word and I make the call." She lifts her phone. Her lips press into a thin line. "I mean it, Nura. Enough. Get that pill on your tongue. Let me see you swallow it."

I sit at the kitchen table. With unsteady hands, I place one in my mouth. I take a sip of water and pretend to ingest it before stuffing it in my cheek. But it's no use—it's dissolving.

"Was any of it real?" I ask her. "Was Samir?"

"Nura! Samir is my fiancé." She looks offended. "He's the best thing that's ever happened to me."

"So it was only our friendship that was a farce."

"Hey." Her expression softens. "Our friendship *is* real. I care about you, Nura. I do. Can't you tell I'm sick over this? Trust me, I racked my brains for another way—but it's either you or me. And I'm finally starting my life. Samir and I, we're at the brink of our future together. We're going to have kids and I'm going to do things right. I'll be there for my family like my mother wasn't. I can't lose it all before it begins."

"You could have had all that without doing this. You were paying down your debt. You were going to be fine eventually, and—"

My watch buzzes against my wrist beneath the kitchen table. I don't dare glimpse down, but I know who the messages are from. Nina. She's getting frantic. Waiting for me. Wondering where I am.

"Next pill, Nura," Darcy snaps. "Can we get on with it, please?"

"H-how many am I supposed to take?"

"We've got a whole bottle to go, and I'm going to be honest, my patience *is* starting to run out."

I take a sip of water and swallow another. How many of these will it take before I black out? I have to stay conscious. I have to find a way out of this.

My iPhone buzzes. Again. And again. Darcy stalks toward it and glowers. She leans down to read the messages.

"Nina again?" She scrunches her nose. "What's her deal? Are you friends now or something?"

I'm late. I check the wall clock hanging over the back window. I'm twenty minutes late.

Grabbing my phone from the counter, she types in my passcode. Hits the voice-to-text button. "Can't chat," she says. "Something came up."

"It doesn't have to end like this."

"I wish that was true," she says. "This is just the way it has to be."

Under her watchful eye, I take another pill. Is my pulse slowing, or am I imagining it? What comes next?

My wrist buzzes again. Will Darcy notice if I look down? What have I got to lose if she does? I sneak a glimpse at the incoming text.

NINA: Something came up? WTF, Nura? I can still make it for the social hour if you get here in the next ten minutes. Please.

Oh.

"What if I confessed?" I blurt out. She eyes me. I rush on. "A deathbed confession? Instead of an overdose, it could be a suicide. My guilt over my actions ate me alive. I'll say I helped Basit. The other clients. Stole their money. I'll admit to all of it."

"Hope springs eternal, huh?" She gives me a small smile. "You think bargaining with me might buy you time to convince me to change my mind?"

"My family relies on me for their livelihood. I-I want them taken care of when I'm gone. How about this? I'll leave you my business in my confession. In exchange, you look after my family and make sure their financial needs are met."

She regards me suspiciously. "And you trust I'd actually do it?"

"I trust the Darcy I've known for the last six years." My voice wavers. "You're right, maybe you won't honor my wishes, but I have no choice but to try. There's an old-fashioned tape recorder in a cardboard box in the closet there. There's no internet connection on that, so I can't use it to call for help." I point to the coat closet a few steps away. "I'll say whatever you want. In exchange, keep my family safe."

"I'm not sure. . . ."

"I mean it, Darcy. Please. If I've ever meant anything to you, even the slightest bit, let me do this for you, and in exchange, you help my family."

A wave of dizziness washes over me. *Focus.* She's tempted. She glances at me and makes her way toward the closet. She opens the door. Looks inside.

This is it.

Hands trembling, I click Nina's message on my wrist. I hit the voice button.

"Don't kill me, Darcy. Forcing me to take pills in my own home won't fix things. Please help me. You're in danger too. Call the police and this can all be over."

Heart pounding, I hit send.

"Nura—I've been trying really hard to be understanding. I understand your predicament, I'm sorry it has to happen like this, but I'm fucking over it. This—ah—here it is." She pulls out the bulky recorder. "Totally thought you were bluffing." She looks at me with what I can only describe as grudging respect. "You're serious, aren't you?"

"If it helps my family, I'll do anything."

My heart thrums against my ribs. Did the text go through? I've never voice texted from my watch before. I don't dare check now that she's setting the recorder on the table and settling down across from me.

"Go on and take another pill," she says. "This is a deathbed confession. Let's go ahead and get on with the dying."

I do as she says, choking the next pill down my throat.

She pushes the recorder toward me. She nods.

I click the red button.

Please, Nina, I pray frantically. *Please call for help before it's too late.*

THIRTY

"My name is Nura Khan, and this is my last confession."

The old-fashioned tape whirs inside the machine. I'm starting to grow woozy.

She points at the pills. I take another.

"Many people know me from the Piyar app. We help people find authentic connections online. I'm proud of the work we do. But there's more to the story. And the burden gets heavier each day. The truth is, I've been getting greedy. I took on more clients than I could handle. I got sloppy."

She nods and points. I take another pill. The room fades in and out. I keep talking. About how I worked with Basit. Helped Farhan until I couldn't control him anymore.

Darcy reaches over and hits pause on the machine. "This . . . this is great stuff, Nura. Thanks. Do you mind if we close out with Lena and Tanvir's kidnapping? I thought I'd evaded the street cameras when I went to check on them, but I think I was spotted at some point. Luckily, you and I are the same size. I dropped a lookalike of your bracelet near the driveway. Figured once they eventually found it, it'd tie things together nicely, but it'll be way simpler if you just confess that it was you helping Farhan."

Confessing to aiding and abetting the kidnapping of a couple I only ever wanted to help? Will I die knowing that's how people will think of me after I'm gone?

My surroundings grow hazier. If the message didn't go through, then my trade for my family's protection may end up being the only good thing that will come of this.

With shaking hands, I hit record.

"I kidnapped Lena and Tanvir. I guess I've been unraveling for a while." She nods at the last pill. I pick it up and take it.

"I leave my business to Darcy Jacobs. She can steer the agency in a better direction. I only ask that she care for my family. To provide for them. They are blameless. I bear all the fault."

My stomach heaves. I lurch forward as though I might vomit, but nothing comes out. Darcy shuts off the recorder. Her eyes well with tears.

"Nura. Thank you. Really. You're a true friend to the end. Whoa. You look pretty out of it. Let me move you over to the sofa. It'll be more comfortable. I'll be right with you until you go."

My elbows slump on the kitchen table. My head rolls to the side. I've lost count of how many pills I've consumed at this point. I couldn't move even if I wanted to. Darcy's speaking, but the words don't reach me. Her nails press into my skin. I'm being dragged by my underarms. Off the chair. Toward the sofa.

"We'll miss you at the wedding," Darcy's voice says from afar. My knee bumps into the sharp edge of the coffee table. "I'll have your family there. Lilah can be the flower girl. We'll have a moment of silence, in your memory."

She heaves me onto the sofa. Covering me with my favorite throw. I remember the last time I slept here. That late, rainy night I lay across from Azar. His voice growing groggier as we talked, until he fell asleep. I'm so grateful for the last two nights. So grateful we cleared up our decade-long misunderstanding. I can't believe I'll never see his face again.

Darcy's still talking. At least I think she is. I don't hear her anymore. I hear nothing at all. Is this how death works? Slipping you in phases from the living world to the beyond?

There's a loud bang in the distance. Someone coming to save me? Or a frantic hallucination of my dying mind? Turns out you don't lose hope for rescue, all the way until the end.

But not all stories have happy endings.

Sometimes you play the cards you're dealt and lose.

THIRTY-ONE

I awake in a fluorescent-lit hospital. Once again, bright lights above make me squint as I come to. Once again, I wear a thin fabric gown. Azar's face leans over mine. There's a halo of light around him. His hand rests on the bed railing. His beautiful, worried face. His mouth relaxes into a smile when I gaze up at him.

"I'm alive?" The words come out between a croak and a whisper.

He grips my hand in his. "It's over."

A button pings. There's a flurry of movement. People checking my eyes. My pulse. My temperature. A doctor in a white coat hurries inside, clipboard in hand, PIEDMONT HOSPITAL embroidered on her lapel.

"We had to pump your stomach," she explains. "You were coding when they found you. They had to administer naloxone. You've been in an induced coma for the last three days while we got your system cleared up."

"A coma," I repeat, dazed, trying to compute all the words coming at me.

The doctor tells me I'll be in the hospital at least a few more days while they monitor me. Make sure I'm all right. I *am* all right, she assures me.

The doctor glances at Azar. "Should we let the police know she's awake?"

"Let's give her a little more time," Azar says.

"Where's my family?" I ask when the doctor leaves. "Are they okay? Are they safe?"

"They're fine," he says. "It's six o'clock in the morning. Visiting hours start at eight."

"*You're* here."

"I'm a doctor."

"At Piedmont?"

"Nope. Just abusing the hell out of my privileges so you're looked after by someone who cares about you around the clock. Fucking hell." His smile fades. "I still can't believe what almost happened."

The hospital door handle turns. Nina, Khala, and Lilah burst in. Yep. Figured they wouldn't listen to visiting hours.

"We sped over as soon as Azar texted us that you were starting to come to," Nina says. "And don't worry about Gertie, she's with us."

"Thank God you're okay." Khala maneuvers her wheelchair toward my bed. Takes my hand and kisses it.

I lock eyes with Nina. "You got my text."

"That was the creepiest message I have ever received in my life." Nina shudders.

"There wasn't . . . there wasn't anyone outside the house? Someone threatening you?"

"What?" She frowns. "No. I reached your place a few minutes before the cops. Fiona broke the door down. Darcy actually tried to jump out your window. Sorry about the broken glass on your rug, by the way."

"Broken glass is the least of my worries." I try to sit up, wincing at the pain in my stomach. Darcy. I can barely think about her without my heart twisting. I can't begin to process the enormity of her betrayal.

"What . . . what happened to her?" I ask.

"She's in custody," Azar says. "That's all I know. We've been more focused on you."

"I made you cards," Lilah sings.

"Whoa." I laugh as she flings ten different construction-paper notes folded in half at me. Each one is filled with stickers and marker and crayon hearts. "Maybe we can tape these up on my walls. They'll definitely cheer me up."

After my aunt, niece, and cousin leave to get some food for us, I'm able to brush my teeth and change into clothing Khala had brought from my home. Then it's back to me and Azar. The sound of a monitor beeps in the background. Carts rumble as they glide over vinyl flooring outside the room. Tree branches scrape against the window across from me.

"I'm assuming you have to get back to work?" I tell him. "I'm okay. I don't need babysitting."

"You never need babysitting. Can't I take a day off and be here because I want to?"

"Fair enough. I could use some distraction."

"Well, here's some distraction: There's something I wanted to talk to you about."

"Is it a heavy conversation?" I ask. "I'm not sure I can handle anything serious at the moment."

"Well, it's pretty serious. Can't wait."

"Uh-oh."

"I think I'm ready, Nura."

"Ready?" I look at him.

He nods somberly. "For your matchmaking services."

I watch as a smile starts to spread across his face. "Is that right?"

"When it's time, it's time."

"What exactly are you looking for?"

"Off the top of my head?" He frowns. "She should be five foot six. Dark hair. Loves good food, and her family. She should never have met an iron she knows how to handle. Says she likes to run, but curiously almost never runs."

"Hey!" I swat him. "I resent that."

"I wasn't done." He pulls down the railing. "She's got to have a laugh that makes a bad day right. And a mouth I very much want to kiss right now." He gazes down at me. "Any leads?"

"I might know someone."

"Yeah?"

"I think you just might love my suggestion."

"I think I most definitely do."

I kiss him. The stubble from his jaw, unshaved these past few days, brushes against my skin. My breath hitches as he kisses me harder. It's the kind of kiss that melts everything else away, the kind of kiss that sets the world aright. He slides onto the bed next to me. I rest my head against his chest.

"Why did we wait so long?" he asks.

"Better late than never."

He wraps his arms around me. He doesn't say anything because he doesn't need to. Later today, I will have to speak to the police. Eventually, I will need to sort out my business and what it looks like on the other side of this ordeal. Right now, this is enough.

One Year Later

"I appreciate you doing this, Nura," says Logan.

"After all your help, I'm glad you're here to share how the whole saga unfolded with me," I say.

"But a 60 *Minutes* interview"—Logan nods to the bright lights in the distance—"that's going to get a lot of eyes."

"The public interest feels bottomless at this point," I tell him. "Hopefully once I've said my piece on the air, I can at least *start* putting it behind me."

Though this will never be behind me. Never fully.

A woman in black hurries over to adjust my mic as we stand at the side of the set. Multiple lights are trained on the couch where we'll sit for the interview.

"No one told me I'd need sunglasses," I joke.

"You're going to do great," she says. "I heard we had to squeeze you into the schedule for this week because you're going on your honeymoon next week?"

Cartagena, Colombia. Though I won't tell her that. Can't risk the public finding out now that the media follows me everywhere. Instead, I simply nod.

"The matchmaker getting matched. And after all the weddings you planned, yours will be the talk of the town!"

I raise an eyebrow, but I say nothing. The truth is, Azar and I tied the knot last weekend in a simple ceremony. There had been no white horses. No gondolas. No florists. No planners. It had been an exchange of vows at the mosque followed by dinner with our families and a handful of friends, including Genevieve and Borzu. Khala even danced. Her leg has healed, and her health is holding up.

It was absolutely perfect.

I see the interviewer who will be quizzing Logan and me on what everyone calls the trial of the year. She's already settling down before the bright lights. She's in a smart skirt suit. She promised she would be gentle, but she'll inevitably press on wounds that have yet to heal. *Do* wounds like these heal? I'm still waiting to find out. Even one year later, thinking of Darcy's betrayal brings tears to my eyes.

The Piyar app continues to run at a steady clip. I'd expected a huge backlash, and there has been some, but the news stories of Darcy's trial only served to increase the traffic to our site. My inbox has never been more full.

The trial concluded a few weeks ago. She was charged with kidnapping and bodily assault. Attempted first-degree murder. The jury found her guilty. Sentenced her to life in prison with the possibility of parole in twenty. Not to mention what's in store for her with the investigation around Farhan's death, which has just been reopened.

"It's showtime," the woman says.

"Ready?" asks Logan.

Absolutely not. But I also know it's time.

It will record tonight.

It will air tomorrow.

Maybe it'll land Logan a book deal. A movie. A show.

What am I hoping for? Peace.

My watch buzzes on my wrist.

Azar.

You okay?

More than okay. I tap back a heart emoji, then walk with Logan toward the seats across from the interviewer's blue couch, into the light.

ACKNOWLEDGMENTS

Writing a book takes a village, and I am so grateful for my community.

Thank you to everyone at Ballantine Bantam and Dell and Random House as a whole. Anne Speyer, I've treasured our time together and am grateful for your sharp insights and guidance to get this book where it needed to be. Wendy Wong, thank you for all your support, I'm excited for our partnership together. Anusha Khan, I appreciate all your help along the way and feedback on earlier drafts of this manuscript. Thank you, Cindy Howle, for your fantastic copyedits. Kelly Chian, your production editorial magic is much appreciated. Thank you also to Jennifer Hershey, Kara Welsh, Kim Hovey, and Kara Cesare. For this lovely cover and the interiors, thank you Cassie Gonzales, Aarushi Menon, and Jo Anne Metsch. Thank you also to Jordan Hill Forney for everything.

Infinite gratitude to The Book Group and especially to my incomparable agent, Faye Bender. Your creative feedback, your encouragement, and your advocacy mean everything to me. Thank you also to William Morris Endeavor and in particular Hilary Zaitz Michael and Sanjana Saleem.

Thank you to dear readers who looked at earlier drafts of

this story along the writing journey: Huda Al-Marashi, Marcy Franck, Ayesha Mattu, S.K. Ali, Sarah Branham, Deborah Halverson, Krishna Kasturi, Mina Kasturi, and Anil Suryaprasad. This book would not be the book it is without your invaluable feedback.

A special shout-out to Tracy Lopez for reading *multiple* drafts of this book. You have been my writing partner from the start. I can't imagine writing any book without you.

Finally, all my love to you, K, for your love and support which nourishes my soul. And to my boys: You are my everything.

The
Matchmaker

Aisha Saeed

RANDOM HOUSE BOOK CLUB

Questions and Topics for Discussion

1. The modern world of dating has introduced new ways to meet people. What do you think about matchmaking? Would you rather meet someone organically? Would you sign up for Nura's matchmaking services?

2. A central theme of this story is love: platonic, familial, romantic. How do Nura's relationships shape her choices? In what ways does her perception of love influence her professional path and personal life?

3. Community is an important element in this novel. How is the sense of community both a source of support and a potential source of conflict for Nura?

4. Nura doesn't see matchmaking as a job but as her life calling. Is there something in your work life or otherwise that you are equally passionate about?

5. In what ways does the concept of family extend beyond biological ties, and how does this broader definition of family impact Nura's choices and her sense of belonging?

6. Consider Darcy's desire to have a traditional South Asian wedding and wear desi clothes. Is this an example of cultural appropriation or appreciation? How can we differentiate between the two?

7. Nura's discovery of the truth about her parents and their past comes as a great shock and forces her to question her identity. Do you believe that learning where you come from can affect the person you are? How might Nura's life

have diverged had she been aware of her family's past? Would she still have pursued a career in matchmaking?

8. Nina and Nura have a complex relationship. Why do you think Nina held resentment toward her? Do you think Nina's disapproval of the agency is justified?

9. In what ways might Darcy and Nura be two sides of the same coin? How do their perspectives differ on the importance of family?

10. If Nura and Azar realized their mutual feelings for each other and got together back in college, how might their lives have been different? In what ways did waiting a decade to confront their feelings contribute to their personal growth and development? What factors do you think gave Nura the courage and confidence to finally be honest about her feelings?

11. Khala created a strict set of rules to safely matchmake and ensure that history wouldn't repeat itself. Can you think of a rule you might consider adding to protect the integrity of Piyar?

Listen to Aisha Saeed's playlist for

THE MATCHMAKER

1. "You Me Bullets Love" by The Bombay Royale
2. "Every Breath You Take" by The Police
3. "no body, no crime" by Taylor Swift
4. "Someone Like You" by Adele
5. "Empty" by Ray LaMontagne
6. "Swept Away" by The Avett Brothers
7. "One Way Or Another" by Blondie
8. "What If You" by Joshua Radin
9. "Hold On" by Alabama Shakes
10. "Ship To Wreck" by Florence & The Machine
11. "I Want You To Love Me" by Fiona Apple
12. "Don't Let Me Be Misunderstood" by Nina Simone
13. "evermore (feat. Bon Iver)" by Taylor Swift
14. "Maroon" by Taylor Swift
15. "Say Something" by A Great Big World
16. "Maar Dala" by Kavita Krishnamurthy and KK
17. "I Will Wait" by Mumford & Sons
18. "Don't Panic" by Coldplay
19. "Stressed Out" by Twenty One Pilots
20. "Set Fire to the Rain" by Adele

ABOUT THE AUTHOR

AISHA SAEED is a *New York Times* bestselling and award-winning author of books for younger readers, including *Amal Unbound, Written in the Stars, Yes No Maybe So* (co-authored with Becky Albertalli), and *Forty Words for Love. The Matchmaker* is her debut adult novel. She lives in Atlanta, Georgia, with her family.

AishaSaeed.com
Instagram: @aishacs
X: @aishacs

This book was set in Fairfield, the first typeface from the hand of the distinguished American artist and engraver Rudolph Ruzicka (1883–1978). Ruzicka was born in Bohemia (in the present-day Czech Republic) and came to America in 1894. He set up his own shop, devoted to wood engraving and printing, in New York in 1913 after a varied career working as a wood engraver, in photoengraving and banknote printing plants, and as an art director and freelance artist. He designed and illustrated many books, and was the creator of a considerable list of individual prints—wood engravings, line engravings on copper, and aquatints.

RANDOM HOUSE BOOK CLUB

Because Stories Are Better Shared

Discover

Exciting new books that spark conversation every week.

Connect

With authors on tour—or in your living room. (Request an Author Chat for your book club!)

Discuss

Stories that move you with fellow book lovers on Facebook, on Goodreads, or at in-person meet-ups.

Enhance

Your reading experience with discussion prompts, digital book club kits, and more, available on our website.

Join our online book club community!

f **g** randomhousebookclub.com

Random House Book Club ™

Because Stories Are Better Shared

RANDOM HOUSE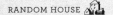